Wild Highland Magic

Lisa Ann Verge

WILD HIGHLAND MAGIC

She Can Read Every Mind, Except His

Gifted with faery blood, Cairenn is blessed and cursed with the ability to read minds, until a naked, half-dead Highland warrior washes up on the shore of her remote Irish island. Challenged by the wall between them, she nurses him back to life as she tries to pierce his thoughts without succumbing to his charm. For only a fool would fall in love with a man whose world she cannot inhabit, and whose heart she cannot know.

About the novels of Lisa Ann Verge

"Let yourself be swept away by the utterly enchanting atmosphere of a best-loved fairy tale. As always, the author delivers a book that is uniquely wonderful."
–RT Book Reviews

"Lisa Ann Verge is on the verge of climbing to the top of this genre, a position she definitely deserves."
–Affaire de Coeur

***Don't miss Lisa Ann Verge's other magical,
adventurous, historical romances!***

The Celtic Legends Series: Boxed Set
TWICE UPON A TIME: Book One
THE FAERY BRIDE: Book Two
WILD HIGHLAND MAGIC: Book Three
THE O'MADDEN: A Novella

Romantic Journeys Collection: Boxed Set
HEAVEN IN HIS ARMS
HER PIRATE HEART
SING ME HOME
THE CAPTIVE KNIGHT

The Cabin Fever Series
ALONE WITH YOU: Book One
LOST WITH YOU: Book Two
TAKEN WITH YOU: Book Three

Also available--the Novels of Lisa Verge Higgins

THE PROPER CARE AND MAINTENANCE OF
FRIENDSHIP
ONE GOOD FRIEND DESERVES ANOTHER
FRIENDSHIP MAKES THE HEART GROW FONDER
RANDOM ACTS OF KINDNESS
SENSELESS ACTS OF BEAUTY

CHAPTER ONE

Inishmaan, 1276

The man lying upon the shore was as naked as the day he was born.

Cairenn stood amid the boulders on the far edge of the beach, shading her eyes against the midday sun. When she'd first headed down the hillside, she'd thought the thing cast upon the shore was nothing but driftwood. As she came closer, what she'd assumed was a branch resolved into an arm, what she'd guessed was the trunk of some ship's mast turned out to be his broad, muscled back.

Now, standing only a dozen yards away, she no longer doubted that a full-grown man lay face down on the sand.

Her young companion, Seamus, clambered down the rocks to stand beside her.

"That man," Seamus said, "he must be cold,

don't you think?"

The boy blinked up at her with close-set eyes, all innocence.

"I imagine he is, Seamus."

"Why is he out here like that?"

She wondered that herself. Finding a body upon the shore wasn't so rare a thing for Inishmaan, since the island felt the full brunt of the North Atlantic Ocean. But generally men washed up only after a gale, when ships sank beyond the horizon and the tides washed the bodies onto the nearest land they could find. There'd been no gale recently. She couldn't imagine what tide had brought him here.

"I think," she said to her young friend, "that the sea just gave him up."

"Oh."

Cairenn knew he didn't really understand. Seamus was a special boy, different from his brothers and sisters. Soft-bodied, and with a face that caved in a little by the bridge of his nose, everyone dismissed him as the village idiot. But she judged people by a different measure. Seamus's mind was as pure as the ringing of a harp's string. It worked in straight, simple lines, shrugged off tangled complications, and favored sunshine and laughter.

Now she glanced back at the man exposed on the sand and, contemplating what she had to do, felt a strange mix of anticipation and unease. On this very strand, several years before, her own sister Aileen had been kidnapped by an outsider and swept away to Wales. It would be too much of a coincidence for such an event to happen twice—but she couldn't ignore the possibility that this man might be sleeping or even playing dead.

But no man could play dead around her, for she had the power to read minds.

So she cast her thoughts out in the way that no one else could. In the next cove, she sensed a lone fisherman coming in with a haul of mackerel. Around the cut of the cliff, an O'Dunn boy felt grumpy because he'd been forced to haul seaweed up the cliff. She sensed anger in the caws of the birds and, just off shore, the curiosity of a herd of seals bobbing in the surf.

But in the body of the naked man only yards away, no life flickered.

"Seamus," she said, drawing his attention away from the corpse on the strand, "I need you to tell my father about this."

"But we're going on an adventure! I'm going to show you how I row my boat over the waves!"

Her gaze drifted to a nook between two rocks where a little skin-covered boat was stowed. It was Seamus's own coracle, gifted to him by his father when the boy finally learned how to navigate the dangerous surf. Seamus had been bursting with pride that he'd passed his test. She'd used his enthusiasm to convince him to show her this new trick, and to take her on an excursion, maybe as far as Galway.

Now she wondered if the entire world conspired to keep her from ever stepping off the island.

"We'll do it another time, Seamus." She

reassured him with a smile. "For now, we have to take care of the man who washed up here."

His brow crumpled. "Will the doctor make the man better?"

"No, but he'll see that he's tended to." The islanders bore witness for any seamen who washed on shore, speaking a few words and then burying them above the high tide line. "I'll keep watch over his body so that the sea doesn't pull him back. Can you do this for me?"

A bright light filled his mind, the joy of helping others. He was already halfway to the slope when he shouted, "I'll run fast!"

The sand sank beneath her leather boots as she headed for the body. The booming crash of the ocean echoed against the backdrop of the cliff. Spray misted her cheeks, caught in billows in this hollow carved out by the sea. As she came closer, she realized how big the man was, far bigger than he'd looked from afar. He had shoulders like a bull.

Over the years, several bodies found on this strand had been of strange, different kinds of men. There were fantastical, lushly mustached people that Da had called Spaniards, heavily-bearded pale creatures he called Vikings, and once a tall, unnaturally thin man with skin the color of peat that Da had called a Nubian. Now as she looked upon this man's water-slick hair, the wonder of his back, and the long, strong length of his legs plastered with seaweed, she thought he looked like a *selkie* who'd clawed himself up to land in order to take human form.

She glanced around the cove in search of his

black sealskin, realizing the moment she did so that she'd been listening to too many of her brother Niall's stories.

Foolishness.

She leaned over to peek at the man's face, but first she saw his wound. She dropped to one knee and plucked away a thick piece of seaweed that clung to his shoulder, revealing an angry, ragged slice and purple, mottled skin.

She wasn't a doctor's daughter for nothing. She recognized a stabbing when she saw one.

Murdered, then.

A terrible chill shot through her. Da had always warned her that outsiders were a strange, violent folk. Proof frequently came by boat when men wounded by sword or mace or axe found their desperate way to his sickroom. Still, she couldn't help but feel some sympathy for this outsider who'd had his life shortened before its natural time.

For he was not an older man. She could see that in the smoothness of the skin around his eyes. To better see his face, she came around to his other side. She wondered what kind of strange work he'd done to have built a body such as this. She wondered if, somewhere far away, a young woman stood staring out at the sea, pining for him.

Crouching down, she dared to slip her finger under a lock of hair that covered his brow, relieved to see that the rest of his face was untouched by the ravages of the sea. She pushed his hair aside to see his features better.

For a breathless moment she gazed upon him. A snatch of her brother Niall's poetry came to her, from the story of Deirdre of the Sorrows.

I would have a man like that
Hair like the raven
Cheek like blood
His body like snow

As handsome a man as she'd ever seen lay before her. His brow was painted with salt-stains, his lashes sand-flecked.

Then he opened his eyes.

Lachlan thought he was still on the ship. He felt it rocking beneath him, tilted up at the bow at an alarming angle. Though the sun was too bright for his eyes, he heard a crew close around him, grunting and shouting at each other in garbled Gaelic.

His mind wasn't working well, but he reasoned that if he was still on the ship, then he hadn't been stabbed. He hadn't been pushed overboard. He hadn't felt the pressure of the ocean squeeze the air out of his lungs as he sank, watching the ship's keel recede by the watery light of the moon.

But he couldn't still be on the ship, because after a time the rocking stopped and he was in a dark place. Some crew of brutes was pressing him down. He could barely breathe as someone stabbed him with sharp, thin knives. His head swam but the pallet beneath him didn't, and the contrast confused him. The room he was in was too hot.

He was pulled into a dream that was a memory.

He heard seabirds. Sand tasted gritty in his mouth. Something warm and soft floated over him. The faint fragrance of spring flowers emanated from that warmth, reminding him of the verdant hills around Loch Fyfe. His mind grasped that memory, tried to draw closer to it though it was like pulling a hemp-line attached to an anchor without the gears to ease the lift. The warmth he sensed burrowed near him and brought comfort. He stretched for that with all his might and suddenly found himself blinking against a light so bright that it stung his eyes.

He tried to focus on the creature leaning over him, haloed by the sun.

I'm dead, he thought.

I'm dead and this is heaven.

"No, you're not dead, young man. Though considering what you've been through, you should be."

Lachlan froze at the deep, unfamiliar voice. His sight cleared and he realized he wasn't staring at the face of the creature of his dreams, but instead at the figure of a tall man towering over him, grinding something in a small bowl.

Lachlan started to sit up but pain speared through his shoulder. He eased back down on the pallet.

"A wise decision," the man said, not pausing in his grinding. "After we brought you up from the strand, I had to pull pieces of linen out of your shoulder. You'll be glad to have slept through that."

Shooting pains stole the air from his lungs. He slipped his good hand over his chest and felt rough linen bindings.

"The wound is deep." The man scraped around the inside of the bowl. "Fortunately for you, whoever wielded that blade missed the vital arteries."

A memory returned, of a trample of feet, a surprised shout, a blur of faces, a burn through his back, and then weightlessness until he hit the cold sea.

"Do you understand me?" The man paused in his grinding. "*Parlez-vous français*? Do you speak English? *Sprechen sie Deutsch? Hablas Español? Vôce fala Português?*" A strange spark lit his eyes. "*Türkçe biliyor musun?*"

Lachlan's tongue was swollen and dry. "I understand you."

"Ah. A Scotsman."

The man sounded disappointed. Lachlan tried to take the measure of the stranger. The man wore the simple woolen tunic of a farmer or a sheep-keeper, but something about the way the man carried himself spoke of a more martial livelihood.

"You're on the island of Inishmaan, one of the Aran Islands," the stranger said, anticipating his question. "I am Conor, the island's surgeon, apothecary, and tooth-puller, when necessary."

Lachlan didn't know the place, but he had cousins in Ulster. Even with his senses so addled he realized this man was Irish.

The doctor said, "We found you washed up in a cove like a piece of flotsam. The fishermen brought you to me. Another hour upon the strand and you'd be dead."

He muscled up some spit to moisten his tongue.

"How . . . long?"

"We've been fighting to keep you alive for a week."

A week.

Panic flashed through him. He struggled to sit up.

"Don't be foolish." The doctor placed a solid hand on Lachlan's good shoulder. "If you move too quickly, you'll tear open the stitches again. I've had a devil of a time keeping that wound closed."

The wound pulled and tugged, a pain that made beads of sweat pop out on his forehead. A week gone already, and who knew how long it must have taken the ocean currents to drag him to this shore.

He remembered the last time he saw home, riding out of the keep with his father's hopes heavy in his heart.

"I have to get back," he said through gritted teeth. "My father will think I'm dead."

"If you don't let that wound heal, you *will* be dead." The doctor increased the pressure on his shoulder. "Trust me, your father will be elated at your resurrection."

The doctor's grip was implacable, but it was the black scrim starting to wink before his eyes that felled Lachlan. He sank back on the pillow breathing as heavily as if he'd rowed the whole white-capped distance between Derry and Loch Fyfe.

Damn it.

"Not a simple sailor, are you?" The doctor released him and frowned. "A Scotsman builds shoulders like that by wielding a claymore."

Lachlan used the excuse of his weakness not to respond. He wasn't so dazed as not to realize he had to be discreet. He didn't know who this man was, or whose side in the conflict he might be on, or even if he knew anything at all about the clan war brewing.

"Trouble then," the doctor grunted at his silence. "Should I send men to watch the shore? Against the enemies who'll return to finish the job?"

Lachlan remembered the sound of the assassins laughing just before the ocean swallowed him up.

"There'll be no trouble." His lips stuck to one another. "They think I'm dead."

He should be dead. He'd been stabbed, thrown overboard in the middle of a gale, yet woke to find himself alive in a room with a wary Irish physician. He struggled against the darkness, thinking *I must get back.*

The assassins believed they'd murdered him.

So the next man they would murder would be his father.

CHAPTER TWO

Cairenn hesitated outside the stone outbuilding where her father tended his patients. He was the best doctor in all of Ireland. She knew this because it was always the sickest, most desperate people who found their way across Galway Bay in little coracles to hire donkeys to carry them to the heights of Dun Conor. People doubled in agony, cut apart by war, groaning under sicknesses no one could see, half-mad in the mind.

She could always feel those minds, whether she wanted to or not. They roared in pain and anguish. Many a night she'd scurried away from the bed she shared with her sisters, fled the house, the courtyard, and the whole stone-walled fort. She'd rather shelter in the caves on the north of the island than sleep within mind-hearing distance of that bloody room.

Now, standing in the white sun in the middle of the courtyard, she spread her thoughts into the sickroom. She sensed a pair of swallows nested in the thatch, warming a clutch of eggs. She sensed one of the house cats cleaning its paws in a patch of sunshine. Blocking out her father's presence, she stretched her mind and probed every corner of the room until she could sense the buzzing of a bee just outside the window, the rustle of a mouse amid the straw in the corner, all the tiny tickles of life that made her head hurt. But for all her probing, she sensed no other human life in that room except her father.

Not even the one she knew lay on the pallet inside, living and breathing when he shouldn't.

The emptiness disturbed her more than a hundred thousand bloody screams.

"There you are, Cairenn."

Her father stood in the doorway. He'd been waiting for her help in the sickroom, but she'd dawdled while she helped Ma clean up the midday meal.

"Why are you standing there?" he said. "Are you going to come in here and do your father's bidding?"

"I'm not my sister," she said, feeling her chin pucker. "I've no gift of the healing hands."

"I know very well that Aileen is an ocean away." As always, when he spoke her sister's name, it came with equal measures of pride and melancholy. "And you know that I called you for other reasons. It's not a healing that our patient needs now."

Her father slipped into the dimness of the room, expecting her compliance. She swallowed the fear and made her way across the bare stone of the courtyard like the dutiful daughter she was supposed to be. She stepped into the cool shade of the building and grasped the doorjamb against the smell of the place—tart herbs and peat smoke and, underneath it all, the copper-tang of blood.

She couldn't help herself. The nothingness on that pallet was like a void she couldn't stop peering into. But sending her mind toward the outsider was like tripping into thin air.

"This man you found," Da said, casting a hand toward the pallet, "is no wayward sailor caught up in a brawl, I can tell you that."

No, Da. No, he isn't.

"I didn't want to talk about this over dinner and worry your Ma. Asking you to help me with his bindings was a pretext to get you in here."

"I can tell you nothing about his mind." That, at least, wasn't a lie. "He was so far gone when I found him on the strand, that I felt nothing but his pain."

"And now?"

She hesitated. To tell her father that she sensed nothing in the body on the pallet was to speak of impossible things. Every creature had a life force, right down to the moth that just fluttered out of the folds of the cloak hanging on a hook by the door. Something was terribly wrong—either with this man or with her gift. In the agitated mood her da was in, she wasn't ready to confess to either.

"He's just dreaming," she said, tripping on the lie. "He's having cold dreams of being in the ocean."

"Look deeper."

A knot tightened at the nape of her neck. She knew Da was just worried about the danger this man could bring into their home, but she couldn't help thinking about other times when he got angry at her, mostly when she blurted truths best kept to herself. Once, she'd unwittingly mentioned in her father's presence that Niall had been sneaking down to a crofter's cottage to lay with a fisherman's wife. Another time he was furious when she refused to blurt truths he demanded to know—like who broke a clay vessel of oil amid his medicines. So often she felt like either a stubborn keeper of secrets or a tattler of terrible truths.

She did have one crazy-mad idea about why her gift was failing her, but she wasn't quite ready to blurt out that the man on the pallet might not be human.

"He's hardly conscious," she said, buying time. "You're asking me to look through the blackest of fog."

He frowned but did not contradict her. As his impatience ebbed, she read the root of his worry.

She blurted, "You think the murderer will come looking for him here."

"Someone tried to kill him for a reason." He ran his hand down his face. "I wager it wasn't for his clothing."

"Surely that happened on some ship at sea—"

"How far off shore could that ship have been, if a half-dead man made it to the strand alive?"

Cairenn pulled on her own fingers, worry filling her up. Da's doctoring brought many an outsider to their door, and each time was a risk. Da seemed normal enough to those who didn't spend more than a couple of hours with him. But her family was not like other families, just as Inishmaan was not like other islands. It would not behoove them to have outsiders returning to the mainland telling tales about Ma with her strange eyes that could see the future, or Aileen who could heal a wound with the pass of her hands, or Niall who could cast a spell with his music that would make you do things you shouldn't.

Fairy-gifts from the *Sídh*, all of them. But many an outsider might call such doings witchcraft. If her family wasn't careful about how they dealt with strangers, all the O'Conors of Inishmaan could end up burnt at the stake.

Her father said, "I've told the islanders to keep quiet about him, especially to say nothing to strangers."

"But you can't imagine that old Domnall won't blabber about the man found on the beach," she said, speaking her father's own concerns, "once he gets some ale in him after his next catch."

"Which means I've got business by the strand, and it cannot wait." Da pushed away from his trestle table, littered with bowls of herbs, and reached for his cloak. "Stay here and watch the man. I need to know who he is and how he got here. When he opens his eyes, you'll be able to see his mind more clearly."

Cairenn dropped her gaze to her clenched hands. Father knew her talents all too well. When she looked straight into a person's eyes she saw their thoughts and emotions and dreams and memories. Most often, the rush of those thoughts assaulted her, sometimes to the point of pain.

Da had his hand on the door when he paused, sensing her discomfort. "Are you all right, *a leanbh?*"

"I'm fine, Da."

She didn't dare tell him that she had already looked straight into this man's midnight-blue eyes—and sensed absolutely nothing.

Again in his dreams Lachlan remembered the sound of seabirds, tasted the sand in his mouth, and felt a warm body near him. He breathed deeply, wanting to draw closer to the source of the comfort. He lifted himself up and then a searing pain jerked him awake.

Gasping, he saw above him the underside of a thatched roof. In a rush he remembered where he was.

Stabbed. Cast overboard. Found on Inishmaan. Ireland.

He heard a small, muffled sound. He turned his head and saw a woman perched on a chair several yards away, her fair hair glowing in the light pouring in through a small window.

His heart pounded. He didn't want to blink, lest she disappear as she had all the other times in his dreams. As the seconds slipped by, she remained in his sight, poised as if at any moment gossamer wings might spread from her back.

I'm dead and this is heaven.

She went still, and that's how he knew he'd spoken aloud. Her bright, wide-set eyes were a shade of green he wanted to see better. Fair hair spilled over her shoulders, so long that the curls brushed the seat of the chair she was perched upon. Her feet were pale, delicate, and bare. He saw the tension in the curve of each arch.

In silence she focused on him with unnerving intensity. Leaning forward, she fixed her gaze as if she were trying to burrow through his skin and bones. Perhaps this was what it was like to be judged. He didn't think he had that much sin upon his soul, no more than any man who'd had the advantage of spending several formative years unchaperoned under the Roman sun. But still, her gaze was unnerving.

He shifted his weight on the pallet. At the movement, the woman startled off the chair, knocking it over beneath her.

"Don't go." His hoarse shout caught her just as she reached the door. "Stay—please."

She hesitated, one hand flat on the door. The thought came to him that an angel would have flown through the window, or disappeared in the blink of an eye, and yet here this woman stood with her hands splayed against the latch, a latch made of iron, and most otherworldly creatures couldn't abide the touch of iron.

Human, then.

How far his mind had drifted into delirium that he fancied she was anything but.

"Water," he said, pitching his voice low so as not to frighten her again. "Will you bring me some, lass?"

She was a slight thing, a wisp of a woman in a tunic the color of blueberries. Her ankles were so slim he thought he might be able to curl his thumb and forefinger around one. She pattered to the table where the doctor kept his things. She sought a clean cup, knocked over a wooden one, before finding a vessel that met her standards. She lifted a pitcher and filled it up, water splashing all over. She held the cup with two hands in front of her as she came around the table.

She hesitated more than an arm's-length away.

"I'm no threat to you," he said, keeping his voice low. "I'm hardly able to rise from this pallet."

The bones of her clavicle rose and fell. She seized a hollow reed left on the bedside table and dropped it into the water. The cup shook as she stretched it out to him.

He winced as he took it, for even that slight movement tweaked his wound. He slipped the reed between his lips and took a good pull. The water was cold and spring-fresh. Strength surged through him with each sip.

She whispered, "Why are you here?"

Her voice was low and husky. As she waited for an answer she grasped her own knuckles.

"It was the tide that brought me here." He met her gaze. "It was you who found me."

"You remember."

"As if I'd dreamed it." A pretty dream, but nothing compared to the reality standing before him. "I have you to thank for my life."

"'Twas nothing but a coincidence that I was

there—"

"If you hadn't been, I'd be dead," he interrupted. "Buried on the beach or sucked back into the sea. And that would have been the end of Lachlan of—"

Loch Fyfe.

He caught himself before he spoke the words. Best not to say too much about his identity, lest those who'd set out to kill him return to see if they had finished the task.

She said, "You don't remember where you're from." It was a statement, not a question.

"My memory is fever-addled, it'll return in time. Tell me your name, lass."

She shook her head once, with vehemence. "I know what you're after."

He hadn't a clue what she was talking about. "What kind of curse do you think I could put upon your name, while I lie here with all the power of a newborn?"

"You'll steal my name," she said. "And then you'll steal my soul."

Her words gave him pause. He wondered if she were touched in the head. Though the thought of stealing this beauty away, touched or not, certainly had him imagining what pleasures could be had with claiming her.

Yes, clearly, he was feeling better.

"I don't like the sea," she said, flexing her elbows like an agitated bird. "I don't like the darkness beneath, and how cold it is, and the thought of the creatures of the deep."

Her words were odd, but he played along. "I'm

not so fond of the sea myself, after the time I spent bleeding and sputtering and trying to stay alive in it."

"Was it a harpoon, then?"

His mind went blank.

"Your wound." She patted her own shoulder, three swift little pats. "Was it a harpoon that struck you so deep?"

A tattered memory returned of three men on a dark deck, the flash of moonlight off a blade. "A sailor's knife, I think. Bought and paid for by my enemies, to prevent me from doing what I was bid."

"Your enemies." Her brow knit, deeper than before.

"It's no secret that I have them. Most stabbed men do. But my enemies are unlikely to find me here, if that's what you're worried about. To them, I'm good and dead."

She mimicked the words *good and dead,* confusion wrinkling her brow.

"But I'm alive," he said, "and I'd give a king's ransom just to know your name."

"I won't tell you." She walked in a tight little circle, turning away from him, and then turning back, distress in every movement. "I've been thinking of this and thinking of this until I came to only one conclusion that made sense," she said, "but I still can't find the proof."

"Proof?"

"I've searched the whole shore where you washed up," she said. "I've been down there twice at low tide to look in the hollows between the boulders, to check every crevice for what you've left behind."

"You shouldn't have troubled yourself. I had nothing on me but what I wore and the sea stole that."

"Exactly. I went looking for your *skin*."

It was fruitless to parse meaning, so instead he tried to make a joke of it by gesturing to his naked chest. "I've got plenty of that, lass."

"I went searching," she continued, speaking as if to a stubborn toddler, "because I know you'll need your skin when you return to the sea."

"Well," he laughed, "I wouldn't want to lose it—"

"Don't be joking," she said. "I'm no fisherman's wife lonely on the strand with her husband six months out to sea."

Unmarried, then.

He felt a kick of pleasure.

"I know what you are, Lachlan, or whatever your true name is." She stepped back. "I know that you're a selkie."

CHAPTER THREE

To Cairenn, it made perfect sense. When the angels fell, some fell on the land and some on the sea. The angels on land became fairies and those in the sea became selkies.

She knew the fairies were real enough. She knew them by the feel of the little whirlwinds that caught up in her skirts. She knew them by the distant sound of pipe music she heard over the waves. She knew them by the gift of foxglove she found growing around the dolmen stones on the height, a place where nothing green should ever grow.

But she didn't feel their fairy minds, not like she sensed the minds of every other creature in the world. Her thoughts passed through them as cold as if they were ghosts.

So it made sense to assume this man spit up from the sea was a selkie. It was the *only* thing that made sense. But the look that passed across

Lachlan's face when she made the accusation was the same maddening, bemused, condescending little smile that everybody bestowed upon simple Seamus.

Then, suddenly, that look was gone.

"I know of selkies," he said, in a low, lilting voice that spoke of serious contemplation. "My people tell tales of them."

She thought of his people and imagined sleek dark bodies rolling and gliding under the waters.

"My clan lives close by the water," he said, "on a river that spills into the North Sea. When I was a child, seals used to come upriver with the first winds of autumn to bask on the rocks off shore. They'd bark all the night long."

His rumbling voice flowed over her like the warm June sun, and she took that as yet more proof that her suppositions were right. Selkie men were the sirens of the sea, more handsome than any human man, once they shucked their slick skins. And could there exist any man more handsome than this one, with his powerful shoulders, with his dark hair splayed over the pillow, with his long legs outlined against the blanket?

"I have a half-sister," he continued, turning his head on the pillow so that he was staring far beyond the thatched ceiling. "Elspeth is a mite younger than you. Last time I saw her, she wrapped a chain of foxglove around my wrist. She said it was a fairy-bond, and it meant that I had to come back."

The timbre of his voice made her feel that he wasn't lying, but, then again, maybe she was just becoming ensnared. "It must be difficult," she said, "finding foxglove at the bottom of the sea."

His lips twitched. "Do I remind you so much of a seal, lass?"

She wouldn't look down the long, strong length of him, no, she wouldn't. "Once you shed your skin," she said, "there's no knowing."

"It's true I have cousins on the Orkney Islands who claim they're descended from the *Finnar*. They were magic folk. Every once in a while, a child of that branch of the family is born with webbed feet." He raised a hand and spread his fingers. "Webbed hands, too."

She didn't like the sly lift of his smile. "You're mocking me."

"Teasing," he corrected. "Maybe a little."

His eyebrows twitched, and a muscle moved in his cheek, and his eyes gleamed, and a strange uncertainty washed over her. She'd never had to look this hard at a person's face to puzzle out what they were thinking, for she had her gift that could see right through such nonsense. How strange it was to be forced to do as her siblings did—attribute someone's true intent by the bend of a brow or the flicker of a lash. What a risky, terrible, unreliable way to communicate.

"You're teasing me," she said, "just to get me off the subject. Do you deny that you're a selkie?"

"It's a fanciful notion, lass, and I think you know it."

She did, but she wasn't ready to embrace that truth. To admit he was human was to admit that her inability to read him was a failure of her gift.

"You're fresh out of your skin," she argued. In

some of Niall's tales, a selkie who'd shucked his skin sometimes forgot that he belonged in the water. "You think you're human now, but at the first sight of the sea you'll remember."

"Help me up then," he said. "Selkie or no, I've got a powerful urge to see what's outside that window."

She hesitated. The window was only a few steps from the pallet, but for him to see the ocean from it, he'd have to be out of bed.

She said, "My father doesn't want you to stand up yet."

"Your father," he said, wincing as he swung his bare legs out from under the blanket, "is not here."

"Don't be foolish." She looked away from the flimsy linen braies that covered his loins. "I don't have the strength to hold up a man of your size—"

"I've been stabbed in the back, not in the legs." He paused while sitting at the edge of the bed. "Your hand, lass."

He was already half up off the pallet. In her mind she saw him keeling forward, crashing to the floor, ripping open the stitches under the wound while the linen that bound it turned black with blood.

"Stubborn selkie," she said, as she reached for him. His hand was warm, firm and so much bigger than her own. She allowed him to draw her close, but once within the circle of his warmth, she shook free of his grip. She slipped her arm behind his back and slid under his good shoulder to brace him. "You don't listen to what's good for you."

"It must be because of all the water in our

ears."

She couldn't laugh because her cheek was pressed against a powerful chest that smelled of medicine and sleep and sea-salt and man. The closeness addled her in the same way the dolmen stones on the height addled her when she dared to creep closer, stealing her senses and making her feel dizzy and tingly at the same time.

"You're a wee bit of a thing." He tucked her under him as he rose to his full height. "I'll try not to crush you with my fins."

"Full of teasing, you are."

She glanced up to meet his gaze and that was a terrible mistake. The face that looked down upon hers was so very human. His unshaven jaw was rough with bristles. Shadows gathered under his cheekbones and in the divot of his upper lip. A crescent scar pulsed white against the skin on his temple. His nose and cheekbones sported a faint, boyish scattering of freckles. And those otherworldly eyes, those deep, deep, blue eyes fringed by dark lashes . . . she felt as if she were falling into them, even though she was looking up.

Still, beyond the gleam of those eyes, she sensed nothing, nothing, a darkness like the bottom of the sea.

He whispered, "Don't be frightened of me, lass."

She *was* frightened, for that was exactly what a selkie would say when he came upon shore seeking the lonely girls, longing for love. Niall's stories teemed with selkie men glimpsing a sore-hearted woman on the strand and feeling the pull of that lonesomeness. And hadn't she been the solemn one these past years, staring out from atop the cliffs, watching wistfully as ships sailed out of Galway Bay?

She must have been a bright, glaring beacon, standing alone on that strand.

Then the sound of the sea drew his attention away. He took another step toward the window. He put very little weight upon her, but she felt every bit of it, his muscles moving in strange and wondrous ways.

They reached the window and the salt breeze hit them.

Her home of Dun Conor stood at the height of the island. Because of the fierce winds, it wasn't the best place to build a home, but her da had chosen it the moment he brought his bride to Inishmaan. He'd raised this fortress upon the ruins of some ancient stronghold that had been here for as long as the islanders had memory. The fortress had high walls to cut the wind coming off the Atlantic. This window gave a view of the nearby island of Inishmore as well as the turbulent channel between.

As soon as Lachlan caught sight of the white caps of the churning sea crashing against the rock below, a shock bolted through his body. She felt it as surely as if it shot through herself.

He murmured "by the *Dagdá*" in a voice full of awe and disbelief.

Her heart did a skitter-skip. Hadn't she known this would happen? The minute he laid eyes on the waters of his home the longing would overwhelm him. Her sister Aileen would call this *hiraeth*, a wistful nostalgia for something that was lost combined with a yearning that would not let go.

"I'll find your skin," she said, as her throat closed up. "I'll find your skin and you can go back home to the sea."

"You mistake me, lass." His weight began to bear down upon her. "Those waters are home only to the dead."

She stared at the churning channel and a strange chill went through her because she knew that he spoke the truth.

"I will go back to the sea," he said darkly, "but it'll be upon a ship." He turned back to the pallet, sweat beading on his brow. "And when I do, I'll go with a sword gripped in my hand."

"I spoke to the boy last night."

Cairenn looked up from pouring ale and froze under her father's steady blue gaze. An image flashed through her father's mind—Lachlan on the pallet with his dark hair spread across the pillow.

"His name is Lachlan," she stuttered. Every man was a boy to Da, who'd lived more years than he could count. "I told you that yesterday."

She'd told Da that Lachlan was Scottish from a place on the shores of a tributary to the North Sea. She'd told Da that he'd been stabbed on a ship, and that he was determined to wreak vengeance on somebody. As soon as Da had come back from the alehouse, she'd told her father everything she knew—except that she couldn't read the man's thoughts. She couldn't confess that then, for her brothers and sisters had been swarming around them, their minds hungry with curiosity.

Her father continued, "I heard him shout in the middle of the night and went to find him collapsed by the window. A few more days and I would take out those stitches, but he's determined to rip them himself."

She put the pitcher of ale on the table and slipped onto the bench. Her brothers and sisters were lined up on the other side, stuffing their mouths with whitefish as they watched them with that preternatural sense that something was about to happen. Something was about to happen, indeed, but if she had her way her siblings wouldn't be around to witness.

"Our stranger was staring at the sea," Cairenn said, focusing her attention on the little ones, "because I think he's a selkie."

She heard them suck in a collective breath, but what she sensed the strongest was the burst of light in their minds, a mixture of fear and rising excitement.

"Cairenn." Her father's voice was a warning.

"He came from the sea, didn't he?" She leaned in to her younger sister, Dairine. "How else could he have survived the surf otherwise?"

Little Dairine nodded, her mind full of innocence. Her two younger brothers stared with their fingers in their mouths, their thoughts whirling. Fiona was at that awkward age when growing girls feign constant disinterest, but her mind was open and waiting.

Little Dairine whispered. "Is it true?"

"I think so," Cairenn said, knowing the lie wouldn't hurt. "His skin is hidden on the strand somewhere. It'd be a slick black skin that he'd pull over him to swim back into the ocean with his brother and sister seals."

Maybe it was the lie that brought her mother's attention from the hearth where she poked at the whitefish she'd roasted upon the stones, or maybe it was just her mother's special sense of knowing. "The first of you who finds that skin," her mother announced, "will receive some sea-treasure from the selkie, no doubt."

In a flash, her brothers and sisters shoved the last of dinner in their mouths and dashed out the front door.

Cairenn gave her mother a grateful smile. Her mother's most powerful gift was a heightened sense of knowing the present as well as the future, so her mother understood Cairenn's intent hardly before she did herself.

"Niall." Her mother eyeballed her eldest son, still digging into his fish. "You go with your brothers and sisters and see that they collect winkles while they're searching."

Niall kicked up to alertness. "But—"

"Would you have Dairine drown while racing out to the rocks?"

Niall suppressed a sigh and cast Cairenn a resentful glance. In her mind she heard his voice as clear as a bell. *Your fault.* He shoved the last of his dinner in his mouth, swung his leg over the bench, and strode out into the sunshine.

Only when she heard the last of their voices

fade did she place her knife on the table and break the expectant silence.

"Da," she said, "I can't read the mind of this stranger."

She didn't have the courage to look at either of her parents, though she felt her mother's gaze upon her. Since the first day she discovered her gift, falling to her knees in agony on the Galway shore, Cairenn had always considered her talent more of a curse than a blessing. What advantage did it give her? Unlike Niall, she could not go to the heights and play the music that flowed in her. Unlike Aileen, she could not go to her father's side and use her gift to heal people. All she could do was pierce the veils of human thought and suffer what she was forced to know.

She couldn't even leave the island.

"Cairenn," her father said, his mind straining with patience, "a wounded man often loses his memory. A knock on the head, a swelling under the skull, and then all is fog."

She saw her father's vision of Lachlan, buoyed on the waves, knocked up against the great boulders in the channel.

"It's not like that, Da."

"His mind is as battered as his body." He picked up a piece of fish and weighted it between his fingers. "You should learn to recognize this."

"When I look at him, I cannot see a thing beyond his eyes."

Her father frowned. "Is that what this selkie foolishness is about?"

"Have you another explanation as to why, with

him, my mind is blind?" She'd not soon forget the feel of his muscles moving against her as he stood by the window. "For I'd like to hear it, I would."

She regretted the sharp words the moment they left her mouth. She did not make it a habit to speak to her father so, but her frustration was like a screeching flock of seagulls in her head. This gift that shackled her to this island had only one, single benefit—using it, she could keep her family safe by knowing the thoughts and intents of the strangers who ventured to their home. Without that benefit, what use was it?

What use was *she*?

Her mother's hand fell upon her head. She glanced up and wished she could read her mother's mind and see the fate that her mother kept secret from her.

"It's not easy, this gift you have," her mother said. "Even in the best of times, you see only the darkness, the sins, and the lies that men try to hide."

Sean the fisherman's envy over his cousin's coracle. Sean's wife's lustful thoughts of Padraig of Inishmore. Tadgh's theft of coins from the roof-thatch of the hut of his own blind grandmother, coins spent on whores and ale in Galway. Men undressing every woman they look upon, bending them down in their minds. Women slashing the faces of rivals with their kitchen-knives.

She shook her head as if that would help shake her free of the things she wished she didn't know.

"You've grown wise these years," her mother continued, "and have learned to keep your counsel. This is a thing not many with your gift would be able to do."

"Niall appreciates it," she blurted. In her mind, she could already see him sneaking around to the widow's hut by the sea.

"Perhaps we have been unwise, Conor." Her mother brushed her hand over Cairenn's hair as if she were Dairine at bedtime. "Perhaps we shouldn't have kept Cairenn safe on this island for so long, away from other people, strangers and mainlanders."

Cairenn felt her heart leap.

"You did not see her collapse that day." Her father frowned. "You did not try to staunch pain for which there was no visible wound."

Through Da's mind she saw herself, barely thirteen years old, collapse on the mud of the strand outside Galway, her eyes rolling so that nothing showed but the whites. Through his mind she saw that her face had been the color of a gray, salt-stained sail. All that she really remembered was a cacophony of thoughts exploding from the city of Galway and funneling into her brain with such force that she'd felt as if her skull would explode from the inside. In the days that followed, pain was her only companion, until she finally came to a shaky alertness on the pallet that Lachlan now inhabited.

That was when her father stopped taking her to Galway, or even allowing her off the shore.

Funny how the one thing you're forbidden to do becomes the thing your heart longs for the most.

"She was young, Conor," her mother said quietly. "Her gift was new."

"And still is," he countered.

"How will it mature, if you don't let her test the limits?"

"I will not lose another daughter, Deirdre, I will not."

Her spirits sank. She knew Da had her best interests in mind, but she could not deny her yearnings. Unless Cairenn could find another moment to talk Seamus into going on their adventure, she'd be spending her days walking the length and breadth of Inishmaan—the whole stretch of her whole world—only to experience in other people's minds the places she could never see.

Her mother said, "Maybe our new patient can be of help."

Cairenn sensed a thought passing between them, high above her, moving so fast that not even she could catch it. It was like that with her ma and da. People in love had a special way of communicating that had nothing to do with fairy-gifts and everything to do with the kind of trusting closeness that she would never have.

"A blade needs a whetting stone, yes?" Her mother turned her swirling gaze on Cairenn. "Maybe your whetting stone is this Scotsman."

CHAPTER FOUR

Black spots appeared in his vision as Lachlan slumped into a sitting position on the peat-pile just outside the sickroom. The doctor would probably blister him for disobeying orders, but he was tired of lying about. He had to get out of the dim room. He had to feel the sunshine on his face and know he was living on the earth. He had to get strong soon, so he could return to Scotland, tell his father he was alive, and unmask the men who wanted them all dead.

Then he saw an angel emerge from the darkness of a doorway to drift like a feather across the courtyard. The sea breeze batted tendrils of her pale hair out of its braid. Her tunic, in a deep shade of sea-blue, flattened against her legs. Cowhide shoes covered her feet. She hesitated as she saw him sitting there, but not for long. The color in her cheeks deepened as she approached.

She held out a bowl. "I've brought you some

dinner."

He slipped his palm under the bowl to take it, by happenstance brushing her fingers with his own. She snapped her hand back.

He said nothing but couldn't ignore her reaction. He usually didn't strike fear in women. In fact, the looks he usually got were of a much more flirtatious type. Then again, this was no dark-eyed, dusky-haired, Italianate *mignotta* standing before him. But he couldn't imagine what this woman might fear, considering his weakened state.

Well, he was sitting here shirtless in nothing but his braies.

He pulled the bowl onto his lap. "Fish, I see."

"Aye. A selkie's favorite."

"I prefer herring. But I'll just get that for myself once you find my skin."

"It may be sooner than you think." She tipped her head toward the opening in the stone gates. "My brothers and sisters are off looking for it now."

"I saw a horde of them shouting as they raced out of the courtyard a while back. Are they all your siblings?"

"Seven out of eight are living here now. There may soon be a ninth, with the way my father looks at Ma."

If she looks anything like you, lass, I've no doubt of it.

"My older sister is gone off and has started a family of her own." She tugged at the hem of a tightly-laced sleeve as if she wanted to pull the cloth over her fingers. "She lives in Wales now, married to one of Prince Llywelyn's knights."

He raised his brows. Wales was far from these islands. Prince Llywelyn of Wales was currently engaged in a battle with the English for control of the marshes. How a lass from such a remote place became the wife of a knight was a tale he'd very much like to hear.

"The reason why my brothers and sisters ran," she said, still fussing with the sleeve-laces, "is because they expect a gift from you if they find your skin."

His lips twitched. "So you have the whole brood convinced, then."

"I did what I must to get them out from underfoot. My mother ordered them to collect winkles while they were looking."

"I don't like winkles." He dipped his fingers into the bowl to scoop up some of the fish. "Too much trouble to break the shells. And the shards get caught in my whiskers."

There it was, a ghost of a smile, flittering across her face, causing her eyes to arc in something like humor.

A beginning.

He bent his head to dinner. The meat was sweet, roasted, and seasoned liberally with pepper. Somehow it didn't surprise him that Conor of Inishmaan would have a supply of the rare spice. The food melted in his mouth and brought with it a blind hunger. When next he looked up, his fingers were greasy with oil and the bowl was empty.

She raised a finely-arched brow. "You'll live, I think."

"Your father says as much."

"You're pale as a fish's belly."

He suppressed a laugh, because laughing tensed the muscles of his ribs, and that pulled on the wound. "My skin was once a lot darker," he said, "but it's been years since I basked under the Roman sun."

"Rome?" She perked up. "You've been there?"

"I studied there." He probably shouldn't have mentioned that, but she must have figured out by now he was no sheep's herder. "The sun is so fierce it toasts a man brown. I prefer the kinder warmth of your island's sun."

"Well you've lost a lot of blood," she said, once again finding interest in some far horizon. "My father advises rest—"

"—rest, ale, and no sudden movements that could tear the stitches."

"He can be a tyrant." Her voice went soft. "We all dreaded coming to the sick house when we were little, taken by ague, or a spotted disease, or if we broke a bone climbing the cliffs. I can still taste the bitter brews he forced down our throats. Not a twinkle of sympathy."

"Nine children, all living. That's the true testament to his skill."

"He's the best doctor in all of Ireland."

"Spoken with a daughter's pride."

He liked her smile. It made a dimple deepen in her cheek. Her eyes gleamed, even if she cast her fair lashes down in an attempt to hide her humor.

She reached for the bowl. He didn't want to give it to her. She was likely to take it back to the kitchens and leave him sitting here alone. Yet he didn't want to be the man who frightened her, either, so he handed it over and this time made sure not to touch her fingers.

She shifted the bowl between one hand and the other and hesitated, casting her gaze to the kitchens and back.

"It's a fine strong place you live in, so high on the island," he said, with rising hopes that she'd stay a while longer. "Has your family always lived here?"

"My da built it before any of us were born."

He eyed the well-hewn stones of the walls, the close fit of the thatch, and the patterned flagstones of the courtyard that reminded him of Moorish mosaics. "A man of many talents, your father."

"He brought my mother here from France." She wandered closer to the peat-pile like a skittish young mare, curious but wary. "From a place called Troyes. He'd been hired to tend to her because she was very sick. Eventually, he stole her away from her family and married her."

She took a seat upon the peat logs, though at an arm's distance. He felt a charge of excitement far stronger than was healthy for a man in his condition.

"Your home," he said, smelling the brine of the sea and the sun-warmed stones, "it reminds me a little of my own."

"My da says Scotland isn't so far away. He's been to many places."

"I see why he settled here." The Scotland he knew was grim and gray, colored by rising danger, but when he was a child it had seemed a brighter place. He supposed everyone remembered their childhood in such a way. "The light here is white and bright. It seems to come from the air rather than from the sun."

"You'll have to meet my brother, Niall. He's a poet and says things like that all the time."

"You've a brother who's a poet?"

"A harpist, more like. But he tells the tales so well you think you're living them."

"So he's the one who has to answer for putting this idea of selkies in your head?" She flushed a little and it was a glorious thing.

"I can't blame him for that," she said. "And that's enough of your teasing, thank you very much."

He traced her fine profile against the bright blue sky for so long that she turned to him in the stretching silence. She had green eyes like fresh hazel-shoots in the springtime, full of curiosity.

"I have a confession," he said.

She dropped her gaze. "The priest comes to the village near the shore on Sundays—"

"My confession is only for you."

Her throat flexed. "I tremble to hear it then."

"I've been teasing you about thinking I'm a selkie," he said, "but when I first laid eyes on you, I was sure you were an angel."

In the silence that followed he watched the quickening rise and fall of her breasts under the fine wool of her gown.

"Lass," he whispered. "Are you ever going to tell me your name?"

***

"Cairenn."

Her name tumbled off her lips and nothing could have stopped it. She was supposed to be finding a way through the walls in his mind, but instead here she sat on the peat-pile with her heart racing in her chest, snared in a trap of her own making.

She glanced away from the blue blade of his gaze and saw that he'd taken a tress of her hair and curled it around his hand, trapping her as sure as if he were about to drag her into the sea.

"Cairenn."

He gave her name a burr she'd never heard before, a sound that rubbed against her like a cat against her leg.

He whispered, "Does someone own your heart, lass?"

Who could she trust her heart to, when she knew the weaknesses of every man on the island?

"The men on this island must be blind," he said into the silence, "to leave such a beauty unmarried."

"It's a very small island."

"And your father keeps you close."

That much was true, even if she couldn't tell him the reason why. "Doesn't every father keep his daughters close?"

He narrowed his eyes a bit, as if contemplating her question, and then shifted his weight and changed the subject. "On the day you found me," he said, "what were you doing upon the shore?"

She huffed a frustrated breath. How maddening it was not to understand why he bounced from one idea to the next.

"Winkles," she lied. "I was collecting them from the stones."

She certainly wasn't going to tell him that she was coercing a young man to row her off shore just so she could imagine what it was like to venture unafraid into the world.

"Your mother must cook a powerful lot of winkles." He gave her a half-smile that made his eyes laugh.

She shrugged, unnerved. She didn't know what he was thinking, what he expected of her. It was like finding one's way along the cliff side blind, when any wrong move would send her reeling into open space.

Her mother's advice rang in her head. *Learn to read this man, and maybe you'll finally master your gift.*

She took a deep breath. For years she had lived only among her family and the village folk, whose thoughts tended to drift to the caring of the cows, or the flow of the herring. She knew their troubles and their fantasies, their worries and their wishes. Despite her father's strictures, she had learned how to keep to the edge of the village and not be overwhelmed by their chatter. Over the years, their collective thoughts had become part of the sounds of the world, as constant as the rumble of the sea.

She had taught herself how to do that. She'd managed to learn it without collapsing under the assault of their minds, as she had outside the teeming city of Galway. Now her mother believed she could teach herself how to read this man, too.

Perhaps, she thought, all she needed to do was

get a little closer.

She slid down a fraction on the peat pile. She lifted her hand between them, waiting for him to say something or stop her or do anything except stare at her with increasing intensity. When he didn't move, she slid her hand across his jaw and felt the bristle of his unshaven cheek rasp against her palm.

Shock registered in those fathomless eyes, but he did not flinch.

"I just . . . want to check for fever," she said. "Da has ordered me to look after you for now."

Lachlan did feel warm, but that was not what seized her attention. When she touched him she felt an associated softening of his mind, a flexing like the pliability of a new pair of calfskin boots. She dared to mentally probe a little deeper, hoping to find a weakness that would let her slip into his thoughts.

Nothing moved, it seemed, not the scuttling white clouds above, not the breeze that had only moments ago been sweeping across the hill, not the birds nesting in the thatch above their heads. Sound thickened, muffled, as if the sea had receded, and the gulls stilled to glide soundlessly on the updrafts, and all she could hear in her ears was the frantic beating of her own heart.

It was strangely soft, this half-beard beneath her hand. Some of those bristles were dark, some reddish in color, all catching the glint of the sun. A pulse by his ear beat against her fingertip. His lips parted and she saw the gleam of his tongue, but no words left his mouth.

Concentrate.

She was close enough to hear his unsteady breathing and see the pulse in his throat throbbing. She knew she had to look into his eyes but she hesitated to lift her gaze from the fascination of his cheek. Finally she did, and oh, how the flood came. A cascade of sensation that had everything to do with the intensity of his stare, the sudden tightness of his lips, and the flexing of a muscle in his cheek as he searched her face with as much unbound curiosity as she used to search his.

There was no mistaking what he was thinking. His mind was as blocked to her now as it had ever been, but she read with different senses than the one she was trying to hone. He was so beautiful, from the divot in his chin, to the sweep of the scar by his eye, and to the strange beauty of his midnight-blue eyes, dark and full of stars. She couldn't read his mind because she was too busy thinking about what it would feel like if he kissed her.

Suddenly his hand covered hers. He peeled her fingers off his cheek and lowered her hand so it lay, palm up, between them. He scraped one thumb over the tender skin at the inside of her wrist. She felt that touch all through her body.

"Warm," he said, his voice a rumble. "I can feel the rush of your blood."

She felt it, too, throbbing through her veins, making her as breathless as if she'd raced the whole length of Inishmaan.

"It seems, Cairenn, that we're both very human."

CHAPTER FIVE

The palm of her hand had tasted like pepper.

It seemed right that she would taste of a spice that had been harvested in India, carried by camels across Arabia, and shipped to Venice, so that flecks would end up here, flavoring the palm of a woman who did not look like part of this world.

He watched a pulse jump in her wrist where her hand lay in his lap. He glanced up to see a look in those sea-green eyes that spoke of wanting, yearning.

Then a shadow fell over them and Cairenn yanked her hand away.

"You disobeyed my orders."

The doctor loomed before them. The man had a sack slung across his shoulder, and his eyes were as cold as glacier ice.

"Yes, I rose from my pallet." Lachlan kept his voice even because this father, with his anvil of a jaw, looked capable of committing murder. "I thought it would do me good. A man gets soft lying about all the long day."

"Straining what's left of your stitches will delay your healing, and your departure."

"I'll venture no farther than this peat pile."

"You've ventured too far already."

The doctor's nostrils flared. Lachlan realized they weren't talking about his stitches anymore. It had been a long time since Lachlan had had to deal with an angry father, yet he knew the doctor had reason for his fury. Just a moment ago Lachlan had been thinking about unlacing his daughter's sleeves. Just a moment ago, he'd been imagining the feel of her long, white throat and the softness of her skin below the neckline of her blue tunic.

"Cairenn," the doctor commanded, "your mother needs help in the kitchen."

She was up with a rustle of wool and gone across the courtyard like a bird darting out of cover.

To him, the physician barked, "Inside."

The doctor pushed open the door to the surgery, not waiting as Lachlan eased himself up from the peat-pile with a wince. Lachlan figured he would get no sympathy today. He wasn't looking forward to the doctor poking around the sore, itchy wound.

"Sit by the hearth." The doctor settled the sack on the table and pointed to the two stools by the fireplace. "Pray the stitches didn't split from your disobedience."

Using the doorframe and the furniture to brace himself, Lachlan made his way toward the hearth. Moments later the doctor strode up behind him and clattered a tray full of tools on the floor by his feet. They rattled and gleamed. Lachlan felt the cold edge of a knife as the doctor slid a blade under his linen bandages. He flinched from memory rather than pain. He knew this doctor wouldn't finish the assassin's work, even if the man was furious that he'd found Lachlan flirting with his daughter. The doctor was just making his fury known by destroying perfectly good, washable linen.

The doctor flung the bloodstained cloth into the fire, peeling down to the layers closest to the skin. Feeling resistance, the healer tugged on a piece that stuck to the scabs with nothing that approached gentleness.

Trickles of warm blood slid down Lachlan's naked back.

"As I suspected." The healer grunted. "You've split two stitches. And there's new swelling around the needle-wounds."

Lachlan stayed silent, figuring that anything he said would only inflame the situation more.

"The stitches have to go." The doctor leaned down to pick up a tool. "That means that, from here on, nothing will keep the edges of this wound together but the thin skin that's formed in the gap over the past week. A wise man would stay still if he doesn't want to wake up in a puddle of his own blood."

Lachlan tightened his jaw as he felt the tool press against his flesh, tugging a stitch until it burned.

"And now that you deem yourself healthy enough to sit in the sun of my courtyard," the doctor continued, tugging and pressing and yanking, "we'll talk about you writing a letter to the father you've been worrying about, to send a ship to fetch you home."

The words were out of Lachlan's mouth before he even thought of speaking them. "I meant your daughter no harm."

"We're not talking about my daughter."

"She found me on the beach and brought me to you. I am not a man who would repay courtesy with dishonor."

"Lofty words. Easy to say, hard to live up to when the blood runs hot."

Lachlan flinched, for already in his mind lingered an image of the gap of Cairenn's neckline, where he'd seen the soft rise of her white breasts.

"There are a half dozen ships," the doctor continued, "now anchored in Galway Bay, but they are from Castile, Aragon, and London. There are no galleys from the Western Isles of Scotland, but there are bound to be some soon."

Lachlan curled his hands into fists under the relentless probing of that iron tool, but he couldn't avoid noticing that the doctor had pinpointed his homeland. Had he slipped and said something to Cairenn? He didn't remember doing so. Considering the man's facility with languages, the physician may have identified his upland accent to within a few roods of Loch Fyfe.

The thought made him uneasy. "My clansmen trade primarily with Ulstermen," Lachlan said, though this wasn't completely true. "Ulstermen wouldn't take kindly to me doing business with the Galway Tribes."

"So you know Ulstermen?"

"Some." He had cousins among the O'Neills.

"Then it'll be quicker to send someone overland rather than to wait for a galley." The doctor paused to clean blood and fibers from the hooked implement he'd been torturing him with. "You send word to your clansmen, and within a few weeks you'll reach home, resurrected."

Lachlan hesitated. "I've no coin to pay for a messenger."

"People pay me however they can—herring, peat, butter, the promise of favors, the labor of their own hands. Because of this, many men owe me favors." The doctor set to work in Lachlan's flesh again, twisting and tugging. "I can have a message delivered where it needs to go, the sooner to see you home."

Lachlan thought of his own father's distress and worry, but he also thought about the blade plunged in his back, and the three strangers who'd done it. Hired men by the looks of them, but hired by whom?

"So that's how it is." The doctor twisted the hook to snare a stitch. "You want to stay dead."

Lachlan grimaced, sweat popping out on his brow. "If the men who tried to kill me think they've succeeded, they may lay low for a time. Until I can swing a sword, staying dead is the wisest course."

"Death sometimes is. Even if it means great grief for those you love."

Lachlan puzzled over the comment as the doctor tossed the tool onto the tray and reached for a bowl of some greasy-looking stuff. The doctor slapped some on the wound. The pungency of the salve hit Lachlan's nose just as its burn seared into his back. Lachlan stiffened, barely hearing the doctor's sharp words to stay still.

"I take it," the doctor said, "that you don't know who wants you dead."

"Many would profit from my murder."

"That's the way of clans and chieftains, Lachlan of the Western Isles. Is that what you're telling me?"

Lachlan fixed his jaw. The doctor had already guessed that Lachlan wasn't a common yeoman, but now he was guessing something closer to the truth.

"Am I to believe," the doctor said, as he slapped more grease on his back, "that there is not a single friend in whom you can put your complete trust?"

"I trust my father," he said through gritted teeth, "but among those who surround him hides a serpent."

He'd been thinking about this, over and over, since the moment his mind had cleared from the pain. His most likely enemies were among the Campbells or the Lamonts, neighboring clans who were always starting trouble. But any man in the three septs of his own clan—the MacGilchrists or the Ewings or even someone among his own people, the MacEgans—had a motive to see him dead. Including his own Stuart stepmother, who looked at him with acid in her eyes for standing in line ahead of Fingal, his half-brother, her only son.

The doctor said, "I have men whom I trust. I'll order that the messenger speak to your father only."

"Such news can't be contained. Once it's delivered, it'll be a race for who will reach me first, my father or his enemies." The burn of the salve eased, leaving a stretch of his back throbbing. "Sending word of my survival would only put your family in danger, Conor of Inishmaan."

The healer clanked the clay bowl of demonic salve back on his tray and fumbled about for something else.

"Once I'm better, I'll hire onto a ship," Lachlan said, sensing the healer's frustration. "I can pass as a common sailor—"

"With this wound?" The doctor tossed the end of the linen across Lachlan's shoulder. "It'll be weeks before you have full use of it."

"Am I to be crippled, then?"

"You'll be able to wield a dagger eventually. Swinging a claymore will take more time. Pulling hemp ropes? That'll rip the muscle for sure."

"I'll heal faster than you think—"

"I'm counting on that. Until then, you'll stay here until you're stronger or until your secrets wash up on my shore."

"The only secrets I hold, Conor of Inishmaan, are those that will keep you and your family safe—"

"She's not an ordinary girl."

Lachlan swallowed his words. Not just because of what the doctor said, but for the rough, raw way in which he said it.

"I've kept her safe on this island for a long time," the doctor continued, "away from the worst of the world."

He couldn't blame the man for wanting to hide such a beauty from men's eyes, but he knew the doctor would not appreciate hearing such words from him.

"Cairenn can't leave this island," the doctor said, "without experiencing devastating pain."

Lachlan frowned. What strange affliction would bind a woman to a place? No doubt, if he asked, the doctor would spit out some Latin name for the condition, but Lachlan's Latin wasn't so good that he would be able to determine if the disease was real or just a construct dreamt up by an overprotective parent.

"My eldest daughter, Aileen, is off in Wales," the healer continued, as if he were yanking out each word. "It was she who most often helped me in this surgery." The doctor stood up and seized the tray of implements. "Now that she is gone, Cairenn has taken her place." The doctor strode with a heavy tread to his worktable, where he slammed down the instruments with more force than necessary. "I have business on the mainland that will take me away from here for a week or more. When I leave, it will be Cairenn who will see to you. Alone."

The doctor stopped fussing. He swiveled on his heel and fixed his gaze upon Lachlan. Lachlan forcibly tamped down his excitement at the thought of being alone with the green-eyed beauty. It was unworthy to let his thoughts drift in that direction, and disrespectful to both her and the healer. And considering the many obligations he'd left behind in Loch Fyfe, he should know better.

"*When* I am back with my father," Lachlan said, "I assure you that my gratitude will be matched in coin—"

"Don't speak to me of coin."

The doctor yanked open a drawer and seized what lay within. He loosed the string of a rawhide sack and, with one violent sweep of his hand, hurled the contents across the floor.

Coins clattered around Lachlan's feet, coins with the imprint of strange faces upon them, coins of sizes and shapes that he'd never seen, all of them minted of gold finer than much of the jewelry his Stuart stepmother loved to wear.

Suddenly the healer loomed over him. "There are things you are too young to understand, boy. And there are secrets I'm unwilling to share." The doctor leaned in so that there was no way Lachlan could avoid looking him in the eye. "The only treasure in the world is one's wife, one's children, and one's family. All the gold from Persia to Arabia wouldn't meet the worth of a single hair on their heads."

The physician's blue eyes blazed with a fierce light. Lachlan no longer doubted what he'd come to suspect: This healer had once been a knight, a warrior, perhaps even a chieftain. In all ways, a formidable opponent.

"The last time a foreign warrior came to Inishmaan," the doctor said, "he stole away my eldest daughter."

An expression rippled through the fury on the doctor's face, an expression of grief and unbearable loss.

"If you want to repay me," the healer said, "then swear not to do the same."

CHAPTER SIX

"The selkie?" Dairine's gray eyes widened. "He's coming *here*?!"

Kneeling by the hearth in the kitchen, Cairenn tugged at the soaked laces of her ten-year-old sister's pampooties, sensing Dairine's mental squeal of excitement and anticipation. It was good to know that Cairenn wasn't the only one who felt those things when considering their mysterious stranger.

"Aye," Cairenn said, as the sound of thunder rumbled through the thatch, louder than the babbling of their brothers and sisters in the room. "With this storm brewing, am I to leave our guest all alone under a separate roof?"

"But we haven't found his skin yet." Dairine gripped the edge of the stool and leaned forward so no one else in the room could hear. "With the rain coming and the fog sweeping in, he's sure to realize he doesn't belong. He'll rush to the strand and find his skin and go away and then he can't come back for *seven years*."

She caught an image in Dairine's mind of the young girl's frantic search for sealskin on the strand, dangerous forays below the waterline, and squealing races away from the pounding surf. Cairenn knew she should scold her sister for recklessness, but no harm had come of her antics. Dairine's gift seemed to be that she always had an angel watching over her.

"This selkie thinks he's a normal man, remember that." Cairenn slipped one of the wet booties off and tipped it to pour rainwater upon the hearth. "If you say nothing, he'll act just like any other man."

"Like Da and Niall?"

"Aye," she said, then leaned in and whispered, "but with less brooding and dreaming."

As Dairine giggled, thunder cracked overhead, shivering the rushes of the roof. A drop slipped through the thatch and hit the back of Cairenn's neck. Flames jumped under the two pots burbling over the peat fire.

"Speaking of our guest," her mother said, twirling a wooden stake in the soup. "You'd best fetch him now, Cairenn, before you can't get across the yard."

Cairenn put the booties beside the hearth to dry and gave her sister a tweak on the nose. Clambering to her feet, she avoided her brother Niall's eye though she heard his thoughts clearly enough. The moment her da had announced he was off to the mainland and that it was Cairenn's responsibility to see to Lachlan, Niall's mind had it up with mischief. Now her brother was mentally dancing in glee, his thoughts running with ideas for love-match songs to sing once the so-called selkie swept into their presence.

She gave her brother a sharp kick as she passed. He jumped, but then grinned and thrummed a chord on his willow-bark harp.

Outside, the rain fell slantwise. It was hours before sunset, but the world had gone gray. Black-bellied clouds boiled in the sky above. It was an angry summer storm, and she'd seen enough of those to know it would be full of harsh wind and biting rain and earth-shaking thunder and lightning that would brighten the whole sky. The heavenly fire might even touch down, here and there, leaving ashy spots upon the heights.

It would be a breach of courtesy to leave a stranger alone in his room to weather such gales, wondering if the end of days had come. At least, with her family around, she'd be less likely to make a fool of herself as she had yesterday sitting on the peat-pile.

She ran across the courtyard and flung herself into the surgery, pressing the door shut against the wind. Scraping her hand through her hair to clear it from her eyes, she blinked into the room and saw him standing with his back to her, outlined by the red glow of the fire.

Her breath caught. Sporting only his linen braies, his skin was burnished by the firelight. A long furrow defined the valley of his spine, from between his shoulders to just above his braies, a narrow hollow she couldn't help but linger upon.

Such was the shape of the legendary Fenian warriors, she thought, of *Cú Chulainn,* and of Deirdre's handsome Naoise. Her experience was limited, but surely there wasn't another man in the world who looked like this.

She glanced up and felt his gaze like a rough hand on her throat.

"You didn't have to brave the rain." He turned his attention back to the fire. "Your father left me enough food to last days."

"It's not dinner I've come to deliver." She glimpsed an uneaten loaf of oaten bread and a pot of fish stew warming upon the swing arm. "There's a gale coming."

"I hear it." He planted a hand on the stones above the hearth, leaning in. "It reminds me of the winter storms of my home, the way the wind and rain shiver the air."

An image came to her mind of a cold, shroud-covered place, but the image was born of his words, not of his mind. If she did not believe the evidence of her eyes, she would think she stood in this room alone.

She mustn't brood over that now. "We've made a place for you at our table in the kitchen."

"I'll do well enough here."

The muscles of his outstretched arm tightened. She had more than an inkling about why his words were short and his voice tense. Her father had given Lachlan a talking-to after he'd caught them at the peat-pile yesterday. It frustrated her that she didn't know the full of the discussion, for she'd only caught fragments from Da. Da, having *Sídh* blood like everyone else in her family, could sometimes be hazy to read.

Well, Da might want this Scotsman to keep his distance from her, but Da had also demanded that she look after the man.

"I don't think you understand," she said. "The gales sweep in from the far edge of the world. Even the easiest of them can rip the thatch from the roofs."

"A bit of rain won't do me harm."

"I won't leave a guest here while the storm rages. It would bring shame upon my family—"

"I'm an intruder. Not a guest."

"You're my father's patient, and thus far more important than the cows, and we've already brought them in under a roof."

"I'd prefer this pallet than sleeping among cows—"

"Don't be foolish. The cows are in the storeroom that opens to the lee side. We've got a pallet made up for you in the main room with the rest of us."

Heat rose to her cheeks, for in the silence after she'd spoken she realized that they'd be sleeping in the same room together. Her mother would insist that she and her sisters stay on one side of the room and Lachlan and her brothers on the other, but now she couldn't help imagining blinking her eyes open in the night and catching his gaze across the space that separated them.

"I cannot join you," he said, "wearing nothing but my braies."

Lightning flashed bright, painting his all-but-naked body in silver. She stood still while the image burned into her mind until the thunder followed, startling her into breathing again.

"My father," she said, feeling strangely tingly, as if the lightning had hit close, "keeps some of his clothing here in case his tunic gets—" *bloody* "—soiled." She walked behind the table to a chest pushed against the wall. The wet hem of her tunic slapped against the rushes as she knelt. She pulled out a linen shirt and an overtunic. "You're of the same height, so these should fit."

His shadow fell over her. She handed the linen shirt up to him blindly. When he didn't take it from her, she dared to meet his eye.

He tilted his head toward his injured shoulder, his face grim.

Da had told her that it would take weeks for Lachlan's shoulder to heal, weeks before the man could even raise his elbow to the level of his shoulder. Her heart did a skip-jump as she realized she'd have to help him dress.

Better he be clothed, she thought, than standing above her with the firelight gleaming off all those naked, swelling muscles.

She stood to face him, feeling very small in the dark corner of the room. She smelled the pungent herbs from the salve her father used upon his wound. She shook out the linen shirt. The arm-holes were generous, but she loosened the drawstring to make the neckline as wide as possible. Rolling the shirt up from the hem, she stepped closer.

She raised her arms as he ducked. She swept the linen over his head. His soft hair brushed her cheek as he straightened. His gaze was a blade, inches from hers. She didn't need to see into his thoughts to know that he was remembering that moment out in the sun.

She fell back on her heels, stuttering, "The bad arm first."

She tugged the shirt down his arm as far as it could go so that he could slip his hand into the armhole of the sleeve. She couldn't meet his eye, but she saw the tightness of his jaw, and the way a pulse throbbed under the crescent scar on his temple. The muscles of his neck strained as his hand caught on the seams, but with a grunt he slid his arm through.

His other arm slipped through with less trouble. The linen strained across his shoulders and outlined the muscles of his chest. She reached for the overtunic but he snatched it away from her.

"I'm not so much of an invalid that I can't do this myself."

Pride, she thought. She turned back to the chest to let him struggle in privacy.

She put her hand amid the cloth in the chest, seeking a belt, but she hardly saw anything. Her body was cold and hot at the same time, shivery and flushed, and it wasn't because she was still soaked from the rain. It occurred to her that these uncontrollable feelings that flowed through her might be the cause of her faltering extra sense. If she could stop feeling like her heart was in her throat every time he looked at her, then maybe that blackness would shift.

He said, "Well?"

She startled and reached for the first thing she found—a length of hemp rope. As she rose to her feet he lifted his good arm, giving her leave to wrap the rope around him. For all his muscles, he had lean hips. When she tied the belt, there was a lot of rope hanging.

He looked down at himself. "I look like a monk."

Cairenn thought he didn't look *at all* like a monk, though she had to admit that such clothes, on another man, might.

"That rope belt may be from a monk," she said, as thunder rumbled above them. "They still come to the island, now and again. They live in the little rock huts that face out to the sea. They fast and pray and sometimes get sick and need a doctor."

He gestured to the trunk. "Is there a stretch of canvas in there as well?"

"For what?"

"To shield us from the storm when we cross the courtyard."

She hazarded a glance toward the door. "My father left his cloak. We can use that."

He walked toward the door and slipped the mantle off the hook. He took one end of it with his good hand and she took the other. Pressing against his bad arm, she helped pull the billowing wool over their heads.

In the circle of his warmth, she was suddenly reluctant to leave. "I should warn you about my family."

"Why? Have they horns and goat's feet?"

"People think we're odd, living up in this

lonely place on the height." She bit her lower lip, wondering what to tell him without actually telling him. "Keeping so much to ourselves, sometimes we act in ways that outsiders find strange."

"Are you all trying to kill each other?"

"Of course not."

"Then we're sure to get along better than my own clan."

He put an end to the conversation by pushing the door open with his foot. The rain hit them like cold needles as they stepped into the courtyard. Bowing her head against the wind, she curbed the urge to race across the yard in deference to his injury. The door to the main house opened before they reached it—Niall had been watching. They ducked in.

Through Dairine's mind, Cairenn saw the two of them sweep into the room, the black woolen mantle flying around them like a loose seal's skin. The thought was echoed in the minds of her younger brothers whose terrified wonder blossomed like the morning glories that opened at sunrise where they climbed upon the walls. She saw Niall's surprise at the size of the man, his sudden insecurity about being the protector of the household. Her mother's thoughts were guarded but Cairenn felt a curiosity flood through her, and something else, too, something muted but warm that Cairenn could only guess was welcome.

The table was set, the bowls of soup steaming, everything ready, and every last one of her family had been waiting for them.

Lachlan tugged the mantle until she released it.

He caught it with his good hand and hung it on the wooden hook by the door.

"A blessing upon this house," Lachlan said, bowing his head toward her mother, "and all those under its roof."

"A hearty welcome to you, Lachlan," her mother said. "Join us at our table."

There was a great rush toward the trestle table as Cairenn's younger brothers and sisters climbed over one another to take their places, excited and fearful at the same time to be the one who sat closest to the selkie. Her mother sat at one end of the table, her brother Niall at the other. She took the place on Niall's right.

"Lachlan," she said, as she gestured for him to sit across the table from her, "this is my brother Niall."

Lachlan lifted a leg over the bench, "The harpist?"

Niall nodded. His mind was racing, sizing the man up, and cataloging every possible weapon within reach.

"I know a harpist," Lachlan said, "by the name of Donal MacLean. He's famous through the Western Islands. You'll play later?"

I'll play a sleep-song for sure.

Niall's thought was like a slap. There was magic in Niall's music, and her brother was fixing to use it as a weapon.

"Niall plays only if the feeling moves him," she said, giving her brother an eye. "But maybe we can coax him into playing something soft and *harmless.*"

A love song then?

"No."

Lachlan glanced at her sharply, and that's how she knew she'd spoken aloud to Niall's unspoken thought.

"Please," her mother said, drawing everyone's attention. "This soup is best eaten while it's still hot."

Cairenn dipped her spoon and lifted it to her lips like everyone else at the table, but she didn't taste a drop. Dairine quivered beside her like a plucked harp-string and Cairenn sensed the instant her curious little sister couldn't keep silent anymore.

Dairine blurted, "You talk funny, Lachlan."

Her mother tsked. "Dairine—"

"But it's true! It's like he rolls his words in his mouth before he says them."

Lachlan smiled. "You've never met a Scot, little lass?"

"I met a Gascon once," she said. "Ma talked to him, babble babble babble, and it didn't make any sense at all." Dairine's face crumpled in concentration the way it did sometimes when Ma was trying to teach her numbers. "And once Da healed a sailor whose skin was as black as charred peat. He even let me touch his skin to see if the darkness would rub off."

Lachlan's eyes crinkled at the corners. "Such creatures you've had at your table."

"You must be a really good swimmer," her sister continued, "to have made it to the strand the day Cairenn found you."

"I am, though I'm glad to be out of the sea now."

"But why?"

"So I can be sitting near a warm fire, eating this fine soup with kind folk like you."

Will you take Cairenn to be your wife in the sea?

"Eat your soup, Dairine," Cairenn said, before the girl could speak her thought, "and stop asking so many questions."

"But—"

Cairenn raised a brow. Disappointment and frustration rippled through the girl, as well as a bit of rebellion. But though Dairine was reckless, she wasn't thoughtless.

Lachlan ventured, "So your name is Dairine, little lass?"

Her sister nodded.

"I have a half-sister a little older than you. I haven't seen her in a while, she's living with relatives. Elspeth is her name. She's just as curious and full of questions as you are, but she doesn't have any older sisters to boss her around."

Dairine covered a giggle with her hand. Cairenn wrinkled her nose at her playfully, but her mind was elsewhere. This talk of his siblings made her realize how little she knew about Lachlan's larger world. Normally when she looked into anyone's mind, she sensed the nearness of those they loved—parents, siblings, husbands, wives, lovers—so many points of warmth that permeated their thoughts.

In her mind, Lachlan had been as lonely as a

wolf on a mountaintop.

Naill spoke up. "Cairenn tells us that you've been to Rome."

"Did she?" Lachlan's gaze slid to hers.

Dairine piped, "Is Rome under the sea?"

"No, wee lass," he said, his gaze making Cairenn blush. "It's far away from here where it is always warm."

"Da has been to it," her brother Declan ventured from the other end of the table. "He says it's full of roads paved in stone and great bridges and it was a wonder to behold until the Vandals came."

Lachlan's brows twitched. "The Vandals you say? It's been centuries since that happened. Your father looks young for his age."

A joke, she thought, he meant it as a joke, but not a soul at the table laughed. From the cradle, they'd all been taught never to speak a word about their special gifts to strangers, and this kind of talk came perilously close.

Everyone turned at once to Ma as if they'd been the one to say too much. Then a great crack of lightning shook the timbers and everyone startled.

"Tell my brothers what you were doing in Rome, Lachlan," Cairenn said to smooth over the awkwardness. "It'll give them something to think about when they're laboring over their slates."

"I was studying." Lachlan looked from face to face with a deepening line between his brows. "There are great churches full of statues and paintings, and buildings made of massive blocks of stone the likes of which I'd never seen."

Niall said, "Most men go to Rome to become priests."

Wouldn't that be a bad bit of luck for you, my sister, if he were dedicated to celibacy.

"Careful, brother," she snapped, "or I'll poison your soup."

Lachlan watched the interchange intently. "I don't mind the questions," he ventured as a great howling wind rustled the roof. "It must seem like a curious thing, for a man to go all the way to Rome."

Dairine said, "Did you swim the whole way?"

"I took a ship." He gave Dairine a wink. "Easier on the fins."

Niall persisted despite her sharp kick. "So, Lachlan, you're not a priest then?"

"My uncle is a priest. He offered me a place to stay and granted me entry to the best private libraries in the city. I begged my father to let me go. I wanted to study architecture and there was no better place."

Niall's eyes had begun to dance. "So you plan to build a coliseum by the North Sea?"

"Nothing so grand." Lachlan waited until a new roll of thunder abated. "I want to build bridges over estuaries. There are lots of them where I come from, difficult to pass even in low tide. The mud can swallow a sheep."

Dairine said, "What's an estuary?"

"A place where the sea sends a finger across the land," Lachlan said. "It empties at low tide, fills up again at high tide. There are always lots of seals."

I like him. I hope Cairenn marries him so I can

visit the seals.

Lachlan glanced up at her again and Cairenn felt for a moment like he'd heard Dairine's thought—but of course he couldn't have.

"My compliments to you, mistress," Lachlan said, sliding a nod toward her mother. "I haven't tasted such fine soup for years. I like the winkles." He gave Dairine a wink. "I'll have to remember that when I return to the sea."

Dairine pressed close to the table. "So you'll be going back, then?"

"I'll be healed soon. Then this Scotsman will be gone from here and no more trouble to any of you."

Cairenn heard her mother speaking kind words about how Lachlan was no trouble at all, words lost in the whip-crack of another burst of lightning.

But all Cairenn heard was *I'll be gone.*

Her mother stood up. "Will you be having more, Lachlan?"

"I'd welcome it."

Then her mother came to Lachlan's side and did what her mother rarely did. She looked straight into Lachlan's eyes.

Lachlan jolted in his seat. Her siblings went wide-eyed. Cairenn's stomach tightened. What was her mother doing? He was an *outsider*. She tried to read her mother's thoughts, but the idea had no sooner passed through her mind when Ma broke the spell by patting Lachlan on the arm and taking the bowl to the burbling pot on the hearth.

It had only been a moment, but Lachlan sat blinking, following her mother's path with a confused gaze.

"Your bowl is empty, Niall." Cairenn stood up and swiped his bowl. "I'll get you more."

She joined her mother at the hearth where they stood with their backs to the room. She held out Niall's bowl as her mother began to ladle. Cairenn stretched out her thoughts to read her mother's mind, but her mother spoke first.

"He's a good man, daughter."

Cairenn frowned because she *didn't* know that—not for sure—and wasn't that the root of all the trouble? "What did you see, Ma?"

"You know better than to ask me such a question—"

"Ma." She gripped her wrist. "Tell me what you saw."

Her mother had the gift of the Sight. With one look, her mother could read a man's future—if the man could bear to stand strong under that swirling, unearthly gaze.

"I saw what he'll suffer, my daughter," her mother murmured, "if he persists in his path."

"And?"

Her mother looked up at her and lifted the veil between their minds.

Cairenn heard one billowing word.

Death.

CHAPTER SEVEN

Lachlan stood in the courtyard squinting against the bright sky as he mentally measured the length of the cottage's eaves against the pile of wood at his feet. Beside him, Niall rose up from his knees from where he'd been perusing Lachlan's plans drawn in the dust—sketches for a sluice to capture the moisture dripping from the thatch and shuttle it into a rain barrel.

"We don't have enough iron nails." Niall rubbed the prickle on his jaw. "Can't we tie the gutter to the thatch with rope?"

"Rope will rot in the salt air." Lachlan lifted his bad arm to shield his face from the sun and felt a sharp pinch in his shoulder, where, after a long week of rest, his body's weakness had narrowed and focused. "You'd have to change the rope whenever you changed the thatch. Wooden stakes will do." He toed over a few pieces of the spare wood. "You say you can carve?"

"Six harps, yew and ash and oak." The young man flashed a cocky smile. "Including the one you admired last night."

Lachlan remembered that it had been a fine harp, chiseled with a precise hand. "Digging a channel in a stretch of wood will be cruder work than that."

"It's always crude work when you've got nothing but a block of wood in front of you. I can carve a channel as you direct, especially if it means Ma won't have to lug as many pails of water from the spring."

Lachlan's mind shifted to the problem of the wooden stakes just when Cairenn walked into the courtyard through the cows' shed door. The sight of her blasted all the numbers and sketches and plans right out of his head.

She walked right up to them, all wind-teased hair and rosy lips. "Should I ask what you two are doing?"

Trying to get you out of my mind.

Niall said, "We're building a rainwater sluice."

"Getting out from under chores, that's what I think." She turned her bright gaze upon Lachlan. "So the books in the sickroom weren't enough to occupy you?"

His chest tightened. The dusty, dry tomes in the sickroom that she was referring to were no match for his growing restlessness this week, nor his heated thoughts about this woman. "Half of them are in Greek," he said. "The others in languages I don't recognize."

Her gaze flittered back to her brother. "You

know you shouldn't be whittling away on all this wood without asking Da."

"You know Da won't mind after I tell him it's for Ma's good."

"And you," she said, turning back to Lachlan. "Do you think you're healed enough to drive stakes into mortar?"

He knew he wasn't, but how he itched for the feel of a mallet in his hand. At Loch Fyfe, when his family was besieged by cattle-raiders and highwaymen, worn down by the complaints of clansmen, the gray weather, or a blight upon the sheep, he used to build something in order to occupy his hands, his people, and his mind with something other than claymores and fruitless searches for sly enemies.

"I didn't think so," she said into his silence, "but if you're feeling so hearty, there are other ways to hurry your healing. Today we'll take a walk to the height."

"Listen to you," Niall said. "Da puts responsibility in your hands and suddenly you're a tyrant—"

"And aren't you the one lording over us from the end of the table?"

"I'm man of the house now, and I won't be going on some idle walk—"

"Oh, I wouldn't dream of taking you away from carving, Niall. You stay here and whittle away." She tilted her head to a boy who'd sidled up beside her. "Seamus will be coming along with Lachlan and me."

Niall did not look happy about this. Since the

first night Lachlan had spent dinner with the family, Niall had taken it upon himself to follow Cairenn into the sickroom whenever she brought Lachlan his meals. Her brother loitered while Cairenn changed his dressings. Against his baser instincts, Lachlan had welcomed the young man as a reminder of his better intentions—and his promise to her father.

But the forced inactivity and Cairenn's frequent nearness made Lachlan half-mad with frustration. Niall's complaints about lugging water and the patter of frequent rain upon the thatch had brought to Lachlan's mind this idea for a sluice.

"Come, Lachlan," she said, squinting beyond him to the sky. "There's a skift of rain coming, I can smell it. We'd best go now."

Lachlan eyed the boy who would be a chaperone in Niall's place, a half-grown hulk of a man-child who didn't look like he'd be paying nearly as much attention as a wary sibling. Lachlan's blood surged despite his better intentions, but he couldn't come up with an excuse not to go with her.

She turned on her heel and headed toward the fort's wooden gate. Ignoring the glowering face of her brother, Lachlan set out after her, not watching the sway of her bottom. He didn't watch the way the breeze pulled at her sleeve as if to tug it off her slim shoulder. He didn't notice the way streaks of mud stretched across her sweetly curving hips where she'd wiped her hands, probably after tending to the cows this morning.

The stout hulk of a boy raced ahead, twirling and stumbling and half-dancing like a child set free of his tutor. They followed him through the cow-fields toward the rocky higher places. Lachlan hadn't been out of the courtyard since they'd carried him up the hill to the sickroom, and though he could see the world through the window, being surrounded by all this openness disoriented him.

Up ahead, the boy had already half dismantled one portion of the rock-pile fence to make it low enough for Cairenn to step over. Lachlan strode ahead to join Seamus picking up the fist-sized stones.

"You shouldn't be doing that," she said as she hurried up from behind.

"My arm will be limp as an eel if I don't use it."

"If my da—"

"Is he here, lass?"

"No, but if—"

"Then it'll be our secret."

He dropped to one knee to ease the stretch of his back. The stones were gritty and cold in his grip. Already the walk had done him good, for he could taste the salt in the air and smell the rain clinging to the grass. Even his ears seemed sharpened, for he heard not just the roaring of the ocean but also the lowing of the cows in farther pastures and the screech of a gull as it wheeled on an updraft.

Cairenn passed over the rock wall and Lachlan helped the boy seal it up behind her. He could tell the woman had something on her mind by the way she concentrated on the path as if it would lead to answers. Her back was stiff, her shoulders tense. As he caught up to her, he resisted the urge to recapture her attention by running a finger down the furrow of her back. She was a woman meant to be held and gently mussed and kissed until her lips swelled and she breathed her deepest wanting.

Enough.

He curled his hands into fists. This would end badly if he didn't lighten the air between them.

"It's a fine, lovely day, wouldn't you say, Cairenn?"

"I would, but it's not the fine, lovely day you're staring at."

So she'd noticed. No doubt it was his staring that had made her tense. They'd never be easy around each other if they didn't talk about this thickening awareness between them.

"Talking about the weather," he said, "is just my way of saying what I'm thinking without saying it."

"So it's a lie, then?"

"It's not a lie, lass. Just an easier way of letting my thoughts be known."

"If you want your thoughts to be known then you should speak them. Loud and clear so that everyone can hear."

"The world would be full of fighting and fury if everyone spoke so."

"So what you're thinking will shock me?"

He gazed at the far horizon as he sought a way to get out of this mess of his own making. "I'm saying your father wouldn't like it much."

"Wasn't it you who just reminded me he wasn't here?"

Caught as sure as a fish in a net. "He's a good

man, your father. He saved my life, I owe him my respect."

"Yet you allow your thoughts to run free about things you dare not speak."

"Come now, lass. A man's thoughts are best kept to himself when he's walking with a lovely woman."

Her eyes narrowed in that contemplative, puzzled way. "You're flirting with me, aren't you?"

"You're surprised."

"I know what flirting is," she retorted. "I've seen it happen during the thatching season."

I've seen it happen. Like she'd never experienced it herself. "Are there no men on this island with red blood running in their veins?"

She tilted her head and a little line appeared between her brows. "Is that a compliment? Are you saying—"

"—that you're a fine-looking lass as any I've known, if a bit slow when it comes to flirtation."

"Well, how am I to know what you're talking about, if you veil your true thoughts with false words?"

"The same way a man comes to know the mind of a woman. By getting to know her better."

A blush spread right to the roots of her hair. He watched it rise, then, distracted by the way strands of her hair flew around her face, he became jealous of the sea wind.

He tore his gaze from her and sought the far horizon. He'd spoken too bluntly. The sooner he changed the subject, the better for both of them.

"Wherever you're leading me, lass," he said,

"will there be a pint of ale at the end?"

"Not unless the fairies see to it. We'll be climbing to the dolmen stones up there."

In the distance he could see a lonely structure limned against the sky, two upright stones supporting a long, horizontal capstone. It brought to mind the hilltop at Loch Fyfe, at least the way it had been in his youth. In truth, this whole island stirred up a strange cauldron of youthful memories. There was something in the brightness of the white sun after a gale, the briny smell in the air, the way the rain clung to each blade of grass, glittering in the sideways light of the morning. He could almost imagine he was chasing Fingal and Elspeth across the hills, playing hide-and-seek amid the stones on the council height.

"Lachlan," Cairenn said, in a voice that sounded as if it were forced through her throat. "You're thinking of home, aren't you?"

Yes, but only to distract himself from thinking of what it would be like to kiss her until her knees faltered. "I'm always thinking of home. That dolmen reminds me of the place where my clan chooses their chieftain."

"And you want to go back soon."

"Considering what befell me, I won't rest easy until I lay my eyes upon my father again."

"But isn't it foolish to be eager to return to whatever made a man plunge a knife into your back?"

"Shall I abandon my people to our enemies, then?"

She raised her brows. "You talk of 'your

people' as if you are lord over them all."

He reached for deflection. "Your sister thinks I'm a king."

"That's my fault, because I told Dairine that your father is the king of North Sea seals. I told her that you ran away from your father because the princess he was trying to marry you off to has a chin full of whiskers."

He suppressed a snort. "You do have an imagination."

"But me, myself," she continued, as if he hadn't spoken, "I've been thinking on this for some time now. I can't decide whether your father is a merchant fighting over trading privileges, a baron fighting over borderlands, or the king of a pack of common thieves." She slid that piercing green gaze toward him. "Any of the three could end up in a knife-fight on a sea-bound ship."

He knew he should tell her nothing. He'd kept quiet about his situation for her protection and the protection of her whole family. But if he didn't tell her the truth now—a truth that would put a gulf between them as wide as that between a plowman and a king—he might find himself unable to resist those rosy lips much longer.

"My father," he said, "is a clan chieftain."

He saw her quick little swallow.

"A chieftain, is he?" Her voice was forced. "We've had O'Flaherty and O'Brien chieftains find their way here, and plenty of those English barons and knights sporting tournament wounds."

"Before long, I suspect every outcropping of land you see will be full of those English barons, and they'll be sporting wounds not from tournaments, but from war."

"The English wouldn't dare start a war here. Have you seen the O'Flahertys fight?"

"Irish fighters are fierce. So are the Scots. But when it comes to fighting the English, fierceness isn't enough." How isolated she must be on this island to not feel the encroachment of the enemy that had harried his father's lands most of his life. "The English are united, but the Scots are divided by clan. Our landholdings are small chieftaincies, and every passing of the rod causes infighting. Divided as we are, we'll never hold out against the English, our true enemies."

"Was it an English knife that put a hole in your shoulder, then?"

"Nay, lass. It was a Scottish one."

She gifted him with the sight of her upturned face, those rosy lips parted in surprise, those winged brows raised high.

He was telling her too much. She didn't need to know why someone had aimed a blade at his heart. And yet, when she looked at him with so much concern and curiosity, he wanted to tell her everything.

"When my father became chieftain," he began, "he decided to change the old traditions. No longer would the next chieftain be chosen by deliberation among the brothers, uncles, or cousins of the late leader. From now on, our clan would pass the rod of leadership as the English do—to the firstborn son— and in that way keep the lands undivided and strong."

She mused on this for a moment. "Then your father—"

"—declared me his heir."

Heir to the chieftaincy of Loch Fyfe, as well as the three septs of the clan—the MacEgans, the Ewings, and the MacGilchrists. Thousands of souls and tens of thousands of Highland acres.

Her gaze fluttered away. She buried her fingers in her skirts, worrying the wool of her kirtle as if ashamed of the rough weave. Oh, he'd put a gulf between them, but Lachlan was beginning to wonder if even the width of a sea could stop him from wanting to slide his fingers into her hair and draw her face toward his.

Seamus's voice suddenly carried on the wind. The boy stood by the dolmen stones shouting out a question about a ship in the bay.

She waved at the boy. "There'll be no peace on Inishmaan until I give that boy my attention," she murmured.

In a pensive silence, they strode up the final stretch to the height. Walking by her side, he fell into brooding. It always pained him to think he'd been stabbed by one of his own people. If the men of his clan would just see sense—if they would give up their own greed for power—then they would understand that it was in their best interests to follow his father's lead.

Suddenly he realized that Cairenn was no longer walking beside him. She'd stopped just inside the ring of the embedded stones that dotted the ground around the dolmen.

The color had drained from her face.

He strode back to her. "Lass, what ails you?"

"Nothing." She spoke in a breathy way that made him conscious of the lie. "I . . . just . . . need a moment to catch my breath."

She placed her hand on his chest. At her touch, every muscle in his body came alive.

"Cairenn."

"A pain in the head, no more." Her fingers curled against him, seizing a fistful of his tunic as if she were trying to stay upright. "It will pass."

He stood as still as a dolmen stone as the scent of this woman—rich earth and wildflowers—seeped into his mind. He breathed the fragrance deep and it was like he was taking her inside him, all of her, her softness and her warmth and her wild, sweeping imagination.

He slipped his hand over hers. At his touch, she lifted her face and threw her sea-green gaze at him like a grappling-hook into his heart.

"Lachlan," she said, as if she were calling him from afar.

"I'm here."

"But you're not," she said, her brows knotting as she pressed against him. "You're *not*."

He couldn't help himself. He wrapped his arms around her. He whispered senseless words into her hair as he gazed past the thatched roofs of the distant farmhouses, to the gray sea and the hazy horizon, breathing in the sharp smell of the sea and rocking her to the sound of birds cawing and waves rolling in on the strand far below. He thought about the grim darkness of his own home and the smell of blood on his sword and angry men painted with woad and thatched roofs burning and wondered why he was in such a hurry to return to war when, everyone thinking him already dead, he might very easily make a place here amid peace.

He must have said something, for she looked up and fixed her startled green eyes upon him. He looked at her pale, lovely face and imagined her sitting in a house of wattle and daub that he'd built himself, spinning wool cut from his own sheep. It should be his cows she milked, his table she graced, his bed she warmed.

The oddest feeling came over him. It was as if he'd walked up this slope before, by the music of the surf below, feeling the warmth of the sun beating on the back of his head, following the bright blond head of the woman now pressed against him. It was an unearthly feeling, like the memory of something that had not yet happened but was already burned into his mind.

"Lachlan," she said, his name on her lips pleading. "Don't go."

"I'm right here."

"Stay," she said, as if he hadn't spoken. "Stay here and be safe."

CHAPTER EIGHT

Cairenn gripped his shirt as if it were a rope in a drowning sea. She struggled to read Lachlan's thoughts as the power of the dolmen boosted her gift to painful levels, but all she could read, in this moment, was the expression on his face. After so much study, she could finally identify confusion when it rippled across his wide, beautiful brow.

Of course he was confused by her behavior. He could not hear what she heard, standing on this height so close to the thrumming vibrations of the dolmen stones. He could not feel the pulsing collective thoughts of the people of Galway, the fishmongers bartering for prices, the blacksmiths teaching their apprentices, the millstone workers worrying as the gears slowed. Lachlan could not hear the Portuguese sailors on the ships in the bay jockeying to be the first to visit the whores in the smoky brothels.

Nor could Lachlan hear the thoughts of the Derry men now rowing toward Inishmaan, or the frightful plans of her father sitting at the stern of the galley among them.

"You're shaking." A muscle flexed in Lachlan's cheek. "I'm taking you home."

"No."

His midnight-sky eyes settled on her with an intensity that made her blood rush. When she had made the decision to approach the dolmen stones, she knew that the noise would overwhelm her, but she'd also expected that the borrowed power would make it easier for her to focus on the one man whose thoughts she wanted to penetrate above all others. Instead, tremors shuddered through her, weakening her more every moment she lingered. For people like her, approaching these heights could be dangerous. Daring to touch a sacred stone could mean derangement, disappearance, or even death.

"Cairenn!" Seamus's excitement broke through her shattered thoughts. "There's a funny boat out there. It's got a carving at the bow."

"I can't see it, Seamus."

That was a lie. She could see the boat through Seamus's mind as well as the minds of the men standing on the shore waiting its approach, but her attention was elsewhere. She thought she could sense something in Lachlan, but it was like trying to grab hold of a sea-slick fish in the dark with fumbling hands.

"Come and look!" Seamus's bright excitement blinded her like a candle held too close to her eyes. "Tell me what it is!"

She said, "A moment, Seamus—"

"It looks like a dragon!"

The darkness of Lachlan's mind gave a fraction, like the bowing of a sail in the wind. She sensed his essence billowing around her as she searched deeper—

"No," Seamus shouted. "It's a sea-serpent, curled up—"

"It's a galley," she interrupted, trying to dim Seamus's excitement so she could concentrate. "Men are rowing."

A jolt shot through Lachlan and she realized her mistake. Lachlan raised his head to follow Seamus's gaze. Then Lachlan saw what Seamus saw, and what she herself saw through the eyes of others: A galley of the kind that came from the Western Isles.

But what Lachlan couldn't know, as he released her to get a better look, was that her father had lured this ship to Inishmaan on the pretext of providing medicine for one of the ailing sailors. Her father had tempted these men to these shores, so that the ship, when it left, might carry Lachlan with it.

"Seamus," Lachlan barked. "Take Cairenn home."

Lachlan knew she was following him. He heard her soft footfall and Seamus's galloping one behind him, but he had other concerns on his mind. Urgency drew him down the path toward the shore, to where the galley approached.

But did it bring friends, or enemies?

He stumbled his way downhill, ignoring the way his shoulder pulled and twanged, ignoring weariness from exertion, drawing on what grit was left in him. He paused on the path long before he reached the thatched-roofed storehouses and the one alehouse. Dozens of nut-brown coracles lay pulled up on the strand or upturned above the waterline, attended by groups of fishermen. Squinting against the sun glancing off the water, he watched the galley drop anchor beyond the reef. A coracle rowed out to meet it. He took cover in the shadow of thatch as the pilot boat made its return.

When the little boat dug its keel through the mud, Lachlan saw a familiar figure rise from within. Cairenn's father stepped on the gunwale and leapt to the shore. He paused to speak to a man who followed him out of the coracle, a man wearing a tartan with the O'Neill colors.

Uneasiness gripped him and he ducked out of sight. The O'Neills were cousins to his people, but Lachlan didn't recognize this man. Even if he could identify him, he wouldn't know whether he could trust him. Even with his father's help, Lachlan had never been able to pinpoint the enemies within his own clan, so who was to say that this O'Neill wasn't a friend of the assassins whose knife had found its way into his back?

Lachlan pressed behind the building as he heard striding steps approaching. When Conor's dark figure swept by, Lachlan made sure the doctor was alone and then stepped into the path behind him. The doctor whirled and his hand went to the knife-hilt of his belt.

Lachlan raised a brow. "Expecting trouble on your own island?"

"Old habits die hard." The doctor released his grip and looked him over. "The shoulder heals?"

"Well enough to heft a knife." Lachlan tilted his head toward the shore. "What business do you have with an O'Neill?"

"Your business, Lachlan of Loch Fyfe."

Had Lachlan been stronger, more wary, maybe he could have hidden his surprise. But Lachlan saw from the doctor's face that his own reaction had swept away the last of the man's doubts.

Lachlan said, "You've been busy in Galway."

"The Derry men are talkative in their cups." The doctor stepped up to him, lowering his voice. "Much has happened in Scotland since you left."

The doctor placed a heavy hand on Lachlan's good shoulder.

"Lachlan," he said. "Your father is dead."

CHAPTER NINE

Cairenn knew the feelings that passed through a mind when bad news was delivered—the denial, the shock, the anger—but she could not read Lachlan's thoughts as her father delivered the tidings of Lachlan's father's death. All she could do was watch that beautiful face from where she stood on a ridge of the hillside path. From this distance, she saw him shake his head once, twice. She saw his brows lower as if he didn't understand the words. Then his face went as still as stone.

As her father coaxed Lachlan up the path, she felt a weight of sadness and wondered if it was Lachlan's or just her own. Her arms ached to open to the grieving man but that was foolishness. Her father would never approve of her making so intimate a gesture.

"Lachlan," Da said, as they reached the bend in the path where she and Seamus stood. "I need a word with my daughter. You and I shall speak more on this later. Seamus, go tend to your cows, it's nearly milking time."

Dutifully, Seamus set up the hill toward the pastures above. Lachlan kept walking up the path, his gaze drawn inward where she couldn't see.

Her father hadn't yet said a word to her, but through his thoughts he communicated everything that had happened in Galway. She saw that he'd spent many nights in smoky seaside alehouses, sitting near the Derry men to listen to their drunken talk. She saw her father buy many a drink and venture many a question about where they'd come from.

I've got a daughter in Wales, her lands besieged. Are the English causing trouble in the Highlands as well? Trouble there is, a man had said, *but it's clan against clan and sept against sept. The Campbells fighting the Macdonalds, and the MacEgans fighting among themselves. The chieftain of Loch Fyfe found dead at the bottom of a cliff, only a week after his son disappeared off a ship in the North Sea.*

Cairenn shivered with the impact of the news. "Father," she whispered, "it's too dangerous for Lachlan to leave."

A muscle flickered in his cheek. "So it's Lachlan now?"

She tried very hard not to blush. "He'll return to a place where people want him dead."

"That's his decision. I can't force a man who doesn't want to stay."

And Lachlan wouldn't stay, that much she

knew. With his father dead, she was sure that duty would tighten a fisted grip around his heart.

Her mother's prophecy reverberated in her mind.

Death.

"Please, Father," she said, her mind racing. "You must convince him he's not strong enough to leave."

Da murmured, "So that is the way of it then."

She saw her own face through her father's eyes, a rictus of desperation, yearning, and something else she dared not name. She heard the thought in her da's mind, but she shook her head against it.

"Your mother warned me," he said. "But like all fathers I held tight to the hope that you'd give your heart to someone close—"

"Father, please," she interrupted, unhinged by the word *heart*. "I ask for your help for his sake, not mine."

"I can't help him any longer. But perhaps you can." Da gestured over his shoulder toward the galley moored just outside the reef. "I know the Derry men's words, but not their hearts."

"You wish me to read them." Hope surged up in her so strong that it blotted out all other thought. "But the subject of Lachlan must be the front of their minds if I'm—"

"They'll be in the alehouse soon enough, and so will I. I'll see that the subject comes up again."

She nodded, greedily. She would know if any of those men held secrets, if any of those men had bad intent. She would know, and she would tell her father, and he would convince Lachlan to stay.

A tingling awareness swept over her. She stretched her mind to the Derry man now in the alehouse, and even farther to the men working in the anchored galley. Before she touched those minds, her father stepped close to capture her wandering attention.

"Read those men true, daughter." His face was full of warning. "Even if it means Lachlan will leave on the morning tide."

Hours later Cairenn entered the sickroom to find Lachlan pacing before the hearth. He lifted his head and set his midnight-blue gaze upon her. A quiver rippled through her. Not because she couldn't read his thoughts—those were as fathomless as ever—but because, perhaps for the first time, she could read his face.

Grief was not easy to bury. It sat in the crimped skin around his eyes, in the furrows deepening on his brow, in the bright steady light of warning in his eyes. Warning for what, she could only guess. Grief made men act oddly. Women wept, but men spit sparks.

She swallowed her unease and headed to the table scattered with bottles and unguents and linens. "My father has sent me to remove your bandages."

"Just give me a knife," he said, setting to pacing again, "and I'll cut off the bandages myself."

"Then you'll pull the scab right off and it'll be worse than before." She busied herself searching for a clay pot with the right unguent. "And how are you going to put salve on your own back?"

"Why didn't your father come himself?"

"He's detained at the waterfront, drinking with the O'Neills."

"Still?"

"Do you think he can know those men's minds so quickly?"

"He can never know them, not at all."

Yes, he can, Lachlan. She let her hair fall across her brow so Lachlan couldn't read the bright thought on her face. *Because Da has* me, *and I have a gift.*

You can have me, too.

She squeezed away the thought before she blushed, then she rounded the table and approached. Her heart rose in her throat as he stopped his pacing. She paused close enough to feel the intensity of his presence, a warm and subtle vibration of the air between them. As the silence stretched, a tingling uncertainty weakened her knees as a flush crept up her neck.

So this is what happens to a woman, she thought, when she's falling haplessly in love with a man.

He reached for his rope belt and, with a flick of his fingers, untied it. It thudded to the floor at his feet. Her heart throbbed a painful beat as he then hauled up his woolen surcoat to wrestle it over his head and toss it toward the pallet.

She'd seen many a man undress. The sailors, before they lugged heavy cargo on shore. The villager men at thatching-time, when the sun became fierce. But it was different watching Lachlan reach over his shoulder and grab a fistful of his linen undertunic. As the hem rode up, it revealed the ridged muscles of his thighs, and then the wound cloth of the braies hugging his hips, and, once he lifted his head free, the gleaming stretch of his naked chest.

She swallowed and it was like forcing a goose egg through a stocking. She'd seen Lachlan shirtless often enough but never when he was so upright and bright with strength—and never when she had a specific intent in mind. Unnerved, she dropped her gaze only to find herself staring at a more dangerous place—the stripe of pale skin just above the waist of his braies. She wondered what it would be like to ride her fingertips along that pale border.

The room around her bowed and swayed. The motion stopped when he turned his back to her and dropped down to sit on the hearth stool.

She mentally shook herself and placed her linens and the bowl of unguent on the little table at the foot of the pallet. She couldn't let him affect her this way, not when she was about to risk so much.

She eased the tips of her fingers under the edge of the linen wrappings. Though the wound was healed and the angry soreness long gone, he flinched as though touched by a spark. A long muscle along his side flexed at her touch. She puzzled over these reactions as she plucked at the knot until she pulled it free. To unwind the strip of linen from his body, she needed to reach over his shoulder and across his chest.

A strand of his hair tickled her chin as she leaned in. She smelled his scent—medicinal herbs and sun-warmed linen, and something else, something musky and completely masculine. When she slipped her arm around his other side in order to seize the end of the linen, she pressed a breast against the thick, hard muscle of his shoulder.

A jolt went through him. It reverberated through her.

She eased away from his warmth more quickly than she should have, because a woman needed room to breathe if she wasn't going to see black spots winking before her eyes. She tried very hard to fix her mind on the second layer of unwinding, but she was clumsy about it. When she reached around to seize the growing ball of cloth again, he made a hissing sound and ripped the roll from her hands. He pulled the bandage across his chest with haste and then backhanded the crumpled cloth to her.

By the time the last of the bandages fell away, her heart fretted in her chest like a trapped dove. The urge to race out of the sickroom was countered in strength only by her determination to see this through.

He growled, "Be done with it, lass."

A pulse in his neck throbbed. With his mind closed to her and his face turned toward the hearth, she could only guess why he behaved so. The not-knowing was like an itch she couldn't scratch.

So by desperate instinct she tried once more to read his mind. She pressed as close as she dared as she took some grease on her fingertips and ran them slickly down the wound. His ribs expanded and contracted, the muscles tensing under her hand. In his mind she felt a similar flex in the wall of his thoughts. She tumbled into that soft darkness, like plunging into the depths of the sea, a muffling of sound and sensation, and a warmth—

"Damn it, lass."

He twisted with a grunt. He wrapped his good arm around her waist and hauled her full across his lap. A muscle moved in his cheek as his gaze devoured her. She thought *this was easier than I expected* just before he rasped his lips against hers.

Black spots before her eyes became black stars exploding in her mind and all thought—any thought—every thought—burned to ashes.

She'd been kissed before, by a boy her age whose mind told her that he'd welcome a few moments behind a cottage. The boy's kiss had been clumsy, his hands greedy, and his leapfrogging thoughts so crude that she'd shoved him away before he'd dared to explore where he hadn't been invited.

But this merging of lips bore no resemblance to that awkward moment in the shade of the cottage wall. She tasted Lachlan's mouth and slipped her fingers into the warmth of his dark, dark hair, and realized this was what she wanted since she came upon him wounded and half-drowned upon the strand. This wanting was a force beyond her control, like the tide tugging at her knees. Suddenly she understood the passion of poor lonely Deirdre of all the old stories, meeting handsome Naoise upon the road, then casting aside her duty to king and clan all because of the desire that flowed between her and her dark-haired, ruddy-cheeked warrior.

Lachlan tilted his head and nudged her lips apart. She parted her lips at his wordless command and sensed the vibrations of a moan rumble through him. He captured her tongue and drew it into his own mouth, slipping his against hers in a way that made her quiver and tense all over.

Then, like a flash in the darkness, she heard her name whispered. It was a thought-whisper, not a sound, for all she could hear in the room was the crackle of the peat fire and their mutual breathing. His thought was like a comet shooting through the darkness. Her heart gave a little leap in her chest.

Then his hand slid down her cheek. His fingers grazed her throat. She knew where that hand was going, even before he plunged it beneath the hem of her gaping tunic and took her breast in his warm palm.

She broke from his kiss with a gasp. She arched her neck as all sensation focused on the tightening nub of her nipple against the heat of his skin. His hair, as soft as thrice-brushed linen, feathered against her neck. His kiss was a spark in the hollow of her throat. He shifted his grip then flicked the pad of his thumb over her taut, aching nipple.

She forced his face level so she could look into his eyes. He kept rolling her nipple as his gaze moved from her hair to her lips. She sensed he understood her expression with a clarity far greater than she could glean from his mind. Sitting on his lap, she felt as open and vulnerable as if she were lying naked, splayed on his pallet, her hair spread across the pillow.

There—another flash of revelation in the

darkness—*that* was what he was imagining right now. It was the same thought that filled her senses. This merging of thoughts was a new and strange sensation and she slipped into its current. She toed off her leather shoes, one slipper after the other dropping to the floor.

"Cairenn."

A soft voice in the darkness, a real voice this time, for his breath brushed her skin.

"You're in all my dreams," he said against her throat. "You're in all my waking thoughts."

She kissed him to quiet him. She didn't want to get caught up in words.

"You, and this place," he said, hoarsely, between kisses. "You've both bewitched me."

The word *bewitched* rasped through her consciousness. "There's no witchery in this, Lachlan."

"Then I have no excuse but my own weakness."

"And mine."

He tugged on the neckline of her shift. She lifted one shoulder to let the neckline slide down. His breath warmed her skin. When he pulled back from her kiss, she glimpsed her naked breast set free of her neckline just before his head blocked her view.

The touch of his lips on her breast was like a torch set to a bonfire. She buried her fingers in his hair to control her own shudder of pleasure. He kissed her nipple, open-mouthed, hungrily, and she sensed the teasing graze of his teeth. All the while his hand slid across her body, down her hip, over the top of her thighs and across her knees.

Wool and linen feathered up over her knees. Cool air bathed her thighs. She wanted to say, *take me to the pallet,* so they could have what they both wanted. She wanted to say, *let's lie upon the floor,* but then his fingertips grazed her inner thigh and words became impossible to form.

Through her mind flooded images of all the times she'd gazed unwittingly into the minds of young lovers—seeing their memories of rolling caresses and fleshy entwinements. It seemed she'd always known the mechanics and the variations of the coupling, but she'd never really understood the intensity of all of it until now, this very moment, as she couldn't help but part her thighs to make a straight path for his fingers. He boldly took the invitation and ran a fingertip inside her cleft.

With her lips pressed against his hair she again sensed his thoughts like a series of shooting stars streaking through a dark night, a series of thoughts that matched her own.

I want to sink inside her.

I want you inside me.

I will have her.

Take me.

His fingers settled on a spot and made swift little circles. Her hips quivered and then moved to match his rhythm. Arched on his lap like this she couldn't move as much as she needed to, and beneath the yearning grew a vaulting frustration. She became conscious of the hardness of his sex pressed against her hip. She wanted to touch him, give him the same pleasure he was giving to her, let him know that she wanted to join him the way men and women were made to be joined. She tried to push off his lap—to the pallet, to the floor—to any place where she could open her thighs for more than just his fingers.

But he ignored her wriggling and slipped his slick finger deep inside her.

"Lachlan."

Her cry was a question. His answer was to lower his head and suck her nipple back into his mouth.

His thumb circled the top of her cleft while his finger plunged in and out of her and his lips suckled her breast. Sensation flooded her body while her inner muscles clenched. She'd finally broken through the barriers of his mind to know what he wanted—and she wanted more than anything to *give that to him*—yet what they were doing right now would not bring him the pleasure he needed—

—but it would bring pleasure to her, she thought, as her head fell back, as her body knotted, as her mind went blind.

CHAPTER TEN

When her sweet body finished throbbing around his hand, Lachlan cupped her sex, trying not to think of what it might have felt like to have her body throb like that around his cock. A cock that now stood upright in his braies, with nothing but linen between it and Cairenn's soft, curved bottom.

She reclined in his arms while her lungs worked like bellows. The lass with her slimness and pale-milk skin gave off an air of fragility, but holding her so close, he felt the tensile strength of her long, lean body. Her tapered thighs, the firmness of her belly, the fierceness of her grip. His fingers could still feel the imprint of the moist pressure he'd felt inside her. Where she'd gripped him, his shoulders would bear bruises tomorrow.

How easy it would be to slip off the stool and onto his knees, spread her across the warm hearthstones, and sink himself deep. She would welcome him—he felt acquiescence in every quivering line of her body. She would wrap her slim ankles around his back and her arms around his shoulders and make little, heaving gasps with every stroke. He could bring her to the height of pleasure again and himself, as well, and for a while—a short, brilliant, welcome stretch of oblivion—he could believe that in her arms lay peace and a life of unfurling happiness.

But he resisted the urge, just as he resisted the temptation to place a kiss on the pale, wet nipple within his lips' reach. Instead, he shifted her weight to set her head against his shoulder. Already his troubles were rushing back to him—his father dead, his duty awaiting him. If he took her the way he ached to, he would only add another helping of guilt.

At least his conscience—and her virginity— were still intact. No sooner had the thought passed his mind when she slid her hand toward his cock.

She whispered, "I want to touch you."

"Don't." He seized her hand as his cock strained. "Don't do something that you'll regret when I'm gone."

"I know you're leaving, Lachlan."

He leaned back to see those half-lidded eyes, those swollen lips, now curving in a sad little smile.

"My father," she said, flattening her palm upon his chest, "is even now negotiating passage for you on that galley."

He frowned. "Why didn't you tell me this?"

"I'm telling you now."

Now, he realized, after she'd already offered

her body up to him. That meant she knew he'd have denied her kiss if she had told him the truth earlier.

Then a more alarming thought intruded. "Your father shouldn't be doing this. He can't be sure of the loyalties of those men."

"It's not a matter of loyalty," she said. "The sailors and the captain of that galley, they talk about the MacEgans' troubles like they're gossiping. It's like an overturned wagon on the side of the road: People like to gawp at it before moving on. It's not personal, so they don't care."

"But if they hear my name—"

"They won't hear your name. When you board the galley, you'll be Brochan of the Western Isles. Da made up a story: You're a sailor who was knifed in an alehouse brawl in Galway, left behind with the doctor to heal and wait for passage."

He took a deep, swift breath. Soon he'd be on a ship back home. Soon he would find the man who'd plunged a knife in his back. Soon he would find the man who'd killed his father.

My father, dead.

The thought, like a knock of an iron mallet. Whenever it surged, a darkness crept over him and dimmed his sight and senses. How his palms itched to feel the murderer's neck between them.

"When?" He tightened his grip on her wrist when she hesitated. "When?"

"Tomorrow."

Shock sent his thoughts skipping toward the future. Tomorrow, he would head back to Derry, and from there to Loch Fyfe. But what to do then? Which allies could he trust? Perhaps none, perhaps not even his Irish cousin Angus O'Donnell in Derry. Best to sneak back to Loch Fyfe himself and see who'd seized the chieftaincy. Yet he couldn't just walk through the gates and present himself as the one true heir. His enemy was smarter and slyer than either he or his father had imagined.

My father, dead.

No, he thought with a flinch. He had to hold himself back, seek information, and flush out the enemy before the enemy even knew he was alive—

"Lachlan."

Her call seemed to come from very far away. Her hand had slipped from his grip. She placed it on his cheek and that's when he met her soft, green eyes.

She whispered, "Take me with you."

The sight of her swollen lips and the scent of her skin should have sent more blood to his loins, but her words worked on him like an ice bath. Suddenly he was back in the room with this soft and willing woman, hoping to un-hear what she'd just asked of him.

He never should have kissed her. He never should have rubbed his cheek against her breast. He never should have stroked her into pleasure and made her believe that he could offer her more.

He was a stupid, mindless ass.

"Cairenn." He pressed her away, half off his lap. "You'd best find your own bed."

Her face contorted with confusion.

"I'll be gone from this place in the morning." His heart clenched. "And I won't be coming back."

She pushed off his lap. He let her go. Her skirts

tumbled down her long, bare legs. She took a few uncertain steps backwards and then ventured a hand toward the mantel to steady herself.

He could not look at her for the wrong he was doing.

She whispered, "You're walking into your own death."

"That I already know."

He focused on the flames flickering in the hearth. In the burning coals he searched for absolution for taking liberties he wasn't worthy of from a woman who deserved so much better.

"But," she whispered, "you don't have to. I can help you."

"Your heart is kind." His heart twisted. "But where I am going I'll be in constant danger."

"You don't understand—"

"There's much you don't know." He tried to fill his mind with the duty that called him, not his yearning for the woman standing before him. "Your father thinks he solved my problem by giving me a false name. But I can't be Brochan forever. The ruse will be over the minute I step foot in Derry, or Scotland. Too many men on both sides of the water know me, and I don't know whom to trust."

"There's much I can do—"

"I'll be living like an outlaw." He dared to look at her, but she hadn't yet covered that sweet, swelling white breast, so he looked quickly away. "I'll be camping in wild places, alone. Stealing from travelers. Lurking in alehouse shadows to listen to the talk. It could take me months to know who my enemies are, and, more importantly, who are my friends—"

"I'm the one who told Da about the Derry men."

He frowned. "Told him what?"

"That those sailors are trustworthy." She tugged at her sleeve until she'd covered the breast he could still feel like a soft pressure against his mouth. "I'm the one who knows that they have no bad intent."

"You can't know such a thing."

"Yes, I can." She all but dropped onto the stool on the other side of the hearth. "I know, Lachlan, because I can read minds."

He heard the words but didn't understand them. Not all at once. He heard them, and he knew what nonsense they were, but it took him a few moments of contemplation to figure out what she was really trying to do.

When the assassin's dagger had first plunged into him, Lachlan, in the heat of a brawl, had felt nothing but pressure. Then came a cold, sucking feeling. Then warmth spread across his back—the blood pouring through—before sharpness registered, a slicing pain so agonizing that it had driven him to his knees.

Looking at the hope upon Cairenn's face, he felt like the tip of that blade had just reached his heart.

"I speak the truth," she stuttered into the silence, knitting her fingers together and apart. "I can gather your friends and identify your foes, and tell you the truth in their hearts in an instant. You won't have to be an outlaw living in the rough. I can find out what you need to know. I can identify the man who killed your father."

"Lass," he said softly, "you're calling yourself a witch."

"It's *not* witchery." Her winged brows drew together. "Why does everyone call what they don't understand 'witchery?' Accusations of witchery can get a body burned at the stake. Is that what you'd accuse me of?"

"I know no other word for what you claim you can do—"

"It's a gift I've been given. I did not ask for it. I did not want it. At least . . . not until now."

How Elspeth would have adored this creature of vivid imagination, if Lachlan could have brought her home.

"It's not so strange," she said, clearly sensing his doubts. "I know much about the Derry men I could not know otherwise: I know they work for a man called Angus O'Donnell. In that galley, they've got a hold full of Spanish wines they'll be bringing to his warehouse on the hill beyond the village. The captain, Eoin, has a wife and three daughters, as well as a mistress in Galway. He sails constantly to get away from all of them. He spends sixteen pounds a year on their dresses alone—"

"Enough, lass."

Alehouse gossip, no more. If his heart wasn't so heavy with mourning over his father's death, and if his shoulders weren't crushed under the weight of duty, and if he didn't feel so guilty over what had just happened between them, then he might have given in to her wishes and taken her away with him—just because of the length she was going to, for the chance to live by his side.

Oh, lass, what a wonderful, loyal wife you will be, to some better man.

Instead, he said, "Are you determined to come with me?"

"Yes."

His heart turned over. There was only one reason why a woman would leave her home and her family for a man, but if he heard those words fall from her lips, he'd be lost.

"I will take you with me," he said, a sigh slipping out of him as if it squeezed from the weight of his guilt, "but only on one condition."

In the blink of an eye she was on her knees at his feet, reaching for him. He seized her wrists to hold her still.

"Cairenn," he said. "Tell me what I'm thinking right now."

Her excitement hardened to an unnatural stillness. She stared, wide-eyed, as the light of the flames flickered over her hair. He watched emotions flash across her face: Dismay, disbelief, panic.

"You're thinking that I'm out of my mind," she said, her voice a quaver. "You're thinking that I've made this all up. You're thinking that I'll say almost anything to get you to take me away."

He'd had those thoughts, indeed, but they weren't the ones that he now held foremost in his mind. Everything would change if she could read what he was truly thinking, and they would change in a thousand strange and heartbreaking ways. Still, he couldn't help himself. He mind-spoke those three words again, over and over, distinctly and undeniable, to the woman at his feet staring with increasing desperation.

He whispered, "Try again, Cairenn."

CHAPTER ELEVEN

The truth hovered on the tip of Cairenn's tongue: *Lachlan, Lachlan, I can read all minds—except yours.*

She felt his doubts pulse in the silence around them, broken only by the crackle of the peat in the hearth. Yes, she'd expected a measure of disbelief when she'd admitted the truth, but her fears had focused on alarm, suspicion, or even horror. Against that, she'd prepared herself to prove that her gift was not witchery or the devil's work.

But Lachlan had just dismissed her confession out of hand.

His doubt put a clamp upon her tongue and tightened the growing knot in her chest. If she persisted, he would keep looking at her in this terrible way, a way that made her feel like a poor, lonely little girl willing to say anything out of desperation. She hated how the corners of his lips tilted in a smile that held no joy. Perhaps this was the kind of rueful look that men gave to women to whom they wouldn't make a vow.

Darkness hazed the edges of her vision and with it came a rush of determination. She shot up to her knees and rasped her palms over his unshaven cheeks as she tried to delve into his thoughts. On her tongue danced a dozen explanations. *My family, they all have gifts, you must have noticed.* Her father's face flashed in her mind, his frown of disapproval as she broke the one rule pounded into them since they were old enough to understand why they kept apart from the world.

I can prove it, Lachlan. I can.

But whatever magic had torn through the black cloud of his mind while they were making love had long dissipated. Holding his beautiful face between her palms, she sensed nothing.

Nothing, nothing, nothing.

His hands gripped hers. She could barely see his expression through the moisture filling her eyes. He gently peeled her fingers away from his face.

She must have stood up. She must have turned toward the door. She waited for him to say something, call her back, whisper her name, but silence echoed in her ears as, suddenly, she stood outside the sickroom in the fading of the day, barefoot with her leather slippers in her hands.

The wind cut through the woven fibers of her linen kirtle and turned the trails of tears on her cheeks cold. She stumbled two steps across the courtyard toward the kitchens, the golden glow of light spilling out from around the wattles of the door. Then she stopped.

Her mother's terrible prophecy rang in her ears. *Death.*

So she headed barefoot for the gate, flinging it shut behind her. Her feet swept her to the lonely places, to where the bones of the island poked out from scrubby grass. She let the breeze pound her clothing against her as she raised her face to the clouds tinged pink from the sunset.

Why, why, why? What kind of fate would bring such a man to these shores only to send him away before she understood why his thoughts were hidden? What senseless urge had made her fall in love with him?

She climbed over the rock-pile stiles and strode past the cows, searching the sea for the galley anchored among the other ships. How many years had she raced across the height like this, watching the ships from Galway unfurl their sails to slip out of the bay to places unknown, places she yearned to see, places she could *never* see? All those dreams were futile, for in the crowded towns and villages of the world, the minds of thousands would pierce hers like a thousand iron lances. The old terror shuddered through her. She stumbled as she continued her charge across the patchwork of fields.

This island was her home, but she was a prisoner upon it.

Tomorrow, Lachlan would sail out of her life on that galley moored beyond the reef. She imagined herself standing beside him on the deck while the wind whipped her hair. She imagined him drawing her into his arms, kissing her. She remembered how the world had dissolved around them when they lost themselves in the touch of their bodies and the rushing current of their thoughts.

Then suddenly she noticed a familiar cluster of thatched-roofed houses. She'd run far, farther than she'd thought, far ahead of her own thoughts. For in one of those thatched-roofed houses lived a special young man, a true and loyal friend whose mind rang in simple notes like the sound of a plucked harp string.

Her heart beat in time to her thoughts.

Do I dare?

Do I dare?

Do I dare?

At the break of day, Lachlan stepped outside the sickroom wearing his borrowed clothes. The doctor and his family were gathered in the courtyard. Lachlan clasped the doctor's hand and thanked him for saving his life. The man shrugged as if he'd done nothing more than a simple kindness. The mistress of the house offered up a sack of food and he took it with gratitude. Cairenn's brother Niall, looking like he'd just returned from a night's carousing, nodded a woozy farewell. The younger siblings leapt and played around him, but Dairine clung to his leg. Her shock of hair was baby-soft beneath his palm.

He sought the shadows for Cairenn.

"She's not here," her mother said, intuiting his look. "She'll likely be waiting to say farewell to you upon the shore."

She would not, Lachlan was sure of it, and he

deserved no better. So he slung the sack of food over his good shoulder and trudged out the gate, taking the worn, winding path down to the strand. Whirlwinds kept pace with him, dancing their way down the narrow path like the regrets he could not shake.

Once upon the shore, he roused one of the islanders who slept above the waterline to look after the boats and the fishing gear. The man agreed to bring Lachlan to where the galley was anchored. Lachlan climbed into the little boat and sat so that he faced the island. With every pull of the oars, the sailor propelled him into the choppy bay, through a herd of seals barking mournfully, and farther away from Inishmaan.

He told himself, with an ache in his heart, that he'd done the right thing when he sent her out of his room last night. He should have left this island the moment he could stand on his own two feet. His duty lay in Scotland, where he would grip a claymore once again and wield it with justice. He would heed the call of his duty, even if he'd responded too late to save his father.

But not without one deep, implacable yearning, and a hundred thousand regrets.

The coracle bumped up against the hull of the galley, now bustling with sailors roused to unfurl the sails. As he climbed the rope ladder and stepped over the gunwale, he scanned the men aboard.

Strangers, all of them.

The captain approached, one questioning brow raised. "Brochan?"

"Aye."

"The doctor said you'd pay your passage with work. Sail or oars?"

He rolled his bad shoulder and said, "Sails."

The captain nodded and tossed him the end of a hemp rope to wind about one of the davits. Lachlan settled the clove hitch knot and then a sailor tossed him another rope to secure. Soon the wind caught the canvas as the boat swelled free of her anchorage. The ship tacked away from the island toward the open sea, piloted by the sleek, black bodies of seals rolling in its wake.

As he watched the island diminish, a tale came to mind, a tale Cairenn's brother had sung one evening while the wind whistled through the thatch. It was a story of a man who, while wandering unfamiliar fields, stumbled into a strange place. Drawn by its music, light, and beauty, he stayed to drink the wine and taste the berries and dance in a cloud of happiness. When he finally stumbled out, disoriented and confused, he found that months had passed in what seemed like days.

Lachlan grabbed another rope and turned to a sailor beside him. "Tell me, what is today?"

"It's Saint Brendan's Day. The luckiest day of the year to set sail."

St. Brendan's Day. A month since he'd left his father. Weeks since he'd first seen her looming over him on the strand with the sun haloing her hair.

Not enough time. Never enough time.

On a small merchant boat, where every sailor knew one another and most were related by blood,

Lachlan understood that a stranger was an object of dangerous curiosity. Fortunately, Derry loomed into sight on the fifth day of the voyage, just as Lachlan's glib story about being stabbed in an alehouse began to wear thin.

He helped furl the sails as the men rowed the galley into the River Foyle. The stone monastery of Doire that formed the heart of Derry stood on a rise surrounded by the oak groves that gave the town its name. Clustered against the shore were the usual thatched warehouses and ale stands, a canvas-covered market, and wagons hitched to nags ready to pull casks of Spanish wine and barrels of fish straight to the monastery. His gaze drifted to one of the finer houses on the outskirts, the abode of his distant cousin, Angus O'Donnell of the northern O'Neill.

Angus was the man Lachlan had been sent to contact before an assassin with a sharp blade put an end to his mission. O'Donnell hadn't known Lachlan was coming, so he should be innocent of the whole affair . . . but that was a reedy guess, full of assumptions and suppositions. The only way Lachlan could be sure Angus was truly an ally was to surprise him. Only by looking into his eyes at the precise moment when he found his cousin alive could Lachlan tell whether Angus was thrilled—or distressed.

"So, Brochan." A sailor—Ruari by name—slapped Lachlan on his good shoulder. "What's first for you, an alehouse or whorehouse?"

"It won't be an alehouse," Lachlan said. "In the last one I got a knife in the back."

"It wasn't the alehouse that did that to you."

"Aye, but the ale had something to do with it." Lachlan jerked his chin toward a peddler on the far end of town. "I'll be visiting the ragman. I'm tired of wearing another man's ill-fitting clothes."

"When you're done with that, come to The Goat's Horn. I'll buy you a pint and try to pry a story from you."

"I'll take you up on that another time." Best not to show his face at The Goat's Horn. He'd spent many a rowdy evening there with his cousins whenever he was in Derry on his father's business. "I've got other business in town today that'll keep me sober."

"The only business I know that's better when a man's sober is the kind you'll find at The Good Plough. Ask for wee Maura. She's plump as they come, it's like pounding on a pillow."

"I'll remember that."

He wouldn't, though, because his mind was filled with the memory of Cairenn stretched across his lap, her slender body going tight as he stroked her.

The captain's shout brought him back to the moment. The rowers had eased and men were readying the anchor for dropping. He glanced to the shore and saw two deep-bellied boats shooting off from the quay to meet the ship and take on the cargo. He followed Ruari toward the hatch to haul up the casks of Spanish wine, despite the stress this would put on his twinging shoulder. The hatch gave him a quick place to duck and hide, just in case he recognized any of the Derry men in the oncoming boats.

Suddenly a frightened yelp came up from the hold. The men on deck cackled, because unpacking the wine casks below decks often rousted a herd of rats from their nests, rats that in their panic ran heedlessly over toes and sometimes up legs. Lachlan laughed with them while Ruari, hanging on the hatch ladder, ducked his head to see what was happening.

Ruari gasped, "Holy Mother of God."

CHAPTER TWELVE

When she first grasped the iron welding of one of the wine casks in order to pull herself to her feet, Cairenn felt the shock wave of the sailors' thoughts: She looked like a ghost shimmering up from nowhere.

While the closest sailor juggled his shock along with the barrel he was balancing, she flattened her hands on the casks to try to maintain her footing. She'd drunk the last sip of her water over a day ago, so her tongue was swollen and dry. Her muscles were cramped from the small space she'd fitted herself into. Her legs felt as wobbly as rope.

"Captain, we've got a stowaway," the sailor shouted. "And it's a *girl.*"

The men's thoughts above deck had been burbling at a lowly simmer, but at the word *girrrrrrrl* those thoughts shot to a boil. She winced at the surge, a cacophony that swelled above the rumbling hum of the town of Derry where they'd just anchored.

A second sailor dropped from the ladder and approached. Backlit by the sunshine pouring through the hatch, his face was in shadow, but she knew his name was Ruari. Before she'd made her appearance, Ruari had been dreaming of a fleshy woman that worked in The Good Plough.

Now she made herself concentrate on his thoughts and *only* his thoughts. She had discovered, after five excruciating days trapped in the belly of this ship, that focusing on one man's thoughts helped dim the noise of the twenty-two others. It was like focusing on the chatter of Dairine sitting across from her at the dinner table while her parents and siblings prattled heedlessly all around her—except on ship it was twenty-two times worse. She could only hope that this hard-earned lesson functioned just as well against the threatening hum of the hundreds of inhabitants of Derry, not so far away.

"Come on, girl, you can't stay here anymore." Ruari held out his hand. "Climb over and let the captain take a look at you."

She tried to get a knee on the cask in front of her, but she was weak and her balance uncertain, and she couldn't coax words from her dry mouth. The sailor didn't notice her attempts because his mind was alight with questions. He was wondering who on board would think to hide a wench in the hold for swiving. *It's got to be Brochan. I knew he was hiding something.*

The mention of "Brochan"—Lachlan—made her whole body go prickly with anxiety.

After she made another flailing attempt to climb on top the casks, the sailor finally mustered the sense to roll the barrels away to make a path for her. She stumbled her way out. He grasped her arm to keep her upright. She winced against the light as the men urged her up the ladder onto the deck. She stumbled on the highest rung, but was saved from falling by the grasp of a strong hand. Hauled bodily out of the hold, she closed her eyes against the light until her feet found the deck.

"What the *hell*?!"

She didn't hear the mind but she knew the voice. She looked up into Lachlan's beautiful face, dark across the jaw with unshaven scruff. At the sight of him so close, all the blustering bravery she'd mustered buckled, along with her knees.

"Water." Lachlan's words were clipped. "Don't just stand there, Ruari, fetch a ladle."

She sagged against the grip of his hand. Black spots winked before her eyes. Her knees just brushed the deck. A gentle hand eased her head back as a ladle full of water wobbled before her.

The water tasted sour like vinegar but she drank it deep. As she wiped her lips, into her sight came a pair of well-shined boots just as into her mind came the thoughts of an Irish captain who was supremely annoyed to discover a stowaway.

"Brochan," the captain barked. "You know this woman?"

"Aye."

"I take you on my ship," the captain said, "and you betray my trust by stowing—"

"I didn't stow her." He tightened his grip.

"She's the daughter of the doctor who took me in at Inishmaan. I don't know why she's here."

Because I love you, you stupid fool, and I'm trying to save your life.

She searched for something in his expression—a glimmer of tenderness, an expression of regret—but any warmth was subsumed by shock and a growing fury.

The captain swiveled on a heel, barking, "Who was on watch the last night outside of Inishmaan?"

Ruari and another sailor came forward, babbling their surprise and ignorance. Lachlan drew her upwards until she stood on her own two feet.

He pressed his lips against her ear. "What," he said in a biting whisper, "were you thinking?"

"I was thinking I could help."

"Your father and mother will be mad with worry."

"My mother knows. I didn't tell her, but she knows." She met his eye and dared to break a promise. "She's like me, just with a different gift."

Lachlan's jaw tightened. He straightened up.

"Captain," he said, interrupting the man berating the sailors, "when is your next trip back to Galway?"

"Two weeks."

"I'll pay for her return."

"You have no coin," the captain said. "If you did, you wouldn't have worked that wounded shoulder—"

"I've got resources."

"Do you plan to conjure coins out of your arse?"

"Will you take her or not?"

The captain shook his head. "A woman on a ship is bad luck."

"I'll pay well. In advance." He jerked his head toward the shore. "I have a cousin in Derry. He'll give me coin."

The captain sidled her a look. She could read his thoughts shifting between greed and suspicion.

"The captain won't take me," she blurted, seizing the idea before she lost courage. "No captain will sail on a ship with a witch."

The silence that followed her declaration was so leaden that Lachlan could hear the wine barrels in the hold scraping against one another in the roll of the tidal river. Yet she just stood with her chin raised like she hadn't just confessed to cavorting with the devil.

"She's out of her wits," Lachlan said into the silence. "She was crazy enough before I even left the island." She gasped but he spoke over her. "That's why her father kept her close. Now she's as mad as anyone would be after five days in the hold."

Her slivered gaze defied him but he matched her look with a glare that warned her to say nothing.

"She belongs back under her father's care," he said. "The sooner I get her back, the better."

"Find another berth," the captain said.

"Captain—"

"Off my ship, Brochan, and take your witch with you." The captain gestured to the open hold.

"The rest of you, back to work!"

The sailors wandered back to their posts, but Lachlan saw the looks they gave him and Cairenn. So he curled his hand around her arm and drew her to the gunwale, glancing down to the men in the boat arranging what casks they'd already loaded so as better to balance. Relief swept through him when he realized he didn't recognize any of the Derry men therein.

This was the last of his luck, he was sure of it.

He climbed down the rope ladder and stepped foot on the stowed barrels, waiting as Cairenn, the self-proclaimed witch, followed him down. As soon as he could reach, he seized her by the waist, swung her through the air, and set her down in the boat with more force than necessary.

He sat on a barrel beside her and leaned into her, turning his face so the Derry men in the boat couldn't hear him. "Have you utterly lost your senses, woman?"

"I didn't sit cramped in a stinking hold for five days," she said between her teeth, "just to be sent back home."

"So you declare yourself a witch in front of two dozen sailors."

"I expected them to dismiss my confession." Her throat flexed. "They're outsiders, you're an outsider, and that's what *you* did."

"I am not a sailor." He flattened his hands on the wobbling casks as the Derry men reached for the last barrels. "Sailors won't sail on Fridays because it's thought to be bad luck. They don't like women on board ship because it's bad luck. They won't whistle while at sea lest they whistle up a storm because it's bad luck—"

"—so you decided to tell them I wasn't right in the head." She turned those piercing green eyes upon him. "And that's why my father never let me off the island."

"I'm trying to keep you off a burning stake."

He saw a quiver shudder through her. She turned away. Maybe she wasn't as foolhardy as she seemed.

As the boatmen pushed away from the galley and started rowing toward the quay, he switched his attention to the approaching shore. The sailors would talk in the alehouses. Soon word would spread about an Inishmaan girl—a *witch*—who'd stowed away to chase after a wounded sailor by the name of Brochan. The two of them would be the focus of too much attention. There'd be no careful approach to Angus O'Donnell now. He'd have to drag her to his cousin's door and beg not just for warriors to avenge his father's murder, but also for the coin to send her home.

"Ruari and Tadgh," he said, running his hand across his unshaven jaw, "swore up and down that they didn't see you climb onto the galley. How did you manage without attracting their attention?"

"They were blind drunk."

He raised a brow. "No one could be blind to a beautiful woman climbing down a hatch."

"It was dark, and they were distracted by the barking of the seals and a boat rowing by. While they were, I climbed over the gunwale and hid." She frowned and rubbed her brow as if a headache loomed. "When they fell asleep, I snuck down the hatch and found a space among the barrels."

"Falling asleep on watch is a whipping offense. They'll never admit to it." They'd attribute her appearance to witchery before they'd admit to it, which would give credence to her admission, damn it. "This boat that distracted the men, who was in it?"

"How am I to know? I was at the other end of the ship."

"Don't lie, Cairenn. I know you didn't swim your way out to the galley, not in that rough surf."

"Of course not. That would be madness. Something only a girl who has fits and delusions might do." Her jaw tightened. "Or a witch."

His lips thinned. He did not want to have this conversation about her so-called gift. He'd hurt her enough when he'd called her on her bluff in the sickroom at Inishmaan.

He said, "You had help getting out to the ship. I know it wasn't Niall, he has too much sense. It was another man." He felt a twist under his ribs, a sting that felt suspiciously like jealousy. "Whoever he was, he then distracted the sailors so you could climb on board."

She sat in stubborn silence, plucking at a loose fiber by the knee of her kirtle. He cast back to the few people he knew on the island, trying to think of who would dare do this and risk the wrath of her father. The answer came to him in a flash.

"Cairenn," he said. "Tell me you didn't do this to that poor boy—"

"He's not a 'poor boy.' He's hard-working and

loyal and wise in ways that you or I will never understand—"

"—and he'll do anything you say, even when it's wrong."

"Seamus understands why I did this." Her brow furrowed deeper, and she began to wince as if the sun was too bright. "He *believes* me."

"He's a dead boy the moment your father realizes who helped you—"

"My father will forgive him," she insisted, pressing her fingers against her temple as if in pain, "because my mother knows what I've done and why."

"In the meantime, your father will live with the torment of thinking another daughter has been stolen from home."

"I wasn't stolen." Her voice faltered. "And I'm not lost."

Then she suddenly bent forward, clasping her head in her hands. Her knuckles went white. Alarmed, he ran the back of his hand across her cheek and found her skin clammy and cold.

"Woman, when was the last time you ate?"

She lifted her hand and waved it as if batting away a cloud of flies. He barked at the sailors for food—anything—a crust of bread, a bite of cheese. One sailor paused rowing long enough to pull an apple out of a sack and toss it his way.

He caught it with one hand and held it under her face. "Take a bite, Cairenn. You'll feel better."

"Too many people . . ."

"We're almost at the quay." He stretched an arm across her narrow shoulders as she started shaking. "Come, just one bite."

She shook off his grip and shot to her feet. She looked down at him, her gaze unfocused and wild, before her eyes rolled to the back of her head.

Then she collapsed like a puppet whose strings had been cut.

CHAPTER THIRTEEN

Oblivion was a balm. It was like being dropped into the depths of a calm sea. The noise of the world muffled to nothing. But the very moment she became conscious of the oblivion was the moment she rose out of it like a bubble wending its way toward light.

She drew in a breath as her senses slowly awakened. She recognized the crackling of a fire, a pillow that smelled of fresh goose-down and a mattress that squeaked with new hay. With some hesitation, she turned her mind toward the world around her, anticipating the noise of thousands of thoughts, dreading the pounding that would begin in her temples under that pressure.

But no one was close. The first minds she touched were those of three men conversing on a lower floor. One was a merchant by the name of Angus O'Donnell, and the other two his clerics. Their bellies were full and their wine cups more so, and they all brooded about the witch in their midst.

Witch.

Her eyes flew open. With a start she realized that Lachlan's face was so close that she could see a crease deepening between his brows.

Then the crease softened, as did the expression of worry on his face.

"I've been waiting too long," he said, in a low, rumbling voice, "to see those eyes of green."

Shadowed by his growing beard, the corners of his lips lifted. His eyes were the velvet blue of a sky just before it darkens into night. She opened her mouth to speak but her throat was dry. She licked her lips, and at the motion he reached for a skin of ale sitting on a table beside him.

He pulled out the cork. "Drink."

As she struggled to rise, he slid his arm beneath her. He eased her up as if she weighed nothing and then he lifted the skin to her lips.

The ale tasted cool, like it had just come from a cellar. She drank deeply, so deeply that she sputtered.

"Easy," he said, pulling it away.

His arm felt warm and strong against her spine. His face was close enough that she felt his breath. In her chest came a strange tightness that made her shy. She lowered her gaze to her hands lying on a fine linen covering edged with lace.

"How long have I been . . . ?"

"A day and a little more. Those church bells you hear are ringing for vespers."

She spread the tentacles of her deeper senses out into the world despite the dull ache in her head.

She realized that they were lodged in a place apart from the center of Derry. She sensed the bright stridency of a dense gathering of people, but at a distance. Far enough for her to set it aside, to push it out of her attention. There were others in this building, a dozen souls scattered about. Cooks in the scullery cleaning up from the supper soup and setting dough to rise on the warm mantel. Maids sweeping the dogs out of the main hall. Stable boys dozing in the hay.

A manor hall, then.

"Don't drift away, Cairenn."

He brushed a curl off her brow, a gentle touch that made her long for so much more. She dared to look at him. She resisted the urge to reach up and wind a lock of his hair around her finger. Was it any wonder that a woman would fall so easily under the spell of a man, when his thoughts were hidden and his face so beautiful?

He said, "How are you feeling?"

"Weak," she confessed.

"Five days in the hold without food or water will do that."

It wasn't a lack of food and water that had made her weak, but she didn't contradict him because his words were soft. This was the softness she'd hoped for when she'd first risen out of the hold of the galley. Maybe he wasn't angry at her anymore for daring to follow him, for causing him so much trouble.

She hadn't come here to cause trouble. She'd ventured into this unfamiliar world for one reason alone: To convince him of the truth so she could help him.

Well, maybe there was another reason, too.

She reached for the skin of ale again. She meant to drink slowly, but the ale was fresh and she hoped there was courage at the bottom.

"Easy, lass. The doctor said if you drink too quickly you'll get sick."

"Doctor?" she sputtered.

"Of course I sent for a doctor." A strange expression passed across his face. "He left an herb mixture for when you awakened to help expel the . . . madness."

Her public confession came to mind, and along with it a rush of fear. "Perhaps I should not have started that foolishness."

"Perhaps?"

"I misjudged the sailors. But you gave me no choice."

"And so you took all choice away from me, as well."

He pulled his arm out from behind her. It felt like he pulled away a hundred thousand miles. He sat back in the chair by the bed and crossed his arms. A look passed across his face, a look that she'd seen once before, while he puzzled out the wooden pieces of the rain sluice he'd started to build on Inishmaan.

He passed his fingers through the scruff of his growing beard. "What am I to do with you, lass?"

"You're going to keep me with you," she said, courage rising. "You're going to let me help you find the man who demanded your death."

"Lass, I'd sooner swim the distance from here

to Inishmaan with you strapped to my back."

"You *will* let me stay," she insisted, "when I tell you about the vision my mother had concerning you."

She was disappointed to find no change in his expression, not even the shift of a jaw or the flicker of an eyelash.

"My mother's gift is prophecy." Strange how easily such forbidden confessions slipped off her lips, now that she'd escaped the island. "She took one look at you and saw your future as clear as day."

"A grim one, no doubt."

"Death."

A lift of a brow was his only reaction. It unnerved her that he'd be so unruffled. But, then again, if he didn't believe in her mother's gift, why would he believe in the revelation, even if it was foreboding?

She said, "You can't deny that my mother has unusual eyes. I saw my mother turn her gaze upon you that night, when you first supped with us during the storm."

She thought she saw a flicker of acknowledgement on his face. But when he didn't deny it, she took his silence as an invitation.

"My mother is the reason we live on a place as remote as Inishmaan. I can hide my gift, my older sister and brother can conceal theirs, and my father walks unnoticed in the world. But my mother's eyes mark her in a way that's unsettling to outsiders."

"So she says I'll die," he said, "but death comes to every man."

"My mother speaks not of what will happen in twenty years, but what will happen within weeks or even days."

"She knew the circumstances of my situation just as you did. It's a wonder another dagger hasn't been plunged in my back already."

"I came here to change that fate."

"Fate is unchangeable."

"That's not true." She pressed the heels of her palms against the mattress and pulled her weight up so she was sitting upright, even though it made her head swim. "If you change circumstances, then your fate will follow."

"Or my fate will consume you, Cairenn, and your parents will lose another daughter."

She winced because she couldn't avoid the guilty impact of those words. She remembered how Ma and Da had suffered after Aileen disappeared from the strand. Now that another daughter was gone, Cairenn imagined that her mother had taken anew to rocking by the fire, silent with worry and care, while her father isolated himself in the sickroom crushing herbs in mortars.

He said, "I take it from your silence that you understand why I have to return you home—"

"My mind," she interrupted, "is not changed. If you take me with you to Loch Fyfe, I can tell you whether a man is an ally—or an assassin."

He breathed hard through his nose. "Are you to step between me and a blade then? Or do you think your so-called gift can help?"

She flinched. How very different the world must be to outsiders who knew nothing of magic. It seemed that whenever magic appeared before them, their first instinct was to deny—or to burn.

She had to offer Lachlan the kind of proof that he couldn't deny.

"We are in the home of Angus O'Donnell," she began. "He's your father's second cousin, and one of three men in Derry who run shipping between Cork, Bantry, Kilrush, Galway, Donegal, and up to Scotland and the Western Isles. He ships wine, timber, hides, salt, spices when he can get them—"

"Your mind is quick to pick up idle sailor's talk with you five days in the hold."

She frowned and focused on odd facts, personal ones. "Angus is longing for more pepper on his meat. He has determined that if some comes in on one of his boats, he will keep most for himself, no matter the cost."

Lachlan made a point of glancing at a tray on the table by the bed—his dinner, she supposed, for she had not yet eaten. On it was the remnants of a stew, speckled with dark flecks that looked suspiciously like pepper.

"He had a wife, a beloved wife," she continued. "Everyone called her Aunt Eva but she was Eveline to him. She died from childbed fever after giving birth to his sixth child, a son. He mourns her every St. Stephen's Day by lighting candles in St. Columb's Cathedral."

Lachlan went still.

"Right now," she persisted, sliding toward him, "Angus is lingering in the great hall below with two of his clerics. One of them is from Donegal. He took his orders in Armagh, he's an Augustinian. He wears a hair shirt beneath his cloak and flogs himself during Lent to purge himself of a sin he's never committed but is tempted by frequently. He also has a small dog he feeds from the table. His abbot doesn't approve, but he named the dog after an old Irish deity, Dagdá—"

"A priest's dog with a pagan name? Come, lass—"

"—Angus loved your father like a brother," she said, despite the rising glower on Lachlan's face. "In their youth, they went to war together against the Campbells. Angus would never betray him, nor you, not for all the pepper in the world. I tell you true: Angus O'Donnell is not your enemy."

"Enough."

Lachlan shot up from the chair so fast it clattered backwards. Then he turned on a heel and walked out of the room.

CHAPTER FOURTEEN

*I**mpossible.*
Lachlan gripped the railing of the second-floor balcony and stared down at the great hall below. He saw the clerics Cairenn had mentioned standing up from the trestle table. He heard the rustle of their clothes, the scrape of their feet, and the last-minute orders from Angus as they headed out of the hall. He told himself that noises carried easily in this house. Much of the nonsense she'd just said she could have guessed from things she'd overheard.

The rest she must have made up—like Angus's pet name for his wife and the damn pagan dog.

Pushing away from the railing, Lachlan made his way down the stairs and laid eyes on his shaggy-headed kinsman. How had she guessed Angus's loyalties? Lachlan had learned the truth yesterday when he roughhoused his way into Angus's mead-hall, carrying a woman in his arms. His burly, big-bellied kinsmen had looked at him with the elation of a father glimpsing his prodigal son.

Now Angus bellowed from the head of the table, "There you are, cousin. How fares our madwoman?"

"Delirious." He planted himself at the end of a bench and reached for the pitcher of ale. "Nothing a hearty meal and another night's sleep won't cure."

He poured himself some of the brew while Angus barked for one of the servants to bring a tray to their guest upstairs. Lachlan took a long gulp of ale and remembered how, at Inishmaan, her curious green eyes used to bore into him as if she were trying to penetrate his skull.

A clatter of wood upon stone brought him back to the moment.

"My son," Angus said, tilting his head toward a small boy of about five playing by the hearth. "He likes to destroy castles, mostly Campbell ones."

Lachlan stilled with the tankard halfway to his lips. Somehow she'd known that Angus and his father had fought against the Campbells all those years ago.

He shook off the thought as the tow-headed boy kept trotting his wooden horse around the rubble. "Your youngest?"

"Indeed. Does he not look more like Eveline every day?"

Aunt Eva, for whom every St. Stephen's Day Angus lit candles in St. Columb's Cathedral.

Lachlan took a gulp of ale. There was an explanation for all of this. Magic didn't exist, not without the touch of the devil.

"Tell me," Lachlan said, turning his mind to other things, "have you heard any more news about my father's murder, or what is happening in my clan?"

"I sent two men to make queries in the alehouses, but there are few Scots in Derry at the moment." Angus raised bushy brows as he poured himself more wine from a dusty bottle sitting beside the pitcher of ale. "You should prepare yourself for the worst. It has been weeks since your father's death. I suspect they've called council by now to determine the new chieftain."

"Maybe not." It had taken three tense months before they'd elected his father. "Even if a council was called, it will be a false council, and my arrival will prove it so."

"Your father's decision to change the tradition was never well-received. Many who had nothing to do with your father's death may still welcome the change—"

"Which means that whoever claims the rod at council must be the man who ordered the assassins."

Angus shook his great, shaggy head.

"Why else," Lachlan asked, "would someone murder the head of a clan and his heir, if not to grasp the rod for himself?"

"The men of your clan are not stupid. At council, they, too, will suspect anyone who claims the chieftaincy."

"As they should—"

"But your enemy is sly. He'll make it look like he doesn't want it, as if the responsibility is thrust upon him."

Lachlan paused. How it galled him to think that his enemy might be smarter than he.

He turned his tankard in his hand and watched the rush lights glance off the surface of the ale. He summoned in his mind the faces of the most powerful men of the clan, those most likely to make a claim to the chieftaincy. The list was long. Dermot MacGilchrist, the head of the MacGilchrist clan, had married a Campbell years ago, a daughter of the sprawling, warlike tribe always trying to expand their influence. Callum Ewing, the head of the Ewing clan, had been beaten out by Lachlan's own father when the rod passed over a decade ago. The Lamont clan to the east, always reeving cattle and driving their sheep onto MacEgan pastureland, would revel in the discord. Then there was Lachlan's own stepmother, a Stuart, always casting acid looks his way while she watched over Fingal, her only son.

Fingal, his half-brother, and the next MacEgan in line.

No, not Fingal.

Never Fingal.

"The man who seizes the rod must be the one." Lachlan repeated the words with confidence, all while he worried his fingers through the scruff of beard he'd not yet gotten used to. "He will be the devil responsible for all of this, I'm sure of it."

His cousin nodded. "You must leave for Loch Fyfe as soon as possible."

"I need a day, maybe two to prepare. I have to arrive unnoticed, and that'll take some doing."

"You don't have a day, perhaps not even an hour. I've ordered my servants to keep your presence here a secret, but the fact that you arrived carrying a self-proclaimed sorceress complicates matters. Your witch is the talk of Derry. *You* are the talk of this house. Both of you have to leave before there's a crowd at my door with torches and pitchforks."

Lachlan grunted. If a rumor began that he was still alive, it would reach Loch Fyfe in the time it takes for a man to row across the strait.

"I need men. Arms." He pulled at his borrowed clothes. "A tunic and surcoat of my own."

"Or perhaps the robes of a cleric," Angus suggested, shrugging.

"A cleric? Carrying a claymore?"

"Staying hidden does seem the wiser course. A smaller sword would be easier to hide."

"Angus, I don't exactly look like I've spent a lifetime bent over a scroll out of the glare of the sun."

"Maybe not," he said. "But nobody will notice if you're one cleric among many who just happens to be accompanying a certain Derry merchant on a long-delayed visit to Loch Fyfe."

Lachlan eyed his cousin as the implications sank in. "I can't ask you to do that."

"Sales of wine have dropped off from the north." He raised his tankard and smiled through wine-stained lips. "I need to remind your kinsmen how much better Spanish wine tastes than your wretched ale."

Lachlan frowned. Though his father had sent

him to Angus to gather men to help in his fight, after so much death Lachlan preferred to act on his own. He didn't need another death on his conscience.

"I loved your father, too, Lachlan," Angus said. "Don't deny me this small sip of your vengeance." Then, dismissing all further discussion, his cousin raised one finger toward the balcony of the second floor. "What shall we do with our frail but misguided beauty upstairs?"

At the thought of Cairenn, Lachlan lifted his pewter tankard but it was already empty. He stared at the dregs and tried not to think of the way the sea wind played with her hair. He pushed away the remembrance of the way her hips moved when she climbed to the island's height. He tried to forget what it felt like to burrow against her breasts, to feel her body arch in pleasure under the touch of his hand.

The clatter of another fortress tumbling startled Lachlan back to the great hall, to the cut of the tankard's handle into his fist, and to Angus's piercing scrutiny.

"Who is this woman," his kinsman asked, "who weighs so heavily upon your mind?"

Memories overwhelmed him, of the curve of her neck lit by the sun, the arch of her feet as she crouched, the heavy slide of her braid over her shoulder. Images of her green eyes intent upon him and the intelligence he saw behind them. Her ease with the village boy, the deference of the fishermen, the stories she whispered to her sister to make the young girl burst into laughter.

His tongue felt like lead in his mouth.

Angus said, "Did you make this woman promises?"

"You know I cannot."

"Love comes upon a man quickly, Lachlan." Angus's heavy sigh filled the room. "It flies swift out of the cold, like a sparrow shooting through the mead-hall in winter."

His kinsman may as well have been speaking in tongues for all the sense Lachlan could make of it.

"I can arrange passage for her back to Galway," Angus said. "My ships, and my sailors, are under my orders. They'll do as I say, witch or no."

A pause lay heavy between them. Lachlan knew he should order it done. Cairenn belonged safe in Inishmaan, among her own people.

Then the rapid click-click of a dog's claws drew his attention. A ragged-haired lapdog bounded out of a far corridor toward Angus's son, who shouted in delight.

"Papa, look! It's Dagdá!"

She woke up to the sound of a door closing.

She jolted up from the bed, disoriented in the dimness. Lachlan stood just inside the room, limned by the reddish light of the hearth fire. She hadn't really been sleeping, too tormented by doubts and concerns, but the sight of him made her entire body come prickly back to life.

"You've eaten," he said.

She glanced where he gestured, to a tray with some crusts of bread and gravy leavings. She didn't remember eating and she certainly hadn't tasted a thing.

He said, "Feeling stronger?"

"I'm always strong when I'm alone," she ventured. "It's when there are many strangers around that I weaken."

No more would she bother with lies or evasions, not after the terrible way he'd looked at her.

"Come by the fire," he said, striding to the hearth and gesturing to the stool on the other side. "I can't talk to you while you're splayed in that bed."

Her body tingled from scalp to toes. Staring at the great stretch of his shoulders, she became achingly conscious of the thinness of the linen shift she was wearing, and not a stitch of fabric beneath it.

She pulled the blanket off her knees and swung her legs over the side. She padded to the stool and sat. The fire gave off a strange smell, tarry and harsh, not at all like the fragrance of the peat her father shipped over from the mainland.

"How long," he said, "have you been like this?"

The brush of his gaze made her heart trip and her blood ripple with a sudden heat.

"Since my thirteenth summer." She wished she'd brought the cup of wine, ruby-red, from the bedside table. "My father used to take us to Galway, one or two children at a time, to give my mother some peace. He'd give us a coin and let us wander through the town. I intended to buy some dyed wool for a new tunic. That's what was in my mind as we headed toward the wharf in my father's coracle—until, suddenly, it was like my mind was full of angry bees."

"Like yesterday," he said.

A lot worse, to her reckoning, but she nodded anyway. "I was unconscious for nearly a week. None of Da's medicines worked. When I finally woke up, I heard everyone's secrets as clear as day. For a long time I thought everyone had gone mad, saying such terrible things out loud."

Even now, when she cast her mind into the world, she heard secrets. The stable boy was staring up at the rafters and imagining sneaking into the maidservant's room to slip his member into her from behind. Angus was musing about a widow in town he'd like to swive but not marry. The kitchen cook was growing ever more excited imagining a witch-burning in the square.

She winced at a sudden sharp pain in her hand. She glanced down and saw that she was leaving half-moon impressions in her palm.

"My mother finally guessed what had happened," she said, rubbing at the angry pink marks. "She taught me how to distinguish between what someone says and what someone thinks. So often the two are not the same."

"Tell me how it works."

"I simply hear everything." She wished he would look at her, instead of watching the fire consume the wood in the hearth. "I can hear the cook in the kitchen right now, kneading the bread for tomorrow. She's thinking about her sick daughter." *And whether she should bring her to the burning.* "I can hear three scullery maids in the mead-hall collecting the dishes and chattering about a fair that's coming. The nursemaid is bone-tired and Angus's son Tadgh is being fussy because he didn't eat enough dinner. I can hear Angus worrying about you."

And me.

A warmth blossomed on her cheeks, for Angus believed that she and Lachlan were lovers.

"If I stretch my mind," she said, forging ahead, "I can even hear the people of Derry, every one of them. Most of the time I hear ordinary thoughts—whether they're hungry or something hurts, or what work they must do before the sun goes down, or whether it's going to rain and ruin the crops or whether the herring are running yet." She took her lower lip between her teeth for a moment, debating whether she should tell him more. "Behind that are . . . other thoughts. I can hear who they are, and who they want to be. I sense their wishes and dreams. I know the things they don't want anyone to know, the things they try to hide, and all their sins. The deeper I look into a man's eyes, the more I see."

Lachlan planted a forearm on the mantel, leaning in. "You say Angus is loyal to me."

"When Angus and your father were young, they sailed on a ship past the Island of Skye during a storm, and your father saved him from drowning."

"That's the past."

"Yes, but the memory is often at the front of Angus's mind. He's very aware that were it not for your father, he'd be long dead."

The folds of Lachlan's tunic shifted across his back in fascinating ways. She tried not to stare.

"My father," he said, "told me that story about Skye just once, the night before I last saw him. He was about to send me to Derry to get men and arms to help fight those who were causing so much trouble. He told me that I needed to understand why he trusted his kinsman Angus though they hadn't seen each other in years. He told me that he and Angus never spoke of that incident again—and no one else knew the tale."

Lachlan settled his midnight-sky gaze upon her. A tingle spread through her at the look on his face.

He believes me.

"Cairenn," he whispered, "tell me how this can be."

Her chest swelling with hope, it took her a moment to find her voice. "My father told me that one of my ancestors was a Druid priestess in Ulster. This was a long, long time ago, before all memory, when the veils between the worlds were thin. This ancestor loved a man of the Otherworld—a man of *Tír na nÓg*—and on one Samhain—"

"Stop." He shook his head once. "No children's tales."

His command flummoxed her. Da had told her this story after she'd woken up in the wake of her collapse in Galway. He'd explained everything while making her choke down some foul-tasting tea. His explanation had seemed so logical then—after all, she'd felt the *Sídh* themselves, rising up between the cracks in the stones whilst she wandered the lonely places on high. But then again, that was Inishmaan, which was different from the rest of the world.

Now, here, sitting in this stone-walled room with this strange-smelling wood, she began to understand why Lachlan might think she was telling him a tale fit for the nursery rather than telling him the truth.

"Children's tales are full of magic," she confessed in a small voice, "but this is no tale for the young."

"Cairenn—"

"Are you to close your ears to the only truth I know?"

His powerful chest expanded with a sigh. She saw a muscle flex in his cheek, then he tightened his jaw and nodded.

"This ancestor of mine," she continued, "loved a man of the Otherworld. On one Samhain, when the veils between the worlds thinned, they went to the fires and . . ." Cairenn hesitated. She didn't know if the Scots had the same traditions as the Irish, celebrating the four turns of the year—Beltane, Imbolc, Lughnasa, and Samhain—with fires and dancing and much more in the night, but she had no choice but to continue. "On that night, they created a link of flesh and spirit, fairy and human, which kept the worlds together even as they threatened to drift apart."

She hazarded a glance at him, relieved that he was still listening.

"Fairy blood runs strong," she said. "This is why everyone in my family has a gift. My sister Aileen has the gift of the healing hands, a gift in which my father took such pride. My gift," she said, shrugging, "is the ability to know people's minds."

"You're not one of the wee folk, Cairenn. Any more than I'm a selkie."

Her heart dipped a little at the reminder of her foolishness.

"I can see you," he said. "I have held you in these arms."

With a frisson she remembered his hand cupping her breast, his fingers doing magic things between her legs. Then, as if he could read *her* thoughts, he crossed the three steps that separated them and stood over her, looking down at her with undeniable intent.

"You're human," he said, grasping her face in his hands as she surged out of her seat. "I feel your heart, I see your pulse beating in your throat."

"Lachlan—"

"For weeks I watched you on Inishmaan. I've broken bread with your family. For all this talk of magic and witchery, everything in my heart tells me you are good."

She ran her hands up his arms and felt the hard, flexing sinew under the warmth of his skin. Emotions filled her, making it hard for her to breathe, to speak, to think.

"I made a promise to your father," he said, his brow furrowing, "that I would not dishonor you."

She shook her head, for she'd followed him across a sea to get out from under that protection.

"Angus has made arrangements." His grip tightened. "Take the berth on a ship that he will offer you. Leave me before I do something I shouldn't."

She pressed her hands against his chest. "I want you, Lachlan."

He made a sound deep in his throat. He dragged his hands up through her hair. He was not gentle, not even when his lips fell upon hers.

He nudged her lips open and there was his tongue, probing inside her mouth in a way that made her knees weak. She tasted the ale he'd been drinking. He slung an arm around her back and lifted her against him. Her toes barely scraped the cold floor. Beneath her palms his heart pounded wildly.

She heard him kick something, heard a stool overturn, then the brush of his feet in the rushes. She knew they were moving but could not see where, didn't care, as long as he didn't let go.

When she felt the edge of the bed dig into the back of her knees, he sucked her lower lip into his mouth, then her upper lip, then rubbed his lips against her while she tasted them with a hunger she hadn't had for the bread and the stew.

Dizzy, she pushed him a fraction away in search of the ties of his tunic. He was wearing too many clothes. She wanted to press her cheek against the naked hollow on his chest where his heart lay, slip her tongue across his skin, do all those things that men and women did when passion took hold, so that she could experience that closeness, that joining, and find her way into his mind.

She fumbled with the ties. He took a step back so she could tug at them, watching as she did. He reached between them and yanked off his belt.

Impatiently she pushed the surcoat off him, let it puddle to the floor, and shoved his linen tunic off the swell of his muscled shoulder.

Then her mouth was against that shoulder, gleaming golden in the light of the fire. Warm on her lips, smooth against her tongue, with a strength that flexed under the grip of her hand. She felt a chill on her back and realized he'd pushed her shift off her shoulders. She wriggled her arms out of the sleeves and let it fall, whisper-soft, to her feet.

She'd never been naked in front of anyone but her sisters. Now, upon her toes with the firelight on her skin, Lachlan leaned back so he could run his gaze from her scalp to her feet. His look felt like the brush of a thousand fingers.

His member rose stiff between them. A pulsing thrill coursed through her, settling heavy in her loins.

"Send me away," he said, his voice husky. "For your own sake."

She answered him by scraping her mouth down his jaw, over his neck and collarbone, to where the neckline of his tunic sagged. Seeking beneath the weave, she found the nub of his nipple and did to him what he'd once done to her.

He flattened his hand against her back until, with a groan, he lowered his face into her hair, breathing hot against her ear. He dragged his hands down her spine—long scraping pinpoints where his fingernails rode—until he grasped her bottom with both hands.

As he hefted her bottom up, she felt her cleft open wetly. Oh, how she ached to feel him there.

The world tipped as he hauled her up and stretched her across the bed. She saw the canopy above her and then Lachlan's face as it descended.

He took her hand and hauled it over her head, holding it there. Then he took her other wrist and hauled it up, too, grasping both tightly with one hand. The movement made her arch off the bed, her breasts—her nipples tightened and tingling—pointing toward the canopy. Lachlan lowered his head.

His hot, sucking mouth shot tremors through her body. He tugged and licked and teased her with the edge of his teeth, gently squeezing the whole of her breast in his hand so he could suck more than just the nipple into his mouth. She was vaguely aware that she was thrashing, jerking her arms against his restraint, lifting her legs on either side of him. She loved the pressure of his body against the mound between her legs, but wanted to feel more, wanted to feel *him.*

He slipped his hand between them and slid his fingers along her cleft. She gasped and went still. His lips and fingers did not. He rolled his tongue over her nipple, then exposed it to the cold air, even as his fingers slid down, deeper, spreading the wetness between her legs. He switched breasts as he pressed the butt of his hand against her mound and probed deeper.

With her head thrown back, one thought skittered across her mind—that this wasn't how she'd expected it to feel. Yes, yes, she'd known that there would be pleasure. She couldn't avoid the minds of all the lovers upon Inishmaan. How she'd envied their intimacies, the wholehearted joining, and the simple, trusting pleasure that made lovers temporarily blind to all else but the sensations coursing between them. But she hadn't really understood *this,* the sweet physicality of the act, the intensity of it, the rising ache and the unfettered urge that took her over as surely as a wave sucking her under the sea.

She wasn't even trying to read his thoughts anymore, but she sensed the merging of minds nonetheless. They were in a bright place speaking a language without words.

All of a sudden, he released her wrists. Her fingertips tingled from the tightness of his grip. She lowered her hands, intending to pull him up for a kiss, but already he was trailing down her body. His soft hair brushed her breasts, her ribs, her belly button, where he paused for a moment to roll his tongue in the hollow. She reached for him, for he was going in the wrong direction. She didn't want him to slide off her—she wanted him covering her body. She wanted to bring his loins between hers and open herself for his thrust.

She grasped his head but he slipped out from under her grip. He slid down between her legs even as she struggled to rise up on her elbows. He thrust a shoulder beneath one leg, forcing her thigh high, and then did the same for the other. She glanced down as he spread her legs wide, vibrating with excitement at the sight of him hovering above her cleft. He glanced up at her, his expression unreadable, his hair haloed by the golden light of the fire, and then he pressed his lips *there.*

Later she would remember that first moment and her heart would skitter-pound and the muscles of the inside of her thighs would clench and she'd lose the ability to speak, breathe, think in a moment of bright blindness that would make her stumble to a stop in whatever she was doing. All she sensed was his hair soft against the inside of her thighs and the rough brush of his tongue opening her wide. A pressure built in her body as he plunged his hot, muscled tongue around and between and deep inside her.

Her mind went blank. She arched against his hands before the light in her mind blinded her. Her body convulsed around the pressure of his kiss. She heard herself give a husky shout before she arched up, again, and again, and again, moaning.

Lassitude spread over her. She pressed her cheek against the blanket as every touch of his mouth sent aftershocks shuddering through her body. Cold air bathed her as he pulled away. The mattress sagged as he settled his hands on either side of her, and he drew his body higher on the bed. She felt a hard, throbbing pressure against her belly. He laid his face beside hers, rocking against her abdomen, pushing his forehead into the covers until he stiffened and held his breath. She heard a low groan as something hot and wet bathed her belly. His body went lax while he buried his face in her hair.

She burrowed her fingers in his long hair. The only sound in the room was the harshness of their breathing. With their skin pressed together, she could feel the moisture between them. With that came a quiver of disappointment. She knew what he'd done. He'd spilled his seed *upon* her, so he wouldn't spill it *in* her.

She stared up at the canopy as the implications of what he'd done sank in. It was a strange side effect of her gift that she knew more about the many ways of lovemaking than most married women. As such, she knew that married men gave their seed to the linens sometimes, in order to give their wives a rest between children. But that was the exception. Mostly, it was unmarried men who did this: Unmarried men catching a woman behind a rock-pile fence on a spring day, or cheating on their wives or sweethearts, or coupling with a woman they didn't want to bother with past the one moment.

Men did this, she thought, when they did not want to be bound.

She closed her eyes, not wanting to believe that Lachlan would act so. Then, by habit, she spread her thoughts toward the walls that always stood between their minds—and the darkness she had warred against for so long suddenly crumbled.

CHAPTER FIFTEEN

Her hair smelled like Inishmaan.

With his nose buried in it, Lachlan imagined they were lying upon the windswept heights while waves crashed upon the shore below. In his mind, he carried her there like a bride. He laid her down amid the heather. He peeled her clothing off her body and watched the way the sea mist beaded upon her skin. He licked those beads off her belly and drank where they pooled in her navel. He took her hips in his hands and slipped into her while she arched up off the ground in pleasure.

His cock swelled despite the fact that he was only moments past his own pleasure. She lay warm beneath him, every breath bringing his chest in contact with her soft, pliant breasts. All it would take was a shift of his hips and he'd make that fantasy real.

The idea filled his head and cast a haze across his conscience. He groaned and mustered enough control to roll off her. He seized her hand and pressed her knuckles against his lips, trying to ignore the hollow craving in his heart. Blinking up at the carved underside of the bed's canopy, he counted diamond panels in order to cool his blood, then he squeezed his eyes shut and tried to think of other things—duty, honor, obligations. A vision of her father rose into his mind, whose countenance demanded he do right by the woman who now lay naked beside him.

How could I resist her? He'd been so sure she would come to her maidenly senses once she dropped her clothing. But the woman who'd emerged had not covered her body, had not shrunk with shyness, and had not looked up at him with eyes begging for gentleness. She'd stood with her shoulders thrown back. Her gaze had been a challenge.

An ache reignited in his balls.

Damn it.

He shifted to his side, bracing himself for the sight of her face, passion-flushed, and her lips begging for more.

Instead he saw tears.

He shot up onto his elbow. "Cairenn—"

She pushed away quicker than he could stop her. He reached for her but all he caught was a lock of her hair that slipped through his fingers. She shot off the bed, swept up her shift from the floor, and strode naked to the other side of the room. Stopping in front of a table near the privacy screen, she seized a cloth and dipped it in a bowl of water.

By the bend of her neck he surmised that she

was washing her belly. Her sweet, rounded bottom swayed with every stroke.

"*Mo chridhe*," he whispered. "What's wrong?"

She shook her head once but did not turn to face him. Maybe it was his restraint that had angered her. Maybe he needed to explain that he had held off from spilling inside her so that there would be no complications from their coupling. He had enough experience pleasing willing women, but narrow experience with an eager innocent. Somehow, he'd fallen short of her expectations.

No, he thought. He could still feel her body throbbing against his mouth. That was surely not the problem. Whatever bothered her hung heavy in the silence. He cast back to their previous conversation, wondering what he'd said that had pushed her to tears. He'd given her every opportunity to send him away.

Then a slow, creeping sense of dread took hold of him. He raised his gaze to the curve of her naked back and thought, as loud as one could think, *Turn around, Cairenn.*

She didn't twitch or pause or shift her weight or make any acknowledgement that she heard his thought, but he was not reassured. A woman under the constant onslaught of other people's minds would have long learned how to control her reactions to even the loudest, most sudden thoughts. Back on Inishmaan, she'd claimed she could read everybody's mind *except his*. He'd dismissed her remark because he hadn't believed in her gift. Now he believed in her gift, but was all the more confused.

Why, amongst all the people in the world, would her gift fail when it came to reading him?

He knew the answer. Her gift didn't fail at all. She'd lied to him, because it was easier that way.

"Don't ignore me, Cairenn," he said, trying to stanch a knot of panic as he shifted to the edge of the bed. "I know you're angry."

"Am I?"

"Are you going to tell me what's wrong or do I have to drag you back to this bed and kiss you until you speak?"

She crumpled the linen aside and then spread her hands on the table as if to brace herself. The shift she'd hung over her arm slipped off her elbow to puddle on the floor. He tried not to run his gaze over the swell of her buttocks, to the space between her thighs, and the shadows of her sex, but the next thing he knew he was standing behind her and his hand was reaching for the path his mind had explored.

She flinched and stepped away. She dipped down to grab her shift off the floor, and then held it against her breasts as she turned. Her face was stony. Her eyes gleamed with accusations that made him feel shame for no reason at all.

Then her expression changed. She narrowed that gaze upon him like she used to do on Inishmaan, and her words came back to him with force.

The deeper I look into a man's eyes, the more I see.

Now he understood what this look meant. Without his consent, she was trying to strip him of the privacy of his own thoughts. He became aware of his nakedness with a keenness he'd never experienced, and it was not the lack of clothing that made him feel so.

He said, "Stop."

She startled and the fierceness of her look eased. He was no coward, but he'd rather face the gleam of a claymore in the hands of a Campbell than have anyone see all his sins, weaknesses, and secrets.

Anger rose like bile in his throat. "You lied to me, woman."

"No," she countered. "You lied to *me*."

He clenched his jaw and strode around the end of the bed, to where his clothes lay strewn in the rushes. He wrestled into his undertunic as certainty pinched him. Now she knew everything. Lachlan of Loch Fyfe was no mighty warrior. No great avenger. Few people ever saw beyond his name and the gleam on his fine chain mail.

She said, sharply, "When were you going to tell me?"

"Tell you what?" He'd be damned if he'd speak of such things aloud.

"Are there so many deceptions that you don't know which to choose?"

"At least I can only accuse you of one." He reared up to face her, thankful for the dimness of the room. "In Inishmaan, you told me you couldn't read my mind."

"I cannot."

"You just *did*."

"I did not." Her voice broke and her gaze

skittered away. "At least, not just now, though I tried." She made theater out of the act of shaking out her shift. "Your mind is shut and barred like a fortress again. The only time I can read you is when—"

She hazarded a glance toward the rumpled linens. It took him a minute to realize what she was saying.

She could read his mind while they made love.

He let out a long, harsh breath. No wonder he'd felt such closeness as he touched her, kissed her, made love to her. An intimacy like he'd felt with no other woman before, because she had slipped into his mind.

He shook off the thought and reached for his surcoat. "You should keep out of a man's mind when he's in his weakness."

"Maybe a man should control his thoughts better."

"How does anyone do that? Even the lowest slave considers himself free to keep his own thoughts."

"You speak as if I can choose *not to hear*."

He ran his hand through his hair, flummoxed. "None of this makes sense."

"Magic never does."

"You must know others like me."

"If there are, I've not yet met them." She swept her shift over her head. Her breasts lifted with the gesture, her nipples tight and tilted. "But you haven't yet answered my question."

He had not. He'd been debating how much she could possibly have seen during the time they spent absorbed in one another's bodies. Surely it took more than a few moments to see into the true heart of a man.

So he told her the only truth he knew. "I've never lied to you, Cairenn."

"You made love to me and withheld the truth. That is no different." She curled her arms around the bedpost, pressing her cheek against it. "When *were* you going to tell me about your betrothal?"

His promised bride was beautiful. In the brief moment when Cairenn had been coherent enough to peer into his mind, she'd had only a glimpse of the woman, but the image had burned like a brand. His someday-bride had hair as dusky as a winter night. She had a mouth that always pouted, like she was constantly begging to be kissed. The woman wore a belt of beaten links that hung from a slim waist. Her breasts stretched her tunic tight, and her hips swayed when she walked.

Now, standing before Lachlan, Cairenn felt like a bundle of hay, flat and skinny with poky elbows and knees.

Into the silence he murmured, "I said nothing about it because I didn't want to cause you pain."

"That's not an answer." If he had told her about this woman from the start, maybe she would never have opened her heart. If she'd known he was promised to another, maybe she would have had the sense to stop herself from wanting more. "You kept it a secret on purpose, for your own ends."

"You are my weakness, *mo chridhe*." He

spread his hands. "From the moment I opened my eyes on the strand and looked upon you, I felt like I had died from my old life and awoken to a better one."

Accusations gathered in her throat but never made it to her tongue. She knew, deep in her heart, that she could no sooner have stopped loving him than she could stop breathing. Now his voice was so tender that it stole all the air from the room.

"I tried to tell you," he said. "I confessed to being the firstborn of a noble family. It was a shield I put between us."

"On Inishmaan we walked and talked as equals." Yes, yes, she knew she had no right to feel betrayed, but she couldn't help herself. "I saw you as a man—not a chieftain."

"Would that more people could see me like that."

"The fact that you admitted to noble blood doesn't absolve you," she added. "You kissed me. You *touched* me—"

"I left you behind on Inishmaan." His fingers made tracks as he ran them through his hair. "As innocent as when I arrived."

"Not so innocent as that."

He raised a dark brow. "Should I have cut your heart in two by telling you about Leana?"

The name made her heart stop for a beat, and then another.

"I determined to leave you behind for your own good," he reminded her. "But you stowed away on my ship."

She bruised her forehead with how hard she

pressed it against the bedpost.

"And after I found you stowed away yesterday, I made every effort to get you passage back to Inishmaan. But when I asked the captain of that galley—"

"—I branded myself a witch," she finished, not wanting to listen to the litany of her own mistakes. "I saw her," she blurted. "As you and I lay in bed together. I saw your Leana, blazing in your mind."

"What you saw was regret. Regret that the woman I'm promised to marry is not"—he made a sound, like a choke—"that the woman I'm promised to marry is not *you.*"

It took a moment for the words to seep through the haze of her pain, but when they did, she raised her face to meet his gaze. It would be simple to cross the distance that separated them and press her face in the nook between his jaw and shoulder. But her feet remained flat upon the floorboards, held there by too many weighty certainties.

Oh, Lachlan.

What a bittersweet declaration of love.

And what a fool she had been, imagining that she'd become so good at reading Lachlan's expressions. The way the little scar by his eye whitened when he was angry. The way his cheek flexed when he wanted something he didn't dare take. But for all that, she'd failed at understanding his most important message of all.

He can offer me nothing.

She pushed away from the bedpost and wandered to a fire that couldn't warm her. She didn't have her mother's gift, but right now she could see her own future as clear as day. If she chose to stay with Lachlan, she'd be living in a hut on the outskirts of some Loch Fyfe village. A place where Lachlan would visit her now and again, when his wife and other duties allowed him. Cairenn would live in that hut and hear news about the chieftain's wife bearing him heirs, one after another. Perhaps she'd bear him a child or two of her own, bastards without names. She would tend to them as she waited by the door in the hopes of hearing the hoof beats of his horse coming through the woods. Days upon days passing, months upon months, years upon years, while she lived far away from him, as well as the only family she knew.

Forever an outcast among outsiders.

"I'll take that berth on Angus's ship." The words passed through her throat like sandpaper. "My parents must be missing me."

She heard his weary exhale. This was the kind of trouble that happened when a woman wrapped herself up in dreams and ignored that which is not spoken aloud. This was what happened to a woman when she couldn't see into a man's deepest thoughts.

He said, "I can't let you go, Cairenn."

"Don't say such things."

"Everything has changed."

"Yes. I'm finally the wiser." No more would she stride to the lonely heights and watch the ships sail out of Galway Bay, for Lachlan was the dream she had chased and now that dream was lost. "Tomorrow morning, I'll be on Angus's ship before the people of Derry can even think to build the witch's pyre."

"You'll be on a ship tomorrow, lass, but you won't be apart from me."

She wondered why he persisted when every word was a plunging knife.

"I'm bound to seize back Loch Fyfe," he said. "Your gift will help me do that. Willing or not, you're coming with me."

CHAPTER SIXTEEN

Cairenn sat in the back of the galley, swathed in a woolen cloak borrowed from the wedding-chest of Angus's late wife. She gripped the gunwales of the boat against the surge and lap of the sea. There was little wind, so the sailors had furled the sail. Fourteen men worked the oars in a sea dense with fog. None seemed concerned by the fact that they couldn't see more than a stone's throw beyond the ship's curved prow, and the low silhouette of Derry had long been swallowed by the fog behind them. They just kept working the oars, steady and hard, doing their best to avoid looking at the witch within their midst.

And here she was, with the sea wind in her hair, and a ship rolling under her feet, and an adventure waiting ahead, just as she'd once dreamed. Yet all excitement or joy or even fear was subsumed by the numbness of her heart. Lachlan had left her alone in that bedroom last night, thwarted, aching, and flummoxed by a new, disturbing truth. His sense of duty was a far stronger force than the love he'd confessed.

If he truly loved her, he would have sent her home.

Now she couldn't help but gaze at the man who had broken her heart, for Lachlan stood at the prow of this ship, looking more chieftain-like than ever. As the man most familiar with the crags, islands, and promontories that would make the best approach to the lands around Loch Fyfe, he would search for an anchorage where they could hide the ship in case they had to retreat from enemies. She knew this through the thoughts of the sailors around her, because Lachlan's mind was battened tight.

"Lugh's Seat is coming up fast port-side," Lachlan said, throwing his voice over his shoulder. "Cut to stern, half-speed, drag the blades."

The man behind her worked the rudder as the galley slowed. Energy surged in the oarsmen, who'd been rowing tirelessly in shifts for hours. Their minds swam with a mixture of tingling anticipation and heart-pounding wariness that she suspected all soldiers felt when faced with looming danger.

A craggy rock appeared from out of the fog, the base foamed with the crash of the sea. Seals swarmed over the stone, barking and ducking their sleek black heads as they dove headlong into the surf. Lachlan shouted orders as the galley slipped by only to weave through a series of smaller rocky outcroppings, just as infested. But for the random arrangement of stony islets, she was reminded of

Inishmaan and the other Aran Islands and how they appeared to sailors as their ships tacked their way into Galway Bay.

The fog thinned to wisps as they entered the mouth of a river. Now she could see the sun, a bright white spot in the sky.

"Head to that anchorage," Lachlan said, pointing to a scalloped landing just ahead, a sliver of mud at the base of a wooded slope. "We're in MacDonald lands, but they rarely patrol these wild places."

With a foot on the gunwale and a hand on the curved prow, he twisted to meet her gaze. His face was stone, but his eyes posed a silent question. She cast her mind toward the shore, spreading her consciousness as far as she could. She did the same for the opposite shore, sensing only the seals swimming around the galley, poking their heads above the water in curiosity, as well as the tickling consciousness on land of red squirrels, tiny voles, and a flock of flighty birds.

Her heart lurched when she turned to find Lachlan waiting, but she met those midnight-sky eyes and nodded.

"We'll camp here," he announced. "Tomorrow we'll march out by land."

When the shallow-draft galley pulled close to the shore, Lachlan leapt out and dragged the tow-line to a sturdy tree trunk. The men settled their oars, paddle-up, and then by turns leapt over the gunwale, hauling their packs above their heads. She stood up and headed toward the bow to find Lachlan waiting, his hand held out toward her.

The word *betrothed* was like a wall between them, one that had nothing to do with the black curtain of his mind.

Slipping a strong arm around her back, he swept her up as if she weighed no more than a bag of flour. She may as well have been a sack of supplies for all the attention he paid to her as he carried her to the shore. Absorbed in the pattern of beard now thick upon his jaw, she didn't realize how far he'd carried her beyond the anchorage until he deposited her out of earshot of the men.

He said, "Still no one patrolling?"

She started at his rough voice, so curt. Like he hadn't stretched his naked body over hers last night.

"There's no one nearby." She mentally probed the woods all the way up the slope. "Not as far as I can tell."

"And how far is that?"

Each clipped question was a pinprick that drew another drop of her heart's blood. "I don't know."

"You don't know."

"On the height of Inishmaan, I could hear sailors on the ships that passed to and from Galway." She wished he wouldn't loom so, she could hardly breathe. "But I could see those ships with my own eyes, and I was far away from people like your sailors, filling up my mind with noise."

It was a half-answer, but it was the only one she had. It had never even occurred to her to measure the range of her gift, it was always too broad as it was. Yet he stood before her as if waiting for a better explanation.

She said, "If I were to move farther from those

sailors and foray into the forest a little deeper—"

"No."

"Why? Do you think I'll run away?"

"If you're seen, we'll be forced into a skirmish."

"I *won't* be seen because I will sense *them* before *they* see *me*. That's why I'm here, isn't it?"

He twisted to glance toward the sailors, setting up camp some ways away.

"They can't hear us," she said. "Though they are wondering if I summoned up the fog that shielded our journey, or conjured the seals, and what other witchery I might now be brewing for you."

"In Derry, you told me that those men were loyal."

"They are loyal. To Angus, and thus, by his command, to you. That doesn't mean their minds aren't wild with superstition. Now are you to let me use my gift for our safety, or was your reason for dragging me here just a mockery?"

She imagined she saw a glint of guilt on his face before he turned away, waving to the deeper woods.

"Be off," he said. "But don't wander far."

She turned on one heel and headed away from him. Slivers of pale sunlight cut through the trees to streak the forest floor. She pulled her senses away from Lachlan's shuttered thoughts and cast her mind wildly into the world. She sensed no other life but that of an owl stirring in a hole in a tree and a fox going still as she passed by its den under the wood of a fallen pine.

She continued to walk long after she stopped bothering to listen. These quiet, thick woods bore no resemblance to the windswept heights of Inishmaan, but her soul sensed that it was a lonely place nonetheless. She let her feet lead her. A pang of longing pierced her to the quick, for the warmth of her family's hearth, for the sight of her mother's gentle eyes, for the familiarity of her own people.

She should have realized that the high-born were not like the laboring folk of Inishmaan, who chose as lovers whoever took their fancy. The people of Inishmaan married young, threw up a house, and happily kept a patch of land in order to feed the single cow given in dowry. But the high-born were like the wounded warriors who found their way to Da's sickroom. Coughing blood, they'd brag of their exploits and boast of their ambitions, risking their lives and the lives of their kin for the stupid, blind determination simply to be called "My lord."

What a fool she had been to give her heart over to Lachlan of Loch Fyfe.

She shuffled to a stop in a pool of hazy light. Out of breath, out of reason, she fell to her knees amid a circle of trees. She raised her gaze past the treetops to the endless northern twilight and wondered how she found herself in this strange place, in such a sorry state. Did she ever really have a choice in the matter? Or had her fate been sealed the moment she'd looked upon Lachlan, stretched naked on the sands of the strand?

She remembered the lines of poetry that had come to her when she'd first laid eyes upon him, lines from the story of Deirdre of the Sorrows.

I would have a man like that
Hair like the raven
Cheek like blood
His body like snow

What irony that she was destined for the same fate as the mythical Deirdre, forever in love with a man to whom she could never be betrothed.

A familiar voice rose from behind her.

"I ordered you to stay close, Cairenn."

Lachlan stepped into the circle of oak trees just as she remembered another thing about the doomed Deirdre of the Sorrows.

Deirdre had defied a king for a chance to be with the man she loved.

In the gloaming, she raised her head from her knees and looked at Lachlan with bright, unworldly eyes.

His heart shifted when he saw the determination on that face.

She surged to her feet and headed for him. Orders shouted in his head—*stay safe where you are, little Cairenn*—but they didn't make it out of his mouth. He'd promised himself that he would protect her—from hope, from harm, and mostly from himself. But the sight of her striding toward him with her face alight broke whatever brittle will he'd constructed. Ever since he'd left her bedroom last night, his heart had been full of wanting.

His arms opened for her as she approached, but he seized her shoulders instead.

"Cairenn—"

"You don't love her," she said, leaning against his grip. "This woman you're betrothed to."

He should lie but her eyes wouldn't let him. "I've known her since I was a child. I don't love her in that way."

"Like a sister, then?"

"A bratty, temperamental one. Our betrothal is just a union to solidify the septs of the clan, nothing more."

She tilted her head. "Swear to me it's true."

"To that I'll swear."

"Then I'll be your leman."

Those words shot to his head faster than a dozen quaffs of ale. His thoughts scattered in a thousand directions, muffled under the riotous pounding of his blood. To be a leman, she would entrust her life, her future, and her body to him with no expectation other than what he offered through kindness. His cock tightened, making it all the more difficult to summon his wits and what was left of his tattered honor.

She shifted in his grip and he realized he was squeezing her shoulders too tight. He eased his grip but fixed his will. "You deserve a better fate."

"Yes, I do." Her voice cut like a blade. "I deserve a hard-working husband of my own kind. I deserve a man who will speak vows in public and grant my children his name. But tell me, what chance did I *ever* have for that, with who I am, and all that I know?"

He had no answer for her. She claimed she could not read his thoughts except in a shared bed, but he remained uneasy with her powers nonetheless. How much harder it would be for a man she could read all the time.

"I'll take what the world allows, Lachlan of Loch Fyfe," she said, "if you're still willing to offer me your heart."

In the end, it wasn't just her words that made him surrender what was left of his tattered promise to her father. It wasn't just the sight of her pale, lovely face, or the beauty that lay beneath her clothing. It was the scent that rose from her pale hair, the salt-sweet scent of the open sea that gave way to a fragrance of sun-warmed rocks and crushed grass that gave away to something muskier. Her fragrance birthed fantasies of the life they could have lived on Inishmaan, if he'd had the liberty to choose.

She made a small, gasping sound just before he captured her lips. He pressed his mouth against hers and felt for a moment like they stood upon the height of her island. Nothing existed in the world but the ground beneath their feet and the trees standing like sentinels around them and their bodies so close he could feel the pillow of her breasts against his chest.

She made another sound, a whoosh of breath. Coming up from their kiss he saw the splay of her hair across the grass and realized that he'd swept her off her feet and laid her down beneath him. He looked at her in the hazy light of the lingering northern twilight. He ran his palm across her breast and her body arched, pliant to his touch.

A groan vibrated in her throat, he felt it against his mouth as he kissed the hollow. He loosened the tangle of her laces as he ran his teeth across the wool that covered the nub of her breast. The arch of her back formed a pocket for his hand. Her fingernails scratched his shoulders in the fury to pull away his tunic.

He loosened her tunic enough to yank it down until one sweet nipple strained away from the restricting neckline. He took it between his lips and rolled it around as she gripped his head and shuddered with her pleasure.

"Lachlan."

His balls clenched, for in the speaking of his name he heard how much she ached for him. He gave up trying to pull down her tunic and instead gathered the hem of her skirts until he found the flesh of her thigh beneath. He ran his fingers up until one firm buttock filled his hand. She moaned and her head fell back onto the grass.

Rising up on his knees, he shoved her skirts up. He made short work with his belt and tugged his surcoat and tunic over his head as one. Her hollow belly rose and fell as he eased her knees wider. His cock throbbed when the shadow of her cleft came into view. He seized her by the hips and dragged her body closer to the swell of his shaft.

Then he paused, though the air was cool and her cleft gleamed and his cock pulsed for release. He wanted nothing more than to plunge into her and feel her hot body throbbing around him. He could give her nothing but his heart and the fleshy pleasures of their bodies, so he would make her come—hard, fierce, and often. He hesitated because she was a virgin and deserved a sweeter, kinder loving, but that was in part a lie. There was another reason that held him back from doing what nature demanded.

Once he slipped inside her body, she would slip inside his mind.

What would the woman he loved think when she pierced the shell of his long-blooded name and his Roman education to see within him the dull, ordinary, unlikely warrior?

He had no time to ponder, for her thighs quivered in his grip. He released them and ran his fingers toward her cleft to grant her the release she needed, but she gripped his hand still before he could touch her.

Her eyes were in shadow but her face filled with longing.

"Please," she said, moving his hand away from her sex. "Come inside me, Lachlan."

Her words scattered the last of his reason. He stretched forward, planting his hands on either side of her. He would accept the consequences. Perhaps if she knew the worst, she would revoke her offer to become his leman and leave him for safety as soon as his duty to Loch Fyfe and his clan was done.

So he surged forward until his cock kissed the warmth of her cleft.

CHAPTER SEVENTEEN

Cairenn dug her fingers into his arms as he pressed deeper between her legs. She craved his fullness, even as the pressure became painful. She flinched at a sudden, sharp twinge. He paused, the muscles in his forearms flexing.

In that moment of stillness, their breath rasping, she forced her heavy eyelids open to the sight of his midnight-blue eyes. He watched her as if he were trying to reach into her mind with his own. In the flex of his cheek, and the tiny movement of the muscles around his eyes, she sensed how he struggled to remain suspended when he wanted to sink fully into her. His restraint was a sweet kindness that rippled through her, causing the tingling pain to ebb and her body to soften around him.

She shifted her hips beneath him in unspoken welcome. With a groan, he slid all the way in.

The tight fit of his hot, hard flesh, now

sheathed all the way to her womb, made her arch her neck in pleasure. With her eyes closed and her mind reaching wild, the wall against his thoughts dissolved. She found herself in a place that dazzled with light, a place she knew she shared with him, for they had the same hunger, the same need, the same pressing desire to get closer, ever closer.

He began moving, long, slick thrusts. She dug her fingers into the muscled swell of his shoulders as her blood raced. In her dizzy state, she imagined she could hear the skirl of pipes and the beat of deep-bellied drums, like some memory of a wild Lughnasa evening. The resonance of the thought-dream was like a pounding *bodhrán* whose quickening pace echoed in her heart.

She gasped for more. He was trying to be gentle. She sensed the strain in his mind. But she was done with gentleness.

Lachlan.

She'd spoken with her thoughts but he reacted as if she'd shouted an order. He made a growling sound deep in his throat and shifted his weight to better grasp her hips. Their loins met with each hungry thrust. His thoughts stretched tight and her body responded, her inner muscles closing around him to the point of a deep, unbearable ache. In a breathless instant, the feeling loosened.

An upsurge of sensation poured over her, rising and rising as he continued to thrust. She tightened her grip on his arms and felt his vibrating strength, the power he exerted to send her to greater heights of pleasure. Oh, to be taken like this by this man. Why had she hesitated at all? Why hadn't she tempted him into this on Inishmaan? Wasn't this worth a thousand lonely nights to come?

Through the haze of her own bounding pleasure she felt his thrusting become shorter, more urgent. As the muscles of his arms flexed, she blinked her eyes open to see him throw his head back. His neck bulged as he shouted and spilled into her womb. The essence of him spread inside her, tingling and warm, a powerful new pleasure that made every sensation crash at once.

She rode the curling wave as long as it lasted, lessening bit by bit. When it lapped in gentleness, she drifted down so she could once again feel the bend of the grass beneath her. He stayed stretched up, breathing hard, still inside her. After a moment or two his shoulders bowed and his head fell, his face obscured by the fall of his hair. She reached up to run her fingers through the tangle. She urged his head up so she could look into his heavy-lidded eyes. As she'd done so many times before, she pressed beyond the sight of his midnight-blue eyes into his mind.

Then she fell into Lachlan.

She plunged through his thoughts, feelings, dreams, and memories, a torrent of impressions that passed her like a blur. She had expected to hit the usual resistance when she looked into his eyes, and instead she'd hurled herself face-first through an open door.

As if from a distance she heard him speak her name. That sound helped her focus and eased the headlong fall. His midnight-blue eyes filled her vision as she tried to slow her streak through his mind. She dug her fingers into his scalp. Bit by bit the landscape of his thoughts slowed.

She struggled to make sense of it all.

She struggled to take in the *wonder* of it all.

Lachlan's mindscape was a world without edges, a vast unfurling panorama of memories and dreams and ideas that stretched to an unseen horizon. For a brief moment she swept through a memory of a sun-drenched room where a younger version of Lachlan bent over a parchment, quill in hand, tracing a line of ink against a sharp plane of wood to meet with other lines. Her nose filled with the musty scent of books and goatskin bindings. Then, as if she were no more than a leaf in the wind, she propelled away from that memory into a landscape of a bright, endless city. She chased his attention from stone arches and flying buttresses, to the ribbing of vaulted domes, to the lines of cracks above colonnades. She flew through memories of workmen with wheelbarrows, chipping slate or weighing stones. She tried to absorb all the images of ropes and buckets and men turning wheeled gears to shift materials to the highest reaches of shaking scaffolding, all under a rain of dust.

Then that rain of dust formed into numbers and symbols that reminded her of the odd lettering on some of Da's books. Those numbers and letters and symbols swirled to form calculations that just as quickly exploded and reformed. A hail of other imagery fell, of bricks and forges, of planed wood and stone, of stirred mortar and iron spikes, of levers and shims. Constructs of his imagination shimmered by her like lightning. She saw enormous stones transported across a bed of rolling tree trunks, water works and sluices, wooden pathways through bogs, ditches and canals for draining and making new land.

If she'd tumbled into Tír na nÓg, the silvery Otherworld found under the burial mounds of Ireland, she would have been less flummoxed by the land of the ancient gods with its promise of magical horses, green plains, and endless youth than she was by all of the fantasy machines rampant in Lachlan's mind. Never had she brushed into a mind so free yet so bound to the earth, the stones, the trees, and the incredible configurations that he could craft of them.

An ache pounded beneath her eyes and queasiness seized her, like what happened when she stood too close to the dolmen stones on the height of Inishmaan. She forced her eyes closed, the better to detach herself. Though she'd plunged deep inside the man, she suspected that there were places she'd not yet glimpsed, enough hidden rooms for her to explore for a lifetime. As she'd known from the first time he'd opened his eyes on the strand of Inishmaan, he was different from other men. Today, she understood exactly how different, how wonderful, how complicated.

She let her hands slip off his scalp. She heard him suck in a breath, as if he'd felt something as she'd pulled away. When she finally could master speech again, she would ask him if he'd felt as immersed as she had. Right now, it took all her concentration to settle herself into her own body. She paid mind to the weight of him atop her. She felt the intimacy of him still pressed snug against her loins, where warmth and wetness remained. A fresh tingling awoke in her, the start of new desire.

She dared to blink her eyes open once again. His head hung between his shoulders above her. She stretched up to plant a kiss upon his chest, but he was already rising off his elbows. His member slipped out of her, leaving a hollow ache behind. The cold air chilled the moisture between her thighs as he rolled onto his back. She found herself bereft, blinking up at an oculus of gray sky, rimmed by treetops.

The word *oculus* echoed in her head, and two things struck her at once.

First, that an oculus was a round opening in a building, like a window, or an eyelike design. It was not a word she knew. Somehow, Lachlan had put it in her head.

Second, they had just made love on a lush patch of grass within a perfect circle of oak trees. Her mother called such places fairy rings, powerful cathedrals of the *Sídh,* a place fitting for the sacred.

"So lass," Lachlan said, interrupting her thoughts with a voice that sounded strange. "Now you've truly had your way with me."

She turned her head against the soft grass, watching the way his throat moved. The expression of his profile confused her. His eyes were restlessly seeking something in the high boughs of the trees. His hands lay flat on his abdomen as if he were a man gut-slain, holding fast to his spilling innards.

Confusion seeped through her. He must know that he'd pleased her beyond measure. Surely he could feel how her body thrummed with satisfaction, and not just from the lovemaking.

But of course, she thought. It was the *other* thing that had unnerved him.

She rolled on her side and pressed her body against his, breast to knee, the best way she could think of to express how much he'd pleased her. "Did you feel it," she asked, "when our minds became one?"

A jolt shot through him, and instantly she realized her mistake. Her father and brother had always barked in anger when they suspected she was reading their thoughts. How much worse it must be for Lachlan, new to the experience, to be told so boldly that she'd been rooting around in all things private.

"I felt a lot of things," he said, still blinking straight up at the sky. "After watching you come, my mind wasn't my own for a long time."

A tingling heat swept up her cheeks.

"If it happens only then," he added, "I'd be glad of it. You were all I was thinking of, in that moment."

She'd seen a lot more than his desire for her, and she sensed that realization was the root of his wary, uneasy behavior. She supposed she could play the part of an innocent and pretend that his blind lust was all she'd perceived, but her heart balked at the deception. She hadn't left her home and followed Lachlan into the world only to pretend—as she did with every other outsider—that she didn't have a gift.

"It's true," she began, "that I felt a communion

with you while we were . . . in the middle of things." Why were there no good, loving words to describe what they just did, that breathless merging of their bodies? "But after, when we were both . . . finished, I could read you as if there had never been a wall between us."

"Even now?"

She sent tentacles of thought toward him with care, not wanting to tumble head over foot again. "You're blocked to me now." He let out such a long, deep breath that she wondered how long he'd been holding it. "It's a pity, Lachlan, because even a glimpse into your mind revealed so much good."

He stilled to stone. Undaunted, she ran her hand over his forearm, up past his wrist, to cover his hand with her own. He didn't raise it from his abdomen or make any attempt to grasp it. She twisted her palm so that her fingers lay between his.

"Listen to me," she whispered against his shoulder. "Back on Inishmaan, when I thought about what might be hiding behind the black haze of your mind, I could only guess that you would be like other men, to some degree."

"So I'm to be judged against such a measure."

"There's no judgement in it. I've been seeing into men's thoughts since my thirteenth summer. I know the lusts that drive them, the overriding sense that their members are a grand thing of great wonder to be worshipped—"

"Are they not?"

"Perhaps some are." She smiled at his unsteady stab at humor. "The irony is that most women yearn for a big heart more than a big . . . cock."

He remained as motionless as the church statues she'd seen as a child in the cathedral in Galway.

"It is the way men and women are made," she continued. "I accept that. And since you're the heir to a chieftaincy, I could only expect from what I've seen in the other noblemen that you would have lofty aspirations, bloodlust, even a craving for a crown of antlers upon your head. But Lachlan—" she squeezed his hand "—what I saw defied everything I expected."

His fingers twitched under her grip. Against her lips she felt the slightest softening in his body, a statue shifting into life.

"It was but a glimpse," she hedged, "but I saw you as a boy in your uncle's house in Rome. Your hair was long and coming out of the rawhide tie at your neck. You sat upon two books to reach the desk. Around you were parchments held open with broken pieces of veined marble, and you were drawing lines on a slate. You were sketching an arch of some sort—"

"A bridge," he interrupted. "My uncle had tasked me to measure the forces, to craft the size of each arch."

"Yes." She squeezed his hand again, and this time his palm lifted from his abdomen. "I saw that. It was a lovely memory, but an unusual one to rise to the front of your thoughts in that moment after we finished . . . loving."

His brows drew together. "That time in Rome," he said. "That was the moment I knew—"

He swallowed his words. She wished she could

slip into his mind and see the battle raging inside. But even as the thought passed through her mind, she had a sudden insight into what he meant to say.

"It was the moment you knew what you most desired," she said, a flush rising within her at the implications. "It was the moment you found true happiness."

He turned his head toward her. She met his midnight-blue eyes and the soft expression within them. Suddenly, she didn't mind that she couldn't see his thoughts, for there was something wondrous in this thrumming sense of intimacy that had nothing to do with the certainty that could come with her gift.

"You felt something, didn't you?" she whispered. "When my mind sank into yours?"

"Yes."

A spiral of excitement rose up in her. She'd never had anyone to talk to about her gift. Even her brother, to whom she was closest, shut right up when she asked him too many questions.

She said, "Tell me what it felt like."

"Lass," he said on a hitching breath, "it's not as easy as that."

"Please, Lachlan. I need to know."

He rolled to his side to face her. He ran a hand over the curve of her hip, up and down, sending shivers of sensation across her skin.

He said, "I need you to tell me something first."

"Anything."

"I want you to describe what it felt like when I put myself inside you."

She flushed. "Lachlan—"

"Not so easy, is it?"

The corner of his lips twitched, a soft, teasing smile that made her heart turn over. "If you can make me understand what that felt like, lass, maybe I can answer your question better."

The skin on her cheeks all but sizzled. She had no reason to be squeamish about talking about such things. Hadn't she mind-witnessed half the island of Inishmaan rutting in one place or another? Those fragmented, heated memories always seemed to float to the top of everyone's thoughts. But she didn't have the language to describe such a thing, and her tongue tangled when she tried to summon words. Since being with Lachlan, she'd realized that seeing the act through other people's minds and experiencing it herself were two different things altogether.

So, for a moment, she let herself wallow in the memory of what they'd just done. She envisioned Lachlan looming over her, spreading her legs wide, lodging the tip of his shaft against the ache that had been building up inside her since he first kissed her on Inishmaan. The memory was as visceral as if he were right now tracing his tongue over her hip, instead of his fingers. Her cleft responded in eager anticipation, three hungry squeezes.

His thumb against her lower lip brought her attention back to the moment. He watched her face as he rolled the pad of that thumb across the length of her mouth.

"I felt an ache," she said, when he finally dropped his thumb from her lip. "The feeling was deep inside me, where you . . . put yourself."

"And?"

"I didn't want you to stop moving. Had a herd of wild boar come crashing through these woods, I wouldn't have torn myself away."

She thought she saw desire flare in his eyes, but he made no move to kiss her. The silence stretched, an unspoken command to continue.

"I wanted to open myself wider, to take your . . . cock . . . more deeply inside me." She ran her hand up his abdomen, over his chest, loving the velvet-hardness beneath her palm. "I wanted you to touch me everywhere. My breasts. My . . ." Her breath quickened and she felt another spasm between her legs. "I wanted to savor every stroke and at the same time I wanted you to stroke harder. I wanted to feel you, all the way to the root. I wanted you to tighten your grip on me because that spoke to how hungry you were to have me. I wanted you to stretch over me, cover me, breathe the same air, feel the same tightening. I wanted . . ."

She struggled for the right word. What, precisely, did she crave in those intense moments? Did she want to lose all power of control? Be taken? Possessed? Each word was right, in its own way, but none was perfect.

He said, his voice uneven, "You wanted to surrender."

She breathed, "*Yes*."

The word lingered in the air between them. It rang true, even though unease plucked at her. To give herself so freely was to open herself to a dangerous vulnerability. She felt like she had just opened the deep recesses of her own mind for

Lachlan's perusal.

Then all was a blur as he captured her lips. It was not a hungry kiss, but he made a meal of it anyway. He took her lower lip between his only to release it to capture the upper, and then captured them both with a kiss that left her panting, breathless, hungry for so much more than just kissing.

He pulled away long enough to press his forehead against hers, murmuring half to himself, "Of ten parts, a man enjoys only one."

Her blood thrumming, she did not have the capacity to understand what he said, and hardly the wits to wonder.

"An old myth," he explained. "Zeus argued with Hera about who enjoyed lovemaking more, men or women. They brought in the prophet Tiresias to judge."

Her ears absorbed his words, though her foggy mind did not.

"Women won," he continued. "Your sex enjoys lovemaking ten times more than mortal men. Until now, I would have disagreed."

"But," she stuttered, "you took pleasure, before—"

"Aye, I took physical pleasure. But after feeling you slip inside my mind, *mo chridhe,* I now understand the full pleasures of surrender."

CHAPTER EIGHTEEN

Half the morning they'd been walking, but as long as Lachlan stayed close, Cairenn felt she could wander through these woods forever without growing weary. Though they'd spoken little since they returned to the campsite last night, a kind of communion buzzed between them. She could hardly sense the minds of all the other men trudging the same path because of the warmth she felt whenever Lachlan happened to glance back at her. He would raise one brow and his eyes would twinkle and suddenly she felt as if she were wrapped softly in thrice-brushed linen.

Maybe that's why she didn't notice the troop of men on horses until Angus, at the head of the column, shot up a hand to order everyone to halt. Lachlan turned to her, his eyes sharp with expectancy. That look jolted her out of woolly daydreaming. She focused on the road below and then cast out the tentacles of her mind.

They had been walking on a crooked deer-path atop a low ridge, a safe distance from the main riverside thoroughfare, so they wouldn't bump into other travelers. Now, she could hear the snorts of horses and the jangle of harnesses coming up on the road below. The mind-voices, however, seemed to come from a much greater distance. The discrepancy annoyed her. Were her wits so love-muddled that she couldn't direct her own gift? What a foolish woman she'd be if that were so.

So she banished Lachlan from her mind and focused more keenly on the man on horseback just coming into view through the scrim of trees. That man's thoughts were quiet like the rustle of a squirrel in the litter, but she could tell he was mentally ticking off a list of anxieties.

She caught his name through the mind of the man on the next horse. She blurted, "It's Callum Ewing."

Lachlan stiffened beside her, but she resisted the draw on her attention. The man called Callum was hungry, she realized, but not for food. Some greater trouble gnawed at him.

She said, "He's off to see the Lamonts."

"The Lamonts?" Lachlan blurted. "Are you sure?"

"Of course I am," she said. Lachlan may have muddled her mind a bit with last night's lovemaking, but she'd been reading men's thoughts for most of her life. "Whatever Ewing is planning, he doesn't want to be doing it at all."

"The Lamonts are bitter enemies. No Ewing would ever have dealings with them."

She glanced his way, found him running his fingers through his short beard. Uneasiness made her concentrate harder, but the name *Lamont* came up, over and over, through Callum Ewing's mind as well as through the minds of the others.

"He feels forced to go there." Her temples throbbed with the effort. "He's concerned about how it will affect his clan and his family."

There was something else there, something important, but her attention was pulled away by a curious Angus striding toward them. The black-haired merchant directed his attention to Lachlan as if she were no more sentient than a nearby sapling.

Angus asked Lachlan, "Can you read the heraldry from here?"

"It's Callum Ewing," Lachlan said. "The chieftain of the Ewing sept, bound to my father."

"I know Callum. I've broken bread with that warrior in your father's own house. What luck that we come upon him." Angus took a step down the slope. "Come, let's—"

Lachlan seized his arm. "Callum is on the road to meet the Lamonts."

"That's nonsense." Angus shook off Lachlan's grip. "How can you even know that? Roads go two ways, and the Lamonts are—"

"—enemies to the MacEgans. The Lamont castle seat is six miles further down the coast road, with no paths off it, in the same direction that those men are moving."

As Angus digested this, the merchant's gaze slid to her. He'd never liked the fact that Lachlan had insisted on taking her on this journey. She felt the waves of his wariness like a hot torch. His thoughts kept whispering *witch.*

"That can't be right." Angus pulled his attention back to Lachlan. "Callum Ewing never struck me as a foolish man, nor a man hungry for power. Certainly not a man who would have anything to do with murdering his overlord."

"Our world has changed, Angus."

"Then let's stop him here and find out what he knows." Angus gripped the hilt of his sword. "We'll make him speak the truth."

Lachlan seized Angus's sword arm when the blade was only half out of the scabbard. "I won't make enemies out of those who could be friends."

Angus blew a huff of air. "This journey to Loch Fyfe will not be bloodless, lad. You know that."

"Callum is riding like he expects an attack. They have at least twenty well-armed men on horseback. We are a half dozen men, and one woman, on foot."

"We have the advantage of surprise."

"We stick to the plan, Angus." Lachlan released his cousin and fingered the hilt of his own sword. "You're here with your clerics and a few porters to pay your respects to my father's family. You've brought gifts of wine to make sure the trade arrangements between Derry and Loch Fyfe are still in place with the new chieftain, whoever he may be. Once we are sure we know who the assassin is, only then will I reveal myself."

"If you truly believe that Ewing is off to deal with the devil Lamont," Angus argued, "that's enough to mark him an enemy—"

"Callum Ewing," she interrupted, "is no enemy."

Angus glared at her with fiery eyes. His annoyance was tempered only by Lachlan's expression of growing interest.

"He misses your father." Though the impression was frustratingly fuzzy, it was strong. "He is not the one responsible for his death."

Angus made a scoffing noise. "By God, Lachlan, what does this woman know of—"

"Are you sure, lass?"

Maybe it was the withering blast of Angus's distrust that made her hesitate. Or maybe it was because of the men around them, nervous and excited all at once as they clutched their short swords. Or maybe it was the strange wooliness of her gift this morning. Whatever the cause, uncertainty bit at the edges of her confidence.

This was the first time in her life when her ability to read someone's mind really mattered.

"I'm sure," she said, her nod more confident than she was. "Callum Ewing is an ally."

"Then we go greet him. *Peacefully*." Lachlan nudged Angus forward and pulled his cowl over his head. "Let the farce begin."

Lachlan hung back with the other men as Angus hailed Callum and stepped onto the road, his hands empty and spread wide. The chieftain of the Ewing clan pulled back on the reins, though his horse fought against the restraint.

"Stupid man," Callum Ewing bellowed. "What are you thinking, jumping out of the wood like that in front of twenty-five armed men? Do you know who you're challenging?"

Lachlan watched as two of Callum's fighters kicked their steads to intervene, their swords singing out of their scabbards. By reflex, Lachlan clutched his own hilt in the folds of his borrowed cleric's robes.

"I'm making no challenge, Callum Ewing," Angus said as the fighting men hemmed him in. "I was happy to see familiar colors. I've been wandering in these woods for half a day now, trying to find my way out of game paths and onto any decent road."

Callum kicked his mount closer. "Angus O'Donnell, is that you?"

"Of course it is. Have you gone blind, old friend, not to recognize me, even after all these years?"

Callum raised his hand for his men to stand down. Lachlan loosened his own grip on his sword as Callum's smile twitched under the well-trimmed white beard.

"You've grown a bit since I last saw you, Angus," the chieftain said.

"That I have." Angus laughed and slapped his belly with his palms. It was a wonder to Lachlan that Angus could go from threatening this man's life to bantering with him, all within a few moments.

"And what in God's name are you doing on this lonely stretch of road? It's dangerous times to be wandering, even for an Irish merchant."

"Indeed, so I've heard. So many bloody tales coming out of Loch Fyfe."

"Aye, there has been enough bloodshed and

treachery in these parts to last many a generation."

Callum squinted to where the rest of them waited by the side of the road. By instinct, Lachlan lowered his head so the cowl would cover his eyes, though Angus had assured him that his beard alone made him look more like a French pirate than a MacEgan.

Callum said, "I see you have porters and clerics and plenty of baggage, but where's your cart of wines and spices? And why didn't you bring your ship to port at Bruichladdich or Kintyre?"

"The fog bedazzled my men, sending us up the river rather than up the coast." Angus shrugged. "Not knowing the difference, we scraped the boat on a shallow rock during low tide. We had to row fast to the nearest shore, to a wild place just over these hills."

"You're lucky you weren't routed by the MacDonalds."

"Oh, I trade with them, too, Ewing. The MacDonald has a weakness for the Bordeaux."

Callum's grin widened. "I'd call you a traitor if I didn't like your wine so much myself. Is that where you're off to?"

"No, I'm off to Loch Fyfe," he said. "To pay tribute at the grave of Fergus MacEgan, and bring my greetings to the new chieftain, whoever he may be."

Lachlan didn't have to squint too hard to see the powerful effect the words had on the chieftain. Callum's features spasmed into a grief. This head of the Ewing clan had been his father's good friend, the septs linked by generations of friendship, interests, and occasional intermarriage. The sight of Callum's grief gave credence to Lachlan's decision to put his faith in Cairenn and her otherworldly, inexplicable powers.

"Aye, Angus," Callum said. "You're a far stretch of the legs from where you want to go, at least twenty leagues off. Follow this road whence we came. You'll pass my castle beyond the third bend. Some ways beyond, there's a good place to ford the river to get to the other side. Six leagues through the woods heading north and you'll be in MacEgan lands."

Angus squinted down the road in the direction the chieftain pointed. "MacEgan lands that way and MacDonald lands behind me. Yes, I've got my bearings now." Angus then turned to squint down the other end of the road. "If my memory serves, Ewing, this path leads to Lamont land."

"And to hell, I suspect."

Surely Angus missed his calling as a master player, Lachlan thought, as he watched astonished disbelief cross his cousin's face.

"There must be a story here," Angus said darkly, "if you're off to speak with the devil."

"There are devils enough whence I came." The old chieftain shifted his grip on his pommel. "But when the only MacEgan left standing is an untried young man, and the whole place abounds with murderers, the only path open to an honest man is straight into the devil's arms."

There was one more MacEgan alive, and Lachlan's body tingled with the urge to shout it. If only he could throw off his cleric's robes and make himself known, but Cairenn's fingers curled under his rope belt as if in warning. She whispered something between his shoulder blades. He could not hear the words, but he guessed their substance. He had to stay mute while in the presence of so many men whose loyalties were as of yet unknown.

Then he noticed another rider weaving past the twenty mounted men to Callum's side. The rider wore a plain blue cloak pulled low as though the rider wanted to hide as much as Lachlan did. Lachlan's heart did a hard throb when he saw a pale, bejeweled hand come out from under the blue cloak to yank at the hem of Callum's mantle.

Lachlan's throat tightened. Strange, that Cairenn hadn't mentioned the woman amid the riders. Why had she kept this detail away from him? It would have been just like her to cast him a sly-eyed glance of reproof, or duck her head with hurt, once she knew who rode with these men. Guilt would have needled him, yes, but at least then he would have been better prepared for the complication.

Lachlan watched as the old chieftain turned to Angus after speaking to the blue-cloaked rider.

"My daughter," Callum said, "would like us to offer you and your men an escort to Loch Fyfe."

"My lady." Angus swept down in a bow. "Your heart is very kind."

"Don't be fooled," the old chieftain interrupted. "She knows it's a call to courtesy that I cannot fulfill, for we are expected at the Lamonts' by end of day. The only reason she makes the request is to delay the inevitable."

Angus shook his shaggy head. "What on earth are you planning, old friend?"

"He's planning to betroth me to a new husband." The woman knocked back her hood to reveal the shine of her black hair. "Didn't you know? My father is marrying me off to the Lamont devil."

Cairenn would know the sight of Lachlan's betrothed from a thousand miles. The woman had hair as black as the richest peat, with eyebrows like arched wings. She rode her horse as if she were born upon its back. Anger pulsed bright in the woman's mind, an anger that kissed the woman's cheeks pink and made her lips glisten in the dappled sun.

Leana.

In one buzzing instant, the woman's name was in every man's mind. The surging rise of their attention was like the crack of a wave against a cliff. It was the first strong sense of mental thought that she'd experienced since rising from her camp bed this morning. Even now, standing within a dozen steps of the chieftain and his men, all she could hear were the acid tones of the lady's disdain floating over a collective murmuring of male admiration and lust.

Lachlan didn't move. His stance hardened and stilled in a way that spoke of alertness. Bark bit into her side as she swayed against a tree, the fingers of one hand still caught up in Lachlan's rope belt. She welcomed the solidity of the trunk, for it kept her from sinking to her knees and spilling the chewed-up remnants of this morning's oatcake all over the ground. A screeching sound filled her mind and she mentally scrambled to seek the source. It took a moment for her to realize that the sound was her own heart screaming, now that she was forced to look upon the woman who would take Lachlan away from her.

Around her she heard voices, words being exchanged between the old chieftain and Angus, but it was all like the buzzing of bees beneath the mind-screeching that was increasing the sharp ache behind her eyes. Sweat gathered on her brow, though the morning was cool. The nausea, the headache, the clammy sensation . . . she was thirteen years old all over again, stepping on the shores of Galway.

A tinny voice spoke in her head, *breathe, little Cairenn, breathe. Slowly. In and out. In and out.* Her father's voice coming to her from memory. She took the advice and it helped lessen the edge of the ache in her head and tamp down the nausea. Casting about for a center of focus, she found herself roped as if by the neck by the high, commanding voice of the daughter of Callum Ewing.

"Why the Lamonts, you ask?" The woman's voice was punctuated by the scuffing noise of her mount's hooves. "*I'll* tell you since my father won't."

"Leana." Callum's voice held a warning.

"Angus O'Donnell has asked a question, Father," she said, making the word drip with disapproval. "It would be uncivil to leave it unanswered."

The woman's dark eyes flashed as she wove her horse between the men, steering the fine beast with the lightest touch of her hand. Cairenn would feel this woman's appeal even if she wasn't half-drowning in the rising lust of the men around her, most of whom were widening their stances to better accommodate their thickening attraction.

"With the MacEgans gone," the woman said, her dark gaze steady on Angus, "the Ewings need new alliances. We would go to the Campbells if we could, but they are already inbred with the MacGilchrists. We would go to the MacDonalds, but they are greedy and strong and they'd swallow the whole of the clan in one gulp. The Lamonts can be controlled, my father says. Lamonts, if they overreach, are small and weak enough to be defeated—"

"Enough, girl," Callum snapped. "Get back to your place."

She tossed her head just as the horse tossed his mane. "Have I said something untrue?"

"You do me dishonor."

The woman's mind grew dense with the black smoke of doused intent. The horse grew agitated between her thighs. With a kick, the woman urged the mount to leap forward with a dismissive swish of tail. She headed back to her place amid the riders, while every one of Angus's men imagined plunging their cocks into her.

Lachlan would want this woman, too, she thought, hating herself for her own jealousy. He was a man like all others, and a man didn't need a love match to want to sink himself into a woman. Such a creature had the temperament and the bloodline to breed strong children, determined sons, ambitious and mighty warriors, just what a chieftain needed to continue the ruling family. She glanced at the back of Lachlan's hood, wishing for the thousandth time she could see inside his head to confirm or allay her fears. The only thing she could read was the stillness of his stance.

Then she noticed Angus glancing back at them, his brow raised in some unspoken question.

She tried to read that question, but Angus's thoughts were slippery things, lost amid the waning pitch of her mind's scream and the collective sexual musings of the men. By the movement of the folds in Lachlan's hood, she knew Lachlan had said yes to that silent question. Then Angus turned around, his thoughts retreating from her as sure as if he pulled a basket of eels from her grasp.

Angus planted his hands on his hips and swayed where he stood. "I see now that there's a divine hand in our meeting, Callum Ewing."

"Indeed," Callum said, "I'd welcome God's intervention in the deeds of these past months."

"Perhaps He sent me to remind you that you cannot betroth a daughter to one man, if she's already betrothed to another."

"She was betrothed to Lachlan MacEgan," Callum sighed, "who is now nothing but fish-eaten bones."

"Is he?"

In the buzzing silence that followed, Cairenn pressed her forehead against Lachlan's back, where his shoulder blade flexed. She wanted to feel the warmth of his body before everything ended. She squeezed her eyes shut and breathed the scent of him, of smoke fires and salt air and leather and man. She wanted to feel as if she possessed him, if only for a moment, if only for *this* moment.

"Callum Ewing," Angus chided. "Have you forgotten that Lachlan's mother was half-selkie on her mother's side?"

"If he were alive, selkie or no, he would be here, fighting for his rightful place. He would already be married to my daughter, and I would be the first man at his side. If you know otherwise, Angus—"

"I *do* know otherwise," Angus said. "As sure as I stand here before you, Lachlan MacEgan is alive."

CHAPTER NINETEEN

Once inside the smoky mead-hall of the Ewing castle, Lachlan ducked into the shadows as Angus's men casually swarmed around him in an effort to shield him from prying eyes. The Ewing sept knew that Lachlan was alive and well, but they didn't yet know that he walked among them. To be recognized was to destroy any chance of discovering his enemy before his enemy discovered him, so he had to be as quiet and unremarkable as possible.

With his face low, Lachlan wound his way through the room as Angus's 'porters' and 'clerics' kept pace. A wide trestle table filled most of the modestly-sized hall, but smaller tables had been thrown up around it to allow seating for the new arrivals. He headed toward an outer table where he would be within easy earshot of Callum Ewing, who now brooded over a tankard of ale.

Lachlan swung a leg over a bench and gave

Ewing his back as Angus's men took their places around him, casually brushing mud off their boots. Thus shielded, Lachlan dared to search for familiar faces in the hall. He recognized Leana, of course, looking like the brat he remembered as she pouted on a bench beside a knight who seemed to be ignoring her. He recognized a number of Ewing men, brawny fighters he'd competed against in foot races, caber tosses, and sheaf throws in clan gatherings during spring festivities. He kept looking and looking until he realized that the person he was looking for was Cairenn.

He knew she wasn't here. The minute they'd passed under the portal of the castle keep, a young servant had swept her away. She would not be allowed to bed down with the men, so he assumed she'd been taken to wherever the lesser female guests ate meals and laid their pallets. Her absence was an aching hollow.

His heart squeezed in its cage of guilt. On the road, when Callum had turned his horses and men back to his own castle, Lachlan had turned to Cairenn with a mouth full of comforting words that never left his tongue. The strain on her face had stopped him cold. For long leagues, she'd remained silent and indrawn, allowing no more intimacy than an occasional touch of his hand. It didn't seem right to question what she might be reading in the minds of the Ewing men, not while the subject of Leana remained unspoken between them. Every time he opened his mouth in the hopes of offering comfort, he swallowed the lies.

Someone passed close by his elbow. He ducked

his head and raised his tankard to hide his face and then chided himself for being distracted. With Cairenn away, he had to use his own eyes and ears tonight. When he lowered the ale, he spied a freshly-washed Angus striding into the mead-hall toward Lord Ewing.

"My faithful Angus," Callum Ewing bellowed as Angus approached. "My apologies for riding ahead of you on the road like that, but those woods have Lamont ears. If what you told me is true, then the betrothal with the Lamonts is worthless—and that will not sit well with them. I dared not leave my daughter vulnerable to capture."

"Your swift response gave my mind ease," Angus said. "It proved that your blood runs loyal to Fergus."

"I should strike you down for even doubting it."

Lachlan heard the bench scrape against the straw-strewn flagstones and assumed Angus had taken his seat.

"So tell me," Angus said, pitching his voice louder than necessary, considering Lachlan's position an arm's length away, "has the council met already? Has the rod of kingship been passed on?"

"It has not. There is still no chieftain of the MacEgans."

Angus made a clucking noise. "You'd think whoever the assassins are would move quickly to seize power."

"It's more unnerving that they haven't."

"Another clan could easily swallow yours up if there's no leader to make the call to arms. Is it instability that they crave?"

"I would say yes," Callum said, sighing, "if two councils hadn't already been called since Fergus's death, and a leader all but chosen each time—"

"A leader?" Angus interrupted. "Who?"

"Lachlan's half-brother, the boy Fingal."

Lachlan froze.

"Fingal?" Angus said, his tone an echo of Lachlan's own shock. "But that boy can't be ten or—"

"He's fifteen," Callum corrected. "He's the image of his father, but an idealist, a true believer in man's basic goodness."

An image came to Lachlan's mind of young Fingal clutching a wooden model of a galley that Lachlan had carved for him, complete with oars. Fingal had spent the last years fostered with the MacGilchrists, so Lachlan hadn't seen him since he'd been sent off at the age of nine. He struggled to imagine that his half-brother had grown so much that much older, more experienced men would bow before him.

"Fingal deferred the offer," Callum continued, amid the sound of a knife tapping against pewter. "I thought it a wise thing, at the time. His father's death was fresh, there were murmurings of treachery, and the rumors about Lachlan being lost at sea were just that—rumors. Fingal insisted on delaying the council until Lachlan's death could be confirmed."

"And then?"

"Then the raids began. Cattle stolen, huts burned, crofters killed—"

"Callum, Callum," Angus said, "what made this different from any other day in Loch Fyfe?"

"It does seem like it has always been like this, though that is far from the truth." Callum sighed. "This time, every sept suffered by these raids. So when the second council convened, the calls for Fingal to be named as The MacEgan intensified."

Angus cleared his throat. "Why were you not nominated, Callum? You would have crushed the reivers, brought order—"

"—I was put forth as a likely candidate, as was The MacGilchrist, and the usual motley collection of ambitious thanes supported by their men-at-arms. But Fingal had much support from his mother's allies, as well as others, like myself, determined to honor Fergus's wishes."

Lachlan closed his eyes, trying to imagine his pug-nosed half-brother with the flop of hair across his brow sitting on the dolmen stone amid a circle of warriors, wearing a fur mantle and a white rod clutched in his hand. In his mind, Fingal was still a boy dressing up to play king of the mountain.

Then he thought about the support Fingal might be getting from his mother's people, Stuarts from the mainland. A strong, ambitious clan. Lachlan frowned as his suspicions darkened. When his stepmother had married his father, she'd never taken easily to the fact that The MacEgan already had an heir. His father's young Stuart bride had shot Lachlan many an acid look, especially after the birth of her son.

He turned his attention back to the conversation, which had become more difficult to hear as the gathered men finished their meals and consumed more mead.

". . . have you spoken to the boy," Angus said, "to advise him?"

"I have not spoken to Fingal except during the council meetings, when it is difficult to be heard above so many others. And, with the roads so dangerous, I couldn't ride to him between meetings. Bringing a dozen well-armed guards through the gates at Loch Fyfe might be misconstrued to the point of bloodshed."

"Fergus was right." Angus said in a voice that rippled with regret. "He made Lachlan his heir to avoid all this bartering for kingship. Why did the boy delay the ruling of the council for the second time?"

"I like to believe that the lad sensed there was mischief afoot. But it's more likely that he still believed that his brother would come back from the dead."

"The boy was right." Angus planted his pewter cup on the wooden table. "I've seen Lachlan with my own eyes, living and breathing."

"And Lachlan knows his assassin?"

"They were hired men. He was stabbed in the dark of night and thrown overboard in a storm."

"Where is he?"

Lachlan ducked deeper under his cowl as if someone had just brought a torch to hold over him.

"Come, old friend." Angus made a clicking noise with his tongue. "Lachlan is safer if no one but me knows his whereabouts."

"Are you not dining in my own castle? Did I

not just break my daughter's betrothal to a Lamont on the strength of your word?"

"Yes, the betrothal," Angus said, and misgiving swelled in his voice. "Why the Lamonts, Callum?"

Callum went mute for so long that Lachlan turned his head a fraction, just enough to see the older man's profile from beyond the edge of his hood. He watched the old chieftain raise his tankard to his lips, then, when he settled it on the table, bow over it as if contemplating the dregs.

"It's complicated." Callum's face crumpled in deep thought. "From what I've seen of him, Fingal is a good young man, but he's inexperienced. Whilst enemies still swarm in secret, such a youth cannot hold the center of this clan."

Angus harrumphed. "Good advisors can compensate for—"

"And who is going to advise him? Me? I can't get close to the boy. The MacGilchrist? That idiot has a daughter of Fingal's age, and he has already sought a marriage alliance for his son with the Campbells."

"As you sought one with the Lamonts."

"Better the enemy you know," Callum said, "than the enemy you can't even see."

"Dangerous business, this." Angus slapped his hands free of crumbs. "You should not fail to arrive well-armed to the next council."

"I won't fail," Callum said. "The next council takes place tomorrow."

So soon.

Lachlan stared blindly at the tankard of ale someone put before him, but did not take it in hand.

"It's good that your porters and clerics are already well-armed," Callum said. "Your announcement will certainly cause a stir."

And perhaps make the assassin nervous enough for Cairenn to find him within the crowd. Lachlan hoped she identified the murderers quickly. Trying to remain unrecognized in MacEgan lands would be nigh impossible.

Frustrated, Lachlan ducked deeper under his cowl, frowning at the noise in the room and the chewing and the slurping and the murmurings of the men around him. His mind drifted for a moment to the memory of Inishmaan, of Cairenn's family around the small trestle table, eating fresh fish grilled upon the hearth stones while they bantered and laughed. A weariness settled upon him, bone-deep and out of proportion to the exertion of the march here.

His heart was torn in two. By his blood, name, and lineage, he was duty-bound to travel to Loch Fyfe to seize back what had been stolen from him by treachery and to avenge his father's murder. But his connection to Cairenn was not a simple one, bound up as it was with her gift, his unexplained appearance on Inishmaan's shores, and the unworldly, thrumming communion they experienced when wrapped in each other's arms. Perhaps he was meant to have stayed on that island, to have taken Cairenn to wife, and to live a peaceful life.

Perhaps, for his own sake, he should have just stayed dead.

The rattle of pewter and knives startled Lachlan

out of his thoughts as Callum slapped his hands on the trestle table.

"Let's talk of happier things, Angus." Callum dropped his voice so that Lachlan had to strain to hear it. "Dare I ask after the fair-haired beauty travelling amidst your porters and clerics?"

Lachlan tensed.

"Ah," Angus said. "You've noticed."

"A tender bite, that one, and as shy as a field mouse. She tried to hide herself behind one of your clerics the whole time we spoke on the road. You once favored the buxom and burly, old friend."

"Your Scottish nights are cold enough to freeze a man's balls." Angus shrugged his shoulders. "Should I travel all this way without comfort?"

"At our age, we must find our pleasure where we can."

Angus raised his cup in salute. "Mead now, swiving later."

"Fortunately for you, I've already made arrangements. You'll find your fair-haired little morsel in a storage room by the gates. There, my old friend, you two won't be bothered."

Something was terribly, terribly wrong.

Cairenn paced in the windowless room while the stub of tallow she'd been given when she'd been led to this small space sputtered. She cut a path around the spears, a dented shield, two stools, and a pile of old leather tackle. A straw pallet lay on the floor with linens and a soft wool blanket, her discarded tray of supper beside it. Outside the walls, she could hear the murmuring chatter of the guards, the occasional bark of a dog, and the chuffing and movement of the horses in the stable nearby.

All this she could hear with her ears.

She could hear nothing with her mind.

She clutched her hands to keep them from trembling. This unnerving sensation reminded her of a time when she and her brothers and sisters took to the sea to swim during a rare hot day of summer. Normally, they never dared the surf or the tide because the water was heart-bracingly cold, but that day they'd stripped to their shifts and dived in. The force of the surf tumbled her willy-nilly. When she finally pulled herself onto the strand, she had to tilt her head and slap one ear and then another, dropping her jaw wide to try to dislodge the plug of water within each ear. Every sound had a hollow tone to it, as if she heard it through a narrow, distorted tunnel.

Seeing Leana did this to me. She was convinced it was so. Knowing the woman existed and seeing her in all her glory were two different things. Knowing Leana was Lachlan's betrothed and hearing Callum Ewing re-stitch the agreement in his mind were two different things, as well. That shock was the only explanation for her deafness that made any sense, for although she'd been fuzzy-headed since the morning, everyone's thoughts had grown more and more opaque after that awful moment. All during the long walk to Ewing's castle, she'd felt increasingly alone in the thickening woolliness, no matter how many times Lachlan touched her hand, brushed his shoulder against hers, or laid his lips upon her hair.

She shook her head as if she could shake loose the walls in her mind. She sensed nothing from the people in this castle other than an indistinct murmuring, like the wash of the tide on the strand heard from the height of Inishmaan. What kind of mind-sickness was this? Ever since she'd discovered her gift, she'd wished she'd had any other gift at all—her sister's gift of the healing hands, her brother's gift of music, her father's endless youthfulness—and not to be cursed, like her mother, with a fairy blessing that brought equal amounts of pain. Yet here she was, her gift leaching from her with each passing hour, and what she wanted with all her heart was to have it *back*.

She jumped at a knock at the door, unnerved that she heard such an earth-bound sound without having been warned of the approach by her visitor's thoughts. It could be Lachlan behind that door—or it could be anyone else.

"Cairenn?"

"Come in," she blurted, recognizing Lachlan's voice. She ran her hands over her hair, tangled from distress, and struggled to control herself.

Lachlan stepped in, tugged the cowl off his head, and met her gaze. She drew in a sharp breath. Worry drew lines between his brows and cast a shadow in his midnight-blue eyes, like a cloud covering the stars.

She barely finished speaking his name before his arms swept around her, one hand cupping her head and the other curling around her back. She smelled the scent of the mead-hall in the fibers of his woolen cloak, sweet mead and charred wood and roasted meats. She heard nothing but the beat of his heart through the ear pressed against his chest, and for a moment, she felt blessedly right.

"All day I've been thinking," he said, "that it would have been better had Ewing been my enemy."

"You mustn't say such things."

"It would have set me free from the betrothal." His grip tightened. "Can you forgive me, lass?"

"It's not a matter for forgiveness." She took a deep breath. "I knew what might happen when we came to these shores."

"You were so quiet today."

Her thoughts skittered. "Leana is very . . . beautiful."

"She's a willful half-child, spoiled as the only Ewing daughter. She is not Cairenn of Inishmaan." He lowered his head to speak against her hair. "Cairenn of Inishmaan is the child of another realm who brings magic to my life."

Her knees softened at his words, even as her heart squeezed at the impossibility of any real future. He must have sensed her reaction, for he pulled back to better see her face. He couldn't know her thoughts, of course, but as he looked at her, his smile dimmed and the lines deepened between his brows.

He lifted her chin. "Something troubles you."

She dropped her own gaze, suddenly understanding why everyone found her mind-reading so unnerving. Her thoughts skittered in a dozen directions. She couldn't confess her true weakness. Perhaps this was just a mind-sickness that would pass in a day or two. Perhaps a good night's sleep would cure her. It would be a cruel fate to be robbed of her gift when she finally had a use for it.

"My head aches." The lie tasted bitter. "There was such a crowd on the walk here. Twenty of Ewing's men, plus ours. I'm better at blocking out chatter than I used to be, but it still makes my temples throb."

"I should have left you at Derry." He nudged a tress of hair behind her ear. "I could have protected you from all of this."

How far they'd come that he would swallow her lie without question. "I'd have stowed away if you'd tried."

He laughed. Oh, how she loved the way his body vibrated against hers when he laughed.

"It won't be long now," he said. "We ride for the council meeting tomorrow morning."

Her heart did a stutter-skip. "So soon?"

"Aye." He took her face in his two hands. "Too soon, *mo chridhe*."

"But . . ." She scrambled to find an excuse to stop a meeting of clans arranged long before she and Lachlan had even arrived in Scotland. "But there'll be people from all clans there, yes?"

"Hundreds, from every sept." He tilted his head. "You're worried."

"No."

She spoke the word in a rising tone. His smile was as kind as her answer was uncertain.

He said, "It's true that the council heights will

be as busy as the wharf of Derry. I'll keep you as far from the crowd as I can, but we may have to press close. The most important men will be inside the circle of sacred stones, where the—"

"Sacred stones?" She pressed her palms against his chest. "Do you mean dolmen stones?"

"Aye. On the height above Loch Fyfe is where the clan's leaders are named and given the rod." He drew back another measure. "I told you about that when we visited the dolmen stones on Inishmaan, remember?"

"No, no." Her breath came fast as her thoughts raced. "I'd forgotten. I'd forgotten completely."

"What does it matter?"

"The stones will *help* me."

"Lass, I'm fonder of stones than most," he said, "but how can they 'help' you in anything?"

Lost in her own thoughts she'd forgotten that he wouldn't understand. "Dolmens—all sacred stones—have a magic of their own. They were built on places of great power and resonance, where our world and the Otherworld meet."

He mused for a moment. "It makes sense. Our clan has crowned kings on that hilltop for as long as memory serves."

"When I'm near the dolmen stones on Inishmaan, I can hear men's minds so much more keenly." Her excitement rose. "The rush of thoughts can be overwhelming, even painful." Stories of those who disappeared, became deranged, or even died after touching the stones wisped through her mind but she pushed them aside. "Getting *too* close to the stones isn't a good idea, but if I just edge toward them, the surge of power may help me make sense of the crowd."

He raised one brow. "So that's why you dragged me to the height that day."

She bit her lip, abashed at being caught. "I was desperate for any trick to slip into that mind of yours."

"Sneaky little wench."

"It didn't work." She leaned into him with a smile. "With you, I needed a different kind of magic."

He laughed and then lowered his head. His lips captured hers, warm and full of promise. She fell into his kiss with new eagerness. Mind-sickness or no, the dolmens would expand any power she had left, at least to the point that she could identify his enemy.

He pulled away from her lips and held her face still as he gazed upon her for a long moment.

"Stay with me, Cairenn."

Though she couldn't read his thoughts, she understood that he wasn't just asking her to stay for the night, or the next day, or the next week, or even the next year. No matter what happened tomorrow, he wanted her to stay with him through better or worse.

She brushed her lips against his in silent assent.

Then his fingers made short work of the laces of her tunic as she unknotted the rope belt around his waist. Their simple clothes puddled in heaps. She laughed as they stumbled over them on the way to the hay-stuffed pallet. She tumbled back onto the linens as he cushioned her head with one gentle hand. Rolling to her side, he cupped one breast before lowering his head to rub his bristly beard against her tightening nipple. She grasped his hair, gasping. Then he guided his thigh between her legs so that every tiny movement made her body tighten with delight.

She murmured, "Let me touch you, Lachlan," as she reached down between them.

He stopped her hand with his own. "Lass—"

"I want to touch you like you touch me. I want to taste you—"

"The night is young," he interrupted, raising his head so that the light from the tallow candle fell kindly on his face. "You'll have your turn, I promise you that."

His fingers ran soft across her skin, finding all the aching places. He kissed her throat, her jaw, and then captured her lips only to pull away and trail his mouth across the curve of her ear. With her eyes drifting closed with pleasure, her fingers followed every ridge of his muscles, every smooth plane of his warm skin, memorizing the shape of his body, which she would hold in her mind forever. Finally, she ran her fingers down his chest to where she could feel his heart pounding between them. Pressing her palm against the vibration, she imagined she held that precious heart in her hand.

When she could barely breathe for wanting him, she whispered his name. Seizing her hips, Lachlan rolled on his back, lifting her so that she straddled him. Startled and upended, she flattened her palms on his chest and looked at him in surprise.

"You wanted to have your way with me, lass." He positioned her hips until she felt his hardness press between her thighs. "Now's your chance."

The hollow ache inside her intensified and she realized what she must do. Grinning at him, she began to sink down.

"Easy," he said, stilling her. "I won't have you hurting yourself—"

"I want you," she interrupted, her breath in her throat, as she leaned down so her hair made a curtain around his face. "I want to feel you deep inside me."

She teased him with a slow kiss. His rigid heat impaled her as she lowered herself to the root. His choked moan made her whole body tingle with pleasure.

"Ach, Cairenn," he said through his teeth. "You'll be the death of me."

A laugh rippled in her throat. She squirmed around his shaft, loving the fullness of the sensation. Lachlan inhaled sharply and dug his fingers into her hips. Though her mind had already launched into that bright, white place that she shared with him whenever they merged their bodies, some small thinking part of her noted the thrill of being able to give her man pleasure. His hands flexed on her hips and he pressed his head back against the pallet as she moved in different, exciting ways.

"Cairenn," he said between his teeth.

She laughed out loud and gave way to the will of his hands, finding a rhythm that rippled sensation through her. Her inner muscles tightened around him and, in a breathless moment, unfurled in a sudden, sweet madness.

Shuddering with pleasure, she no longer cared if she never read the thoughts of another living being—so long as she could spin forever like this through Lachlan's sweeping mind.

CHAPTER TWENTY

Rain misted the road on the day of the council gathering. The constant drizzle made the ground soft, the air gray and dim, and the world noisy with the patter of raindrops falling off the leaves in the surrounding woods. The fog was so thick that even the horses sensed danger, for no one could see more than three-horse-lengths ahead on the grimy path that led to the council heights.

Lachlan clutched the hilt of his dagger as he scanned the woods from under the hem of the hood. Tradition demanded that no man bring a weapon to the sacred height, but that tradition didn't apply to the three winding roads that led from each major sept to the hill that was the political center of their combined clan. These roads were bloody with tales of ambushes, of kidnappings, of murders, and so every man in the column rode or walked in tense anticipation of treachery.

Lachlan still did not know what he would do

once Cairenn identified the man who'd ordered the murder of his father and himself. His cousin Angus expected Lachlan to sweep off his cloak, reveal himself, and call out his enemy, claiming he'd been told by the assassins who sank the knife into his back. That was the plan.

But once he made his presence known, his every move as the new chieftain would be watched and noted. He would be swiftly married to the willful girl who used to steal tarts from the kitchen and point a blaming finger at his half-brother Fingal. His visits to Cairenn would be curtailed, always slyly prearranged, like a man visiting a whore rather than the woman he preferred to marry.

His mind resisted that plan.

It was the only plan he had.

He hazarded yet another glance to where Cairenn walked beside him. No doubt it was the rain that made damp tendrils cling to her brow, but she looked pale and wan, as if beset by fever.

Hidden by the folds of his cloak, he covered her cold hand with his. "Any danger nearby?"

She shook her head with more violence than necessary. Then she yanked her hand from his and pressed the back of it against her lips, as if holding back bile.

"What's wrong, lass?"

She splayed the fingers of her hand as if to ward off questions.

He said, "Is it the crowd that's causing you pain?"

"No," she said, her voice strained. "All I hear is a crackling noise, like a thousand bolts of lightning sizzling in the air.”

The hair on the back of his arms rose. “What does that mean?”

“I don’t know.”

His senses sharpened. He peered through the thick fog ahead. He listened to the suck of horses’ hooves in mud, the ringing of harness and shield. He listened harder and thought he heard, from a great distance, the sound of muffled voices.

By reflex he pulled his dagger from its sheath and eyed the woods around them. He said, “We’ll stop here.”

“No.”

“You’re in pain.” She stumbled on a raised stone. He seized her arm to keep her upright.

“I need to be near the dolmen stones.”

“If you can hear the crowd from here, then why—”

“I just need to get closer.” Her voice was reedy, terrified, and determined all at once. “I need to do what I came here to do.”

He cursed himself for not telling Angus that she required a mount. Callum would have accommodated the request with a wink and a smile, and then Lachlan could have brought Cairenn close to the heights and retreated just as quickly. The woman he loved was paying a high price for an end she didn’t want.

As they came out of the wooded path and into the open area that wound up to the council height, the fog began to dissipate in the rising lake breeze. He saw shadowy movement through breaks in its density. He passed vassals holding horses and guards standing over piles of weapons. Cairenn pressed into his side to cover her face. Then they rose above the mist and the crowd came into view.

Into his tunic, she whispered, "Is this the place?"

"Open your eyes and see."

He walked her a few paces out of the line of Ewing horses and men so she could better see the summit, not more than two dozen yards away. There was a crowd, but in gaps he could see the three stone monoliths lying on the grassy height.

"The council height," he said, mentally marking the tartans of the septs. "Where the clan officially decides who will hold the rod of kingship."

"But . . . where are the stones?"

"Look," he said. "There are three of them there, lying in a triangle on the ground."

"But where are the *standing* stones," she said, her voice tight. "The ones that belong inside that triangle?"

"When my father became king," he said, "he had the upright stones moved to the MacEgan castle."

Her breath hissed through her teeth. Her whole body tightened in his embrace, like she herself had turned to stone.

"Tell me it's not true, Lachlan."

He had no time to respond. Around them, the Ewing men were unstrapping their swords, pulled daggers out of sheathes, and tossed maces and shields upon the ground. Callum Ewing and Angus were already heading toward the height, Angus furtively glancing over his shoulder in search of Lachlan.

"We have to approach now," Lachlan said. "Callum and Angus will make the announcement as soon as they step inside the dolmen stones—"

"I can't."

The force of her resistance was strong.

"Lachlan." She looked as pale as death. "I can't hear *anything*."

She did not feel normal. She did not feel *right*.

Noise flooded through her mind, crackling and sizzling like pork fat overheating in an iron pot. No matter how hard she tried to build walls against it, the pressure made rubble of them. She pressed her fingers against her temples and squeezed her eyes shut, tried to breathe through the assault. With every step she'd taken closer to this hill, the cacophony had intensified.

She was certain now: All the mind-trouble that she'd experienced since landing on Scottish shores emanated from this sacred but mutilated place.

"Cairenn?"

His voice rang with wariness and disbelief and her heart squeezed.

"Maybe," he said, "if we drew back from the crowd—"

"It's not the crowd." Every word was labor. "The height . . . it's desecrated."

He blinked in that way he did when she spoke of matters not of this world. She struggled to come up with a means to explain what no outsider was meant to know. Places like this one—dolmens, barrows, sacred heights ringed by oak trees—were hallowed links holding the worlds together. They were meant to be feared and loved and respected and holy. They were not meant to be disturbed by mortal men.

"I told you," she stuttered, "that the dolmens are a portal between this world and the Otherworld. Your father moved that door."

"A door," he said, his voice full of musing. "Thus the two upright stones, a capstone, and a space in-between."

"There may be other stones on a sacred height," she said, "but the source of power is always the portal—"

A shout came from the crowd. The council was beginning.

He said, "I must go."

"No," she said. "You mustn't."

She seized him, crushing two handfuls of his cleric's cloak in her fists. The crowd was a shifting menace atop the defiled hill. The gleam of so much chain mail was like a thousand light-daggers stabbing her eyes. Any or all of those men could be his enemies, planning to kill him the moment he threw off his hood.

"Don't go." She pressed her forehead against his chest. "Stay hidden."

His fingers flexed on her shoulders. "The time has come, lass," he said. "I have strong men all around me—"

"And so many enemies you don't know." She concentrated harder, trying to pierce the rattling din for some insight. "Perhaps, if I could just approach the portal stones—"

"Impossible."

"But you said the portal stones were moved to the castle—"

"—to my *father's* castle," he interrupted, "where every man and woman within will recognize me the moment I cross the threshold." He set her apart a space, forcing her attention to his face. "I cannot turn back from this path, lass."

Words surged to her throat but he leaned forward and pressed his forehead against hers. Swathed in the darkness under his hood, breathing his breath, smelling the scent of wet wool and leather and man, she suddenly found herself in the white mind-place they shared in the most intimate moments of their loving.

"Long before I knew you," Lachlan whispered, and she couldn't be sure whether she heard him with her ears or her mind, "I put my life in the hands of men I considered friends. Today I must rely, as all men must, on faith and trust."

Then, like a light snuffing out, he was gone.

Lachlan strode up the hill, pushing away his worries about Cairenn to concentrate on the danger before him. Her gift could not have failed at a worse time, but he couldn't let himself be distracted by the capriciousness of supernatural abilities or her distress. In this moment, he had to concentrate on what he'd come here to do.

Keeping his gaze down and his head covered,

he circled the outer edge of the crowd until he caught a glimpse of Angus, pacing with impatience. Without disturbing any other men, Lachlan found an unobtrusive spot in the outer circle, one that gave him a good vantage point of the proceedings.

Dermot, the chieftain of the MacGilchrist clan, paced in the open space. A short man with a lion's head of salt-and-pepper hair, The MacGilchrist was the eldest under-chieftain of the three septs, beating Callum Ewing by only a few months. Thus it was his right to be the first to pace around the white rod of kingship lying in the center of the circle, just as it was his right to be the first to speak at council.

"These six weeks and more," The MacGilchrist said, splaying a hand on his chest as he projected his voice over the crowd, "have been trying times for all of us. We've seen a king fallen off a horse, dead in his prime. An heir lost in the depths of the sea. Our lands raided, and our people murdered, all for no reason."

Suspicion curled like a knot beneath Lachlan's ribs. MacGilchrist had always been an ambitious man. Now, scanning the guards standing under the MacGilchrist banner, Lachlan could identify more than one Campbell among them, probably relatives of Dermot's wife. Yet the chieftain's aligning with such a rising clan was a dangerous game, for the Campbells could swallow the MacGilchrist's smaller sept right up, leaving Dermot little chance to ever hold the white rod of overlordship.

Yet many men would be drawn to such strength—even if it subsumed them.

"You men know," MacGilchrist continued,

"that I did not always agree with Fergus MacEgan. His plan to have the chieftaincy handed down through only one family line smacked of selfish ambition. Of plain greed."

A few shouts went up among the men. Lachlan's chest tightened. He found himself reaching for a sword he wasn't wearing, his fist closing on air.

"But Fergus MacEgan," MacGilchrist continued, *"was right."*

The words echoed on the hilltop. Lachlan waited, surprised but wary, for MacGilchrist's next words.

"Already," the chieftain continued, "Wales has succumbed to the might of King Edward. Our Welsh brothers are conquered. What more proof do we need that the English devour those who make themselves weak?"

The men around Lachlan shuffled and murmured. Few of these men had ever traveled farther than Derry or Galway Bay. What went on in the lands beyond the Highlands rarely concerned them.

"Why did the Welsh lose?" the chieftain asked. "Because the Welsh are divided as we are divided. They parcel their holdings among their sons, making those fiefdoms smaller, weaker, and impossible to defend. And we Scots argue with the death of every chieftain, dividing our clans with bitterness, splintering our loyalties."

A single shout came from the crowd. "Do you hold yourself forth as the new king, Dermot? Will we forever have a MacGilchrist to reign as overlord?"

"I," MacGilchrist said, "do *no such thing.*"

The murmuring that began at the accusation died just as quickly.

"I put forward to you the same name I put forward two times before. Fergus's only remaining son, Fingal MacEgan."

A tall, thin man stepped into the circle and commanded the attention of every eye. This young man wore no chain mail beneath his clan's tartan, held secure by the MacEgan brooch. His thatch of dark hair was tousled as if he'd just woken from a long slumber, but there was no sleepiness in his gaze, or in the cut of his bristled jaw, or in the way he raised his hand to acknowledge every man as he swept the entire crowd with a look so penetrating that Lachlan dipped his head so that his cowl would hide his face.

Fingal.

A thousand memories flooded his mind. His half-brother as an infant, placed in his arms, a mewling, red-faced thing. The toddler who leapt for the jingling length of chain mail links that Lachlan hung just out of his reach. The long-legged nine-year-old whose arm strained with the weight of a wooden sword as Lachlan sparred with him in the muddy courtyard.

When Lachlan had first determined to take the rod of kingship, he hadn't envisioned ripping it from the hands of his fledgling half-brother—or the full-grown man Fingal had become while fostering with the MacGilchrists.

"I have news," Callum Ewing bellowed as he

stepped into the circle with Angus at his heels. "News that will change everything."

Lachlan froze at the sound of these words, but his heart shouted *no*.

NO.

CHAPTER TWENTY-ONE

*"**L**achlan MacEgan is alive."*
When Callum spoke those fateful words, Lachlan's cry lodged in his throat. A collective gasp swept through the crowd, but Lachlan could only stand there wishing he could claw the words out of everyone's ears. This announcement had been his plan from the start—but that was before he'd laid cyes upon Fingal.

Was he to fight his own half-brother over a chieftaincy that only duty and birth order compelled him to take?

"It's true," Callum shouted, above the crowd's jeers and doubts and accusations. "Lachlan MacEgan is alive and well."

Lachlan knew he was supposed to be looking around the agitated gathering, marking enemies according to who dissented, but now he had a more urgent mission. He stood riveted, waiting for Angus's gaze to find his.

It did not take long. As Angus swept the crowd with his gaze, he paused for a moment to lock eyes with him. Danger be damned, Lachlan shook his head once, with force, so that Angus could not doubt his meaning.

Angus's brow rippled in confusion but his perusal continued past Lachlan, to encompass the entirety of the crowd. Moments later, Angus's gaze returned in a slow sweep.

When their eyes locked a second time, Lachlan tempted fate by shaking his head once again. He would not—*could not*—do what he'd come here to do, now that he'd seen his half-brother stand like a giant among these men.

"Angus!"

Fingal's voice startled Lachlan. It was octaves lower than he remembered.

"Is it true, Angus," Fingal said, as he swooped like an eagle across the clearing to stand before his cousin. "Is my brother alive?"

Angus nodded his shaggy head. "As surely as I stand here before you."

Fingal embraced his cousin with such force that Lachlan felt his own chest squeeze. Then his half-brother pulled away to search the crowd.

"Is he here, among you? Lachlan! Lachlan, show yourself!"

Lachlan, Lachlan, show yourself!

The words echoed in his head, a memory of a thousand games of hide-and-seek in the deep woods.

I can't find you, Lachlan! Show yourself!

"Your half-brother is safe." Angus placed his

hand on the boy's shoulder to draw his attention. "He's recovering from his wounds in Ireland until such time as he can return. He sent me forth to bring you word."

"Then we shall feast in his honor tonight." Fingal swept up the white rod by his feet and waved it above his head. "This council will be deferred until my father's firstborn returns—"

"Fingal," MacGilchrist interrupted. "How do we know that this man speaks the truth and isn't here to put off what must be done?"

"Because he is my Irish cousin and beyond reproach." Fingal took MacGilchrist by the shoulders. "Be happy, my lord, that this matter will soon be settled as it should be."

A shadow crossed MacGilchrist's face, even as the old chieftain bowed his salt-and-pepper head.

"Now to the castle, all of us," Fingal commanded. "It's time to drink deep and eat our fill. My closest kinsman is alive!"

The crowd dispersed under the power of Fingal's enthusiasm. The men headed to their horses, talking among themselves. Fingal led Angus down the slope toward Loch Fyfe, asking questions Lachlan couldn't hear.

Lachlan kept his head bowed as he turned away and headed to where Cairenn waited at the base of the slope, every step a drumbeat of hope. His breath came fast, and his ideas came faster. His mind tumbled down a future he'd closed off to himself, a choice that, until now, honor compelled him never to consider.

He approached Cairenn, weaving where she

stood, looking at him in pained, silent question.

"Cairenn, *mo chridhe,*" he said, cupping her pale, lovely face. "It's time to take fate into our own hands."

Around the bend, the spit of land that curled into the dark blue waters of Loch Fyfe came into view. At the end of that crescent rose the mighty, square, stone-walled keep in which Lachlan had been raised. It was a formidable defense, guarding the lake from any sea invaders who dared to come upriver into the heart of MacEgan lands.

He supposed he'd always known that his home was also a fortress, but seeing it with Cairenn beside him made him all too aware of how little her people needed such defenses, and of how damned often his did.

"Lachlan," she said, as she faltered in her step. "I can *feel* them."

His heart leapt, for she could only be speaking of the dolmen stones. "Can you hear anything?"

"That strange crackling sound has dimmed." Her brow furrowed. "I feel less burdened by the noise, now that we're farther away from the council height. But I can hear . . . something . . ."

Her words trailed off.

He said, "I'm sure it'll come, lass."

"Yes." She filled the word with conviction. "Perhaps when I get closer."

She dropped her gaze to the muddy ground. How he ached to draw her against him, but an embrace would draw the attention of the men on horseback who cantered by. Some were guards he knew, some were MacGilchrist and Ewing cousins, and others were squires and MacEgan servants. The long, winding path lay before them, crowded with people heading to the narrow causeway that led to the castle. If he made it that far unrecognized, he'd still have to stride under the iron portcullis into an interior courtyard full of stable boys who'd once saddled his horses, laundresses who'd once given him an eye, and long-time guards who used to tousle his hair.

Only then would he reach the mead-hall where the dolmens stood in the midst of his newly-alerted enemies.

"Talk to me, Lachlan." Her face was pale with fatigue, which made her green eyes all the more striking. "Tell me why your father moved the portal stones into the castle."

"He did it after changing the way we choose the chieftaincy." How he longed to run his hand over her soft hair, tucked beneath the hood of her cloak. "My father did nothing without a big, symbolic gesture. This was his way of buttressing his plan that only MacEgans would be chosen as chieftains."

He'd been barely twelve years old when his father had considered the idea of moving the stones. His father soon became convinced that the task would be impossible, but Lachlan's own imagination wouldn't let the idea go. So he stole a fresh lambskin from his father's cleric and sketched how such a feat might be done with rope and rolling logs. His father had been on the verge of beating him for the theft when he paused and examined the sketches. He ordered the work done according to Lachlan's plans. When the project was finished, his father had written to his brother in Rome about Lachlan's further education.

Lachlan liked to think it was his father's pride that had sent him so far from Loch Fyfe—and not the hostility of his father's Stuart bride.

"For both worlds," Cairenn said, "moving those sacred stones was a dangerous thing to do."

"So was his decision," he said. "But my father wanted to make his decree as vivid and memorable as the portal he seized from the heights and erected within his hall."

"Those stones do not belong under any man's roof, Lachlan."

"You are not the first to say so." Back then, his father had had a hard time gathering men to move the stones, and it wasn't just because the septs balked at the idea of dismantling the place where the central council had met for generations. As a boy, he saw the dolmens as fine pieces of building stone, but many of his father's crofters looked upon them with fearful eyes. "It took months of hard labor because my father had so few workers."

"And haven't the years since been full of strife?"

He thought of his childhood before the movement of the stones, when every August the seals swam upriver to loll on the mud flats around the castle walls, and he, Fingal and Elspeth ran unfettered through the nearby woods. Then he thought about the reeving and the skirmishes of the last decade, of all the men who'd died.

"Discord arises from desecration." She curled her hand in his tunic, leaning into him as they walked. "I'm afraid, Lachlan."

Hidden by the folds of his tunic, he wound his hand around hers. "My blade will find bone if anyone seeks to hurt you."

"It's not me I'm afraid for. So uprooted from their rightful place, those portal stones may not help my gift. Then we'll be right in the middle of the mead-hall in full view of those who murdered your father and tried to murder you."

She didn't speak her mother's prophecy in so many words, but Lachlan heard Cairenn's fear that this crazy attempt to take fate in their own hands just might make that deadly prediction come true.

He ran his hand over her hair, knocking her hood off so that her blond tresses shone in the growing sunlight. He'd meant to do it in comfort, but the sight of her bright, beautiful hair sparked an idea.

"Lachlan?"

"What would you think," he said, as he trailed a tress through his fingers, "if I asked you to make use of another of your gifts?"

The sun was halfway to the west horizon when they finally approached the portcullis. Lachlan's gut tightened as he saw guards swarming on the ramparts. Within, the courtyard teemed with boys taking the reins of the horses as mail-clad men dismounted. Through the gate, he recognized Tadgh the blacksmith hammering horseshoes while dogs, goats and chickens roamed freely. Bonnie and Coira came out of the shadows, laundry in baskets on their hips, while Peigi the cook, her apron dusty with oat flour and stained with cooking grease, argued with the fisherman Gilroy over a basket of eels.

When he ducked into the courtyard among Angus's men, all heads turned toward them. Bile burned in his throat, but he kept walking, his cowl low but his eye on the path that led to the wooden doorway of the mead-hall, clear across the yard. The attention felt like a thousand torches thrust close. His skin prickled, anticipating discovery.

But halfway across the courtyard, when no man shouted his name and no hand grabbed his tunic, he realized that his plan was working. He and Angus's men followed in the wake of a beautiful woman, striding without a cloak, her shimmering tresses bouncing upon her pale shoulders and sunlight gleaming on her skin above the scooped neckline of her tunic.

Not a single man turned his face from that vision to settle on the bowed-headed, lowly-dressed porters and clerics following in her wake.

A MacGilchrist warrior taking his ease by the mead-hall door broke into a smile at the sight of Cairenn. He interceded to open the heavy door for her. The man's gaze wandered over her curves with avarice and lust as she passed through. Lachlan curled his hands into fists. He supposed this was the price he paid for arranging to hide behind Cairenn's skirts. It took all his will not to throw the warrior a sharp, well-placed elbow before he himself passed into the dimness of the hall.

Once inside, his unease surged. Men and

servants filled the room. Pewter tankards clanked as they hit wooden tables. The guests shouted to be heard over one another. Several lute players in the near corner battled to play above the din. Crossing to the tables, the wife of MacGilchrist strode by with a flagon of ale in her hand as if she were the lady of the castle, greeting them all as they entered.

That woman's gaze passed over Cairenn without a flicker of interest before resting on the men, "More space in the middle, lads," she said. "And mind you be patient about the ale."

Lachlan dipped his head and stepped behind one of Angus's men. He hoped his beard obscured the cut of his jaw, for MacGilchrist's wife knew the slope of it too well. Whenever she'd visited in past years, she'd taken to searching it for scruff, with a gleaming promise in her eye.

The men in front of him moved forward, so he followed close behind. Beyond the bobbing shoulders, he saw Cairenn heading to the far end of the hall where the dolmens stood, lit by narrow beams of sunlight streaming through the arrow-slits. The crowds impeded the way. Soon he and Angus's men were winnowed into single file.

The light that came through the arrow slits flashed upon Cairenn's hair in intervals, like bursts of golden lightning. The effect had an impact, for as he wove his way through, he could see, even with his cowl pulled low, how heads turned and whispers rose. He took advantage of the distraction to glance quickly around. Against the east wall, he caught sight of Fingal standing and chatting with people at the lower tables. A young girl hovered by Fingal's side, another MacGilchrist if the red hue of her hair was any indication. In the shadows behind Fingal, Lachlan saw his stepmother lurking like a spider.

Sensing attention upon him, he turned his head to face the west wall only to dodge another gaze by turning back east. There was Alan, a Stuart cousin his father had fostered. On the other side was buxom Murdina, hefting a tray of ham above the heads of the crowd. He felt like a man sparring, bobbing his head at every hint of a glance in his general direction. The gauntlet of danger seemed to stretch out forever, all the way to within yards of the standing stones. His back tightened with each step.

By habit, the most honored guests would be seated at the head of the main table. That fact was confirmed as they approached. Angus, catching sight of Cairenn, suddenly shot up off the bench so fast that half the ale sloshed out of his tankard.

"I prefer ale in my mouth, Angus," shouted a clearly drunken Callum Ewing, receiving the full brunt of the spray. "But see how our Irishman straightens up at the sight of his leman!"

Lachlan didn't slacken his pace as he continued on, choking down the urge to make Callum swallow his words.

"Angus, you old dog." If the slurring of The MacGilchrist's words were any indication, clearly the ale had been flowing. "If that's the beauty you're swiving, I'll have a piece—"

"Shut your mouth, old man."

Lachlan started at the sound of the woman's voice behind him. Lady MacGilchrist shoved past, carrying a fresh pitcher of ale and an empty tankard in her pocket.

"Fill my cup, woman," MacGilchrist said, thrusting out his tankard, "and keep to your place–"

"You're a drunken fool who's had enough," she said, stopping short in the lane between tables as the man just ahead of Lachlan squeezed by. "I won't waste the last of this ale on *you*."

Then she swiveled on her heel, skirts swirling. Lachlan froze as he heard the clank of flagon against tankard and the gurgle of ale pouring to the point where a good portion of it splashed all over the floor.

"This ale is for the cleric," she said, blindly thrusting the tankard at him, "who has the wit to stay silent and bow his head. *He* could teach you something about the virtue of holding your tongue, husband."

Lachlan took the tankard in his hand just as a hunting hound emerged from under the table to lick up the ale spill. Lachlan bobbed his head in silent thanks, but, mercifully, the Lady MacGilchrist didn't linger to acknowledge it. She stepped over the dog and swept by him to stomp back in the direction she came. Aware of the attention he was drawing, he didn't waste a moment to sweep past Callum and walk into the clearing in front of the portal stones.

For the lack of a place to sit, Angus's men milled in that clearing. Cairenn stood with her back to the hall, staring up at the stones. Perhaps it was a trick of the light, but the rocks seemed to pulse in her presence. He moved close enough to speak in a whisper.

"How do you fare, lass?"

She took a shuddering breath. He watched the small muscles of her upper shoulders flex and straighten as if she were bracing herself.

"I fare well enough," she said, "for a woman about to take fate in her hands."

She stretched out her arm. He thought he heard a crackling sound as her fingers neared the glittering surface of one of the standing stones.

When she touched the dolmen, the room boomed like thunder.

A white-hot, sizzling sensation bolted through her. A cry rose up but the noise stuck in her throat. One moment she was staring at the vaulted ceiling of the mead-hall and in the next images flooded her mind, crashing over her in a cacophony of sound and color and sensation.

She glimpsed a grass-soft clearing in a circle of oaks. She heard the sound of fairy-music. She saw slim shapes idling among the flowering vines while tipping nectar into wooden tankards. Their laughter made the leaves rustle like the wind. She sensed curious glances upon her and saw a woman stretch out a hand.

Then suddenly she found herself on Inishmaan, racing up the hill to the lonely places. She watched a creature whirl up out of a crack in the ground to fall into step beside her, laughing. She saw herself as if from afar, brooding on a ledge as she gazed upon a ship passing by below. Small shapes sat behind her, mimicking her stance, their pointy chins in their slim hands. She saw her father grinding some herb with mortar and pestle while an older woman in gossamer white stood behind him, smiling a gentle smile. She saw seals upon the shore looking up at her with the faces of men.

Then, with a breathless lift, she was on the council hill above Loch Fyfe and the stones were where they belonged except they were not. What she saw were ghosts of the portal stones, with moisture slipping down their sides though there was no rain. There was no wind, or warmth, or life, either. At the foot of each ghostly stone the earth was churned and red like blood and she heard the slap and clatter of many hands and feet, like a hundred thousand creatures trapped beneath the face of the earth.

Her heart raced so hard it ached. A distant voice warned her to pull her fingers away from the stones but they felt nailed to the surface. The dolmen grew hot beneath her palm. She tried to fight off the power of the assault but it was like pulling a wild wolfhound by a leash. She scolded herself that she'd experienced this feeling before—when she stepped onto the shore at Galway as a girl new to her gift, and when she arrived at Derry, still unused to the rush of hundreds of minds. She mustered what she'd learned from both those experiences, struggling to master her senses so she would not collapse under the beating of so much keen, indiscriminate awareness.

Dizzy and disoriented, she squeezed her eyes shut and willed herself back to the mead-hall. Only when she could feel the ground beneath her feet could she control the power that made her pulse throb painfully and her head swell with bursting pressure. She mentally forced herself back up the path to where she'd first laid eyes upon the castle, when she'd sensed the initial pull of the stones. The portal dolmens had called to her in winsome singing voices that pulsed with longing and pain. Once inside the mead-hall, she hadn't been able to take her eyes off the carved, glittering surface that now lay flat under her palm. So long they'd been bereft of the bright caress of the sun, the gentle watering of the rain, and the feel of the wind flooding over their surface.

The assault eased a fraction. With effort she rose above the mental battering long enough to draw a breath. She began to separate colors from sounds, thoughts from noise, moods from mischief, and doubts from decision. She realized that the chattering she was hearing all around her did not completely emanate from the stone. Her brain was alight with all the noise. It flowed through her from the minds of the people in the mead-hall around her, a cacophony of hopes and lusts and worries and plans—plans—plans.

Lachlan.

Among all those minds she even recognized his, bright and open to her, filling up with curdling worry as he lunged toward her to pull her away from the stone.

I will not fail . . . I must *not fail.*

Even as she became aware of his hands yanking her back, she squeezed her senses to chase down that one whisper out of thousands and isolate that single dark murmur of murderous intent.

In an instant she was sucked into the murderer's mind. She saw thick fingers slip poison in a flagon. She saw the flagon carried through the mead-hall, swiped away from those who would have their cups filled not knowing any better. She saw the flagon taken toward the dolmen stones, and felt the murderer's mind growing blood-dark with intent.

My daughter will be queen.
My daughter will be queen.
My daughter will be queen.

Cairenn watched the flagon tip and the cup filled. Then she saw the achingly familiar face of the man marked to die.

Lachlan watched in frozen horror as Cairenn touched the stone and then shuddered as if in the throes of death. Her head fell back as strange thunder shook the walls of the mead hall. Her eyes rolled up to show the whites.

He lunged and yanked her away. She pitched back against his chest. He gathered her so close that the ale in his tankard sloshed out of his cup. It spilled on her kirtle as he whispered, *"Cairenn."*

He felt a force ripple through her. She wrenched herself from his arms and, swirling, knocked the tankard out of his grip. The shocked, sonorous silence that had settled in the wake of the booming thunder was broken by the clatter of his tankard upon the flagstones, spewing ale everywhere.

Then another sound could be heard, a terrible thrashing and grunting and rattling of claws. Gasps went up at the head table. People leapt up and cleared away. In the space left behind, a hound convulsed on the floor, white froth bubbling around his snout.

"Poison," Cairenn blurted, weaving where she stood. "MacGilchrist's wife."

She pitched forward. Lachlan caught her in mid-fall, his heart stopping. He seized her jaw and raised her lolling head only to see her eyelids flutter closed. His throat tightened and his mind went blank with fear.

A shadow fell over them. He glanced up to see Angus with Callum at his side. The chieftain's eyes widened. Only then did Lachlan become aware of a cool breeze against the back of his bare head, the weight of his woolen cowl upon his shoulders, and the shocked gasps arising in the hall.

The thought passed through his mind like a wisp: He'd been recognized.

He didn't care.

All that mattered was the woman who sagged unconscious in his arms. With the pressure in his chest growing, he dipped down and swept an arm under her knees to lift her into his embrace. He had to get the woman he loved far away from these dolmen stones. He had to take her far from the assault of the thoughts of a thousand curious onlookers. He had to bring her to where she would be safe.

"My tent is in the field outside," Angus said,

his nostrils flaring. "I'll send you a doctor."

Lachlan barely nodded as he turned toward the trestle tables, seeking the straightest path out of the mead hall.

Before him, women clutched their hands close. Knights stared in wonder and placed their palms over their hearts. Servants lowered their gazes, pitched their heads forward, and bent their knees.

He took one step forward and the crowd parted. Bareheaded and barefaced, he carried Cairenn through a sea of bowed heads.

CHAPTER TWENTY-TWO

Lachlan sat on a stool beside the pallet upon which Cairenn lay, gripping his head in his hands. Moments ago, Callum's private doctor—a man Lachlan had never met—showed up at the tent with his bag of powders and nostrums. The doctor declared he could find nothing wrong with the woman, but took out his lance to bleed her.

At the sight of that flashing knife, Lachlan had thrown the man out of the tent. Whatever caused Cairenn to look so pale against the wool blankets, he knew the affliction was of the mind, not the body. No doctor except her own father knew anything about that kind of sickness, and that doctor was across a wide and frothing sea.

He dug his fingers deep into his scalp. By knocking the poisoned chalice out of his hands, she had saved his life. There was always a price to pay to change one's fate, and that price might be too steep to bear.

Come back to me, Cairenn.

He gazed upon her lovely face and willed her to open her eyes.

I need you, mo chridhe.

He heard footsteps outside the tent. No matter how hard he willed it, they did not stop in their approach.

Angus swept the tent flap aside and bent his head as he entered. Callum Ewing followed, looking grave. When a third head emerged—with an all-too-familiar mane of salt-and-pepper hair—Lachlan shot up from the stool.

Rage boiled up inside him and made the edges of his sight go red. Everything around him became a blur of motion until he found himself holding The MacGilchrist up by the throat, pressing him against the center strut of the tent so that the wood shuddered with the force.

"You sent your wife to kill me," Lachlan said between gritted teeth. "A *coward's* way, Dermot."

MacGilchrist sputtered, his eyes wide.

"The men who put a blade in my back," Lachlan continued, the words like gravel in his throat, "and the men who threw my father off the cliff—will you deny that they were all Campbells?"

The MacGilchrist's sharp fingernails clawed against Lachlan's grip, but Lachlan didn't loosen it to hear the answer he already knew.

"The question is," he argued, "whether you sent your wife to do that too—"

"I sent those men myself," interrupted another voice, "because my husband *is* a coward."

Lachlan turned to see MacGilchrist's wife

standing just inside the tent. He stared at her, at her fading blonde hair hanging straggly around her shoulders, at her mud-streaked tunic, at her bound hands. His fury became a wild, hot thing pounding in his chest. He had to dig deep to find what chivalry was left in him so he wouldn't reach for the knife in his boot and take his revenge.

Lachlan loosened his grip on the chieftain enough for Dermot to slide down the wooden post. At least now his good hand was free.

The woman shifted her gaze to her husband where he slumped at the foot of the tent pole. "That man is a lapdog," the woman spat, "always groveling at Fergus's knee. Giving up all hopes of the chieftaincy with a shrug, even after Fergus was dead—"

"You stand before me," Lachlan interrupted, his palm itching for the leather hilt, "and confess you killed my father."

"Your father stole from us and from all generations yet born." Her eyes gleamed. "Yet even with your father dead, I couldn't trust my husband to seize the rod for himself. I had to kill you, too—"

"You stand before me," he repeated, "and confess you sent men to kill me."

"*Yes*." She sneered at him. "*Yes*. For I knew my coward of a husband would put forth Fingal— and fifteen-year-old boys are easily swayed."

The curl of her lip cut the last shred of his patience. He slid the knife out of his boot. The red light pouring in through the open flap glittered on its edge as he strode across the tent to put an end to this.

"Lachlan."

Callum's strong, steady voice broke through the haze of his fury. Lachlan's heaving breath hitched. He scraped to a stop an arm's-length from the woman, an instant from committing bloody murder himself.

Callum loomed beside him. "The chieftain of the clan should render justice in this matter. And it should be done for all to see."

Lachlan tightened his grip on the hilt and curled his free hand into a fist. Callum was right but that knowledge did nothing to master his anger. He made an effort to control his own breathing, to loosen the muscles of his jaw.

"Throw her in a storeroom," Lachlan said. "Bolt the door. After the council has chosen a chieftain, her fate will be the first to be decided—"

"They'll all rise for me," she interrupted, mocking, as one of Callum's men emerged from the shadows to lead her away. "The Campbells will come for me."

"They'll abandon you," Callum retorted. "They know better than to go to war for a woman who killed a chieftain for her own ends."

Lachlan's anger took on an edge of despair. More war, he thought. More bloodshed for the sake of power. Strife and conflict infected his lands, and it wasn't only due to stubborn Scottish pride.

Callum stepped in front of him to seize his attention. "Justice will be swift for her." The chieftain tilted his head toward the tent pole. "But what are we to do with him?"

Lachlan frowned as he turned back to Dermot, slumped upon the ground. Lachlan remembered seeing The MacGilchrist in the mead hall earlier, before Cairenn had touched the stones. Lachlan remembered how his wife had denied him the poisoned drink. He remembered Dermot's stormy look and his wife's quick retreat.

Theater, he thought, nothing more, but the chieftain raised his hands above his head as if he heard Lachlan's thoughts.

"By all that is holy," the chieftain said, "I knew nothing of this."

"You married a Campbell," Callum interjected. "You've always wanted the rod."

"It's not true! I put forth Fingal—"

"Intending him to be your son-in-law," Callum added. "Deny it if you dare."

"Idle talk. Everyone knows that your daughter is betrothed to the MacEgan heir, Callum."

A silence fell in the room. Lachlan glared at the chieftain and remembered a day in his own boyhood when The MacGilchrist had hauled him onto his great palfrey for a ride back to the MacEgan castle, where Lachlan was sure to get a beating for some transgression or another. Dermot had held him by the scruff, but he'd also talked to him about how, as future overlord, he must learn to take his punishment. For someday he would be charged with standing before men to judge them, and punish them, too, according to their crimes.

How Lachlan wished Cairenn stood beside him now, strong and healthy and full of wisdom, to uncover MacGilchrist's lies—or his truth.

"Like your treasonous wife," Lachlan said, "you will be brought before the new chieftain to be tried. In the meantime Callum will put you in one of the upper rooms of the castle where you will stay until the reckoning. Do not break my trust."

The MacGilchrist nodded humbly and stumbled to his feet to follow Callum out of the tent. Angus fell in line and the other men in the tent trailed him out until only one man remained in the deeper shadows.

A young man, Lachlan noticed, with stubble upon his once-soft cheek, who stared at him with grave and solemn eyes.

All Lachlan's anger dissolved. "Fingal."

The young man who was no longer a boy stepped into better light. "I always knew that you would return."

The space between them closed as Lachlan engulfed his half-brother in an embrace, his worries ebbing for a moment under a surge of relief and reunion. He squeezed the boy's not-inconsiderable shoulders, and then found himself grunting as he hefted his half-brother off his feet. Fingal's guffaw bore no resemblance to the mischievous giggle Lachlan remembered.

Fingal pulled away and gave Lachlan a half-smile, his teeth white against the stubble on his jaw. "After all this, I understand why you made your way here in secret, Lachlan. But I can't think of a single reason why you didn't reveal yourself to me and the clan upon the council heights."

"There *is* a single reason." Lachlan gestured to Cairenn sleeping upon the pallet in the corner. "And there she is."

The boy glanced at her. "I don't understand."

"You will, someday, if fate is kind."

"Fate *has* been kind, by returning the firstborn of The MacEgan to take up the white rod as you were meant to."

Fingal's words were buoyant but they weighed upon Lachlan like a mantle of lead. He and Cairenn had entered the mead-hall of his father's house in an effort to change the fate that lay before them, but now, with his brother's fervent gaze upon him, Lachlan began to realize that choosing a different fate for himself meant settling the fate he yearned to reject onto the young shoulders of his own brother.

"Our father's truest wish," Lachlan said, his heart rising to his throat, "was to do what was best for the entire clan."

"It is my truest wish, as well."

"Well then," he said, placing his hands on Fingal's broad shoulders. "You have a decision to make."

The wind off Loch Fyfe tossed Lachlan's hair as he stood within the stones on the council height. It felt strange to stand bareheaded before his people after spending so much time in hiding. He felt their scrutiny upon him, and their assessment, like a hundred thousand lances.

He straightened his shoulders, though it was like shifting the weight of a stone carrier's yoke. Fate was rolling over him faster than he could comprehend, but he was resolved: He would do what duty demanded.

Once silence settled under the wind-whipped clouds, Callum Ewing walked into the circle, his snowy hair oiled and gleaming so that every man could see the tracks of the comb in it. The chieftain stopped in the center, where the white rod lay at his feet.

"These six weeks and more," Callum bellowed, "have been terrible times for our clan."

A murmuring of agreement rippled through the gathering.

"Our lands have been ravished," he said, "our people frightened, and our own chieftain—a good man, a strong leader, and my friend—murdered on his own lands."

Lachlan flinched at the reminder and sensed the same shock ripple through Fingal where his half-brother stood beside him.

"All this," Callum said, "is what happens when we are divided. Fergus himself warned us of this. Fergus himself offered a remedy."

Callum Ewing bent down and took the rod in his hand. When he straightened, he turned toward Lachlan.

"Lachlan MacEgan, the firstborn son of Fergus, is the true heir to the chieftaincy." Callum pointed the rod at him like a sword. "This rod, and the lordship of all of us, belongs to you."

The rod glowed like a beacon. Lachlan walked toward it though he was hardly aware of crossing the beaten grass. Ever since his father had made his intentions clear, Lachlan had known this day would come. He'd never wanted it, but he had envisioned it, the rod stretched out to him like this, glowing as the clouds parted and set the marble surface alight. His visions had never quite gone so far as to see that rod firm in his grip. Not like now, as his palm pressed against its chill girth.

It was heavier than he'd expected.

"Say hail." Callum raised his arms to the crowd. "Hail to the chieftain of—"

"NO."

Lachlan's shout echoed across the hill. "No," he repeated, as a restlessness began among the men. This was the fourth time the council had convened and these men had hoped to return to their homes, and to peace. "Before a decision is made," he said, "heed my words."

He walked in a circle and raised his own voice so that he would be heard by even the farthest man.

"My father, your late chieftain, was a man of great wisdom," he began. "He recognized the kernel of English strength and chose to adopt it, so that we, as a clan, may be stronger." He lifted the rod to show it to all of them. "But are we not Scots?"

A shout of assent rang out, and then another.

"My father settled this duty upon me." He tightened his fist on the raised rod. "But shouldn't I, a clansman just like each one of you, have a say in who shall be chieftain of my own people?"

He stopped in front of his half-brother, whose eyes shone bright.

"As heir, it is *my* choice whether to take the rod," Lachlan said, holding out the scepter to his half-brother, "or to pass it to the better man."

A moment of surprised silence hovered over

the hill. Fingal bowed his head before him, and then raised his beaming face. A shout of huzzah erupted, followed by more. Soon the crowd added the approval of pounding feet and the rise of joyous laughter. Lachlan embraced Fingal, and then separated from him so that Fingal could hold out his hand. With ceremony, Lachlan placed the rod in his palm. Gripping it, Fingal raised it above his head so that all the gathering could see.

Lachlan drank in the sight of his brother and their exultant clan while his chest swelled with pride.

CHAPTER TWENTY-THREE

Cairenn swam up from sleep. The sunlight beat against her eyelids. Somewhere nearby came the shuffling of feet, the rustling of fabric, and a strange, intermittent, scratching sound. As the intensity of the sunlight increased, she moved her leaden limbs and felt the tickle of the wool against her skin. She became aware of something else, too—a presence in the room, a loving warmth that she instantly recognized as Lachlan.

It came back to her, then, the whole crashing weight of the memory. The jolt of force from the stones. The rush of images and thoughts, the sense that her very life force was being drained from her body even as she experienced the whole world with a clarity she'd never known. She remembered the ease with which she singled out the lady MacGilchrist, who watched them from a shadowy corner, willing Lachlan to drink from the poisoned ale. She remembered the ale splashing against her hand and across the floor just before her the world winked out.

Now she blinked against the brightness seeping through the weave of a canvas tent. She opened her mouth to attempt speech, but her lips were dry. Her throat was sore as well, though she remembered, vaguely, the taste of cool water sometime during the night. Along with that memory came the feel of Lachlan's hand cradling her head, his soft voice in her ear, and his lips on her forehead.

She turned her head toward the scratching sound. It came from the tip of a feathered quill being drawn across a surface by the man she loved. He sat upon a stool on the other side of the tent, wielding that quill upon a plank across his knees. As she watched, he lifted something pale and limp off the plank—a lambskin, such as her father sometimes used to write his recipes for salves. His cheeks bellowed—cheeks clear of beard—as he blew upon the surface.

Tears came to her eyes to see him sitting there, looking so well and strong and at ease, his strong knees poking out.

She must have made a sound, for he raised his head. Then he was all motion, setting aside the board, grabbing a cup, and slipping his arm under her pillow to lift her up. The cool liquid was a balm upon her throat. The honey-mead swept through her with tingling swiftness.

When she finished, their gazes touched, and locked. Without effort she sank into that bright place they shared until she was surrounded by the pillowy warmth of his love, edged with a dose of concern.

She whispered, "How long have I been . . . ?"

"Two days." He put the cup aside and pushed her hair off her brow. "You slept most of it, rousing now and again just when I was convinced you were dead."

A flash of memory came to her, of Lachlan sleeping in her father's sickroom while she tried to penetrate his impenetrable mind, also convinced he was dead.

"I hope," she murmured, "that I've been a better patient than you ever were."

His lips tilted in a wry smile. "Surely I was full of patience and virtue in your father's house."

She tried to laugh but it was a dry, husky thing. His shadow fell over her as he placed a hungry spark of a kiss upon her lips.

He pulled away before the tingling faded. "I feared I might never hear your laughter again."

She was about to say *nor I yours* but she could already see in his midnight-sky eyes that he knew. So she did what she wished she could spend a lifetime doing: She looked at him. With her gaze she traced the fall of his blue-black hair across his brow, the faintest of lines on his forehead, a blood-scarred nick that crossed the line of his beardless jaw, and the way his cheeks swelled as a slow smile stretched the corners of his lips.

"We caught the murderer," he said, as he trailed his fingers across her brow. "All because of you."

She lifted her hand to press against his heart

and she felt a pleating of thick, fine wool beneath her palm. He wore clothes she'd never seen before, a plaid of many colors, made of wool frieze that was wrapped many times around him. It was held in place below his shoulder with a large, circular brooch. A nobleman's clothing, rich and fine. She traced the gold scrollwork on the metal as she absorbed the implications.

"Much has changed," she murmured.

"I have so much to tell you, Cairenn . . ."

As he told the story, her mind vaulted out to the world so she saw what had happened even as he spoke it. She saw the Lady MacGilchrist brought into the tent, heard her defend her bloody ambitions. Cairenn sensed her now, pacing and unrepentant in one of the castle's storerooms.

"She paid some of her Campbell cousins to commit murder," she said, startling Lachlan in the middle of his recounting. "But not even her own husband knew what she was about."

Lachlan's gaze rested on her with new intensity. "Your gift is back."

His words gave her pause. Her gift had responded with such alacrity that she hadn't really noticed it, just as one wouldn't notice how one's legs moved when walking. She started to probe the range of her abilities when she mind-stumbled upon unexpected news.

"You are not chieftain," she gasped. "You are not The MacEgan."

His eyes twinkled. "Disappointed?"

"You stood upon the council heights today." She saw him through the eyes of other men, straight and strong and speaking with authority as he raised the white rod. "You had the white rod in your grasp."

"My father desired above all things for the clan to be unified under one lineage, so I took the white rod this day, as I knew I must. Then I passed it to Fingal."

Cairenn tried to read the easy smile that hovered around his lips. His shoulders stretched strong and light, as though the burden of a hundred thousand stones had been shaken off them. "You gave up becoming chieftain of the MacEgans," she whispered. "Overlord of the entire clan."

"I handed the white rod off to a half-brother who stood as an example of wise, patient governance in the midst of bloody turmoil. A half-brother eager to lead, if his enthusiasm is any measure." He raised his brows. "The rod belongs with the true chieftain."

"But, you sacrificed *everything*."

"I sacrificed nothing." He took her hand and warmed it between his. "And I've gained exactly what I've always wanted."

Those words sank deep into her, slipping past walls she didn't even know she'd put up to guard her wary heart. They glided into her with the same ease that she'd always fallen into other people's minds, except that she welcomed this openness, this sharing, with a heart that swelled with a hope that she thought she'd long buried.

"But," she stuttered, "the betrothal to Leana—"

"Broken once again. Callum Ewing will likely have her married to Fingal before the year is out."

"Poor Fingal," she said, sensing the sulky impatience of the girl now pacing in an upper room of the castle. "But perhaps," she added, reading the excitement in Fingal's mind, "that final betrothal shall bring them both happiness."

"Is that hope speaking? Or does your gift now roam so far and wide, and with such precision?"

"My gift is . . . clearer."

The fuzziness and pain, the crackling and sizzling, all the force that had caused her so much pain was gone. The collective musing of the throngs camping upon the plain just outside Loch Fyfe came to her as naturally as if she'd just cocked her ear. Within the castle, she sensed the hurried anxiety of the women roasting meat, the single-minded focus of the blacksmith working in the smithy, the bored stable boys kicking hay in the stables, the guards taking their ease upon the ramparts. She discovered that she could mute the thoughts of one or another group by simply turning her mind away from them, as if she were turning her back on a conversation at a meal to focus on the talk of those on her other side.

Her heart did a little trip-dance. Touching the dolmen stones must have done this to her, though she couldn't imagine why. Whatever the reason, it was as if a great flood had scoured through her head and left her vitally aware, her mind as clean and clear as a newborn babe.

Then she looked into Lachlan's midnight-sky eyes and felt no resistance between them, no mist to shadow his brightest thoughts, nothing to dim the love that emanated from every corner of his vast and beautiful heart.

"I know your mind," she said, a laugh rising, "yet I cannot really read your thoughts, not like others."

"Lass, you've always known my heart."

She did. *She did.*

"But since I don't have your gift," he added, brushing a strand of hair off her brow, "I have to ask you for what I most hope for." He hesitated and took a breath. "Will you still have me, Cairenn, though now I'm naught but a lowly Scot who knows nothing except how to build bridges?"

With a slow, lazy smile she whispered *yes.* Lachlan lowered his head and pressed his warm, hungry lips against hers. She tasted honey-mead on his tongue. She combed her fingers through his thick, warm hair and dreamed of the two of them standing upon Inishmaan with the sun on their faces and her hand lost in the wispy blond hair of a little boy who had eyes like the twilight, so full of stars.

And suddenly she knew the answer to a question she'd asked herself since she'd been a girl, about why any young woman would so willfully hand her heart to a man whose mind she could not possibly know. Love builds a bridge between a man and a woman. It's built out of adoration and respect, and crossed over by trust.

He pulled away with reluctance. "You need to rest, *mo chridhe.* I would have you strong again."

She didn't have to read his thoughts to know he wanted to take her in his arms, run his hands over her skin, and slip his body against hers under the warmth of the blankets. Her heart lightened as if she were one of the birds singing just outside the tent. She felt a billowing joy unlike anything she'd felt since she'd been a child racing across the heights of Inishmaan.

All this thrumming delight felt wonderful, but it also felt oddly *new*. She gave him a look out of the side of her eyes. "What have you done, Lachlan?"

He grinned like a boy and reached back to pick up the lambskin he'd placed upon the floor. She did not have to see it to know what it was, for suddenly in her mind the mead-hall echoed with shouting men sweating in their braies as they yanked upon a tangle of pulleys and ropes.

She caught her breath. "You're moving the stones."

CHAPTER TWENTY-FOUR

Once Lachlan announced that they would be returning to Inishmaan, Fingal ordered a banquet to be thrown in Lachlan's honor.

Cairenn sat near the head of the trestle table, arranged in a different configuration now that the portal stones were already halfway up the slope to the council heights. At first, she felt very much out of place among so many grand people. She sat not far from Callum Ewing and the lion-maned Dermot MacGilchrist, whose newly-humble manner was that of a hound who stayed near his master though he'd been sorely beaten. Summoned from her safe exile with her Stuart cousins, Lachlan's twelve-year-old half-sister Elspeth sat across from Cairenn, peppering her with questions about Inishmaan. At the head was Fingal, who Cairenn discovered to be a focused, intelligent, and surprisingly sensible young man, when his attention wasn't drifting to Leana, his soon-to-be bride, who'd been relegated to the next table to avoid the awkwardness of sitting among two men to whom she'd been betrothed.

Lachlan was a steady, loving presence at her side. All through the boisterous banquet, she made sure that her smile told him how much she adored him. The only thing she regretted was that they could not extend this joy through the night, because the minute she had been deemed healthy enough to emerge from Angus's tent, Angus himself had insisted she be relegated to sleeping in the women's quarters with the other unmarried maidens. There, the beds were stuffed with feathers rather than hay, but without Lachlan, they were not nearly as warm.

The morning after the banquet, she was roused early by a young servant boy. She tossed her tunic over her head, slipped on her leather slippers, and grabbed her sack before following the child out of the room. Lachlan waited for her in the mead-hall amid heaps of snoring men, his own belongings rolled up tight and slung over his shoulder.

"Are we to sneak out," she whispered, once they'd stepped into the courtyard, "without even a last good-bye to Fingal and Elspeth?"

"They'll be down anon, along with Angus." He tugged on her hand. "But there's something I want you to see."

She did not have to guess what he wanted to show her. The creatures had slipped into her dreams last night, and now she heard them barking long before she and Lachlan passed under the raised portcullis to step onto the narrow causeway. Upon the rocks scattered along the shore of Loch Fyfe, hundreds of seals sprawled, raising their heads to the skies.

As she and Lachlan emerged, the seals turned their soft brown eyes toward them. The barking intensified as if the creatures expected them to toss buckets of fish.

She asked, "Do they usually come in such numbers?"

"Never. When I was young, we'd see a family or two in the fall. It was always the same family, so we came to know their markings well. But I've never seen so many."

"But surely," she said, remembering the seals around Inishmaan who loved to loll upon the rocks, their white pups close, "it's the season for them to come to a safe cover?"

"It's not, and the sea's a good league away."

"Well, this crowd seems happy to see us."

"I think they are, lass."

She slid him a glance. "So you *are* a selkie then?"

She'd meant it as teasing, but his expression became pensive. "I've no yearning to dive into the deep, if that's what you're thinking." He slipped his arm around her and drew her close into his warmth. "Not unless you promise to dive in with me."

"It's the high, lonely places I fancy," she said, "though if you're there to keep me warm I'll reconsider."

They stood for a while, basking in the odd, barking praise of a herd of seals. She knew that Lachlan's mind spun with questions and confusion. Like any woman who could read a man's mind, she waited in silence until he was ready to talk.

"All this barking," he finally confessed. "It's unearthing a memory that I'd thought was a dream."

Because he struggled so hard to explain it, she slipped into his thoughts to share in the dream-memory. It was a watery, salt-sea dream. The sharing was so vivid that she found herself rubbing her shoulder where a shadow of soreness throbbed, in the same place where Lachlan now bore his scar. Beyond the pain, the dream-memory was filled with sleek shadows slipping dark through cold waters, and the sense of being bumped toward a bluish light by strong, whiskered snouts.

She said, "You once told me that your mother's people were from Orkney, said to be descended from the *Finnar*. The selkies."

"I'm mad enough to believe it," he said, "now that I've witnessed all that you've shown me since you saved me."

"I don't know if I have an explanation for that dream," she said, "except that it might explain how you washed up on the shores of Inishmaan."

He blinked in that way he did, whenever she was telling him something too far out of his ability to understand.

"All otherworldly creatures feel the power of the dolmen stones," she explained. "Perhaps these seals—and maybe a selkie or two among them—felt the desecration upon the council height keenly, and hoped you, with a bit of their blood running through your veins, might be able to put matters back to rights."

"So they sent me to you," he murmured, "because I couldn't do such a task alone."

She nodded. She was part of this, too. When she'd touched the dolmen stones, her gift had changed profoundly for the better. Perhaps that was the Otherworld's way of showing gratitude for the risks she'd taken, unknowingly, for their sake.

"So what you're telling me," he persisted, as he pressed his lips against her hair, "is that you and I were brought together for some greater purpose."

"Oh, Lachlan. I've no doubt we were."

His nod was thoughtful. She laid her head upon his shoulder, burrowing into his warmth. For a long time, they stood on the causeway with the wind blowing off the lake, watching the seals frolic as the people in the castle behind them woke to the day.

"So today we begin the journey back to Inishmaan," he said into the silence, "and yet we never really spoke about it."

"It will always be that way with us. We know each other's hearts."

"Yet you spent years hoping to leave that island."

"Only because I yearned to find you. Now that I have you, I want nothing more than to live with you among my people."

He grunted. "Your father may greet me on shore with a swinging sword."

"My mother will assure him that all is well," she said, laughing. "And he'll be overwhelmed that one of his daughters, at least, has come back to Inishmaan for good."

In that suspended moment, she thought of her mother and father standing on the height. She thought of Niall strumming a sleep-song. She thought of her brothers and sisters, racing like puppies toward her. She thought of Seamus and his bright, joyous mind. She thought of a stretch of pasture where Lachlan would build their house from the surrounding stones, rigging rain-traps and pulley-systems and new ways to haul the bounty of the sea to the height.

She'd never wanted, so dearly, to go home to the people she loved, with the man she loved.

"I never really asked you to marry me," he said. "Not properly, as a man should."

Her heart brightened as she shared his thoughts. Soon they would be touching each other every night, kissing each other every day, lying naked against one another as their hearts beat as one.

"Oh, I heard you ask," she said, lifting her face toward his, "and the answer is *yes*."

THE END

Turn the page for an exclusive sneak-peek of HEAVEN IN HIS ARMS, a historical road-trip romance by Lisa Ann Verge

"An absorbing, exciting romantic adventure!"
–RT Book Reviews

"Lisa Ann Verge breathes fresh life into the romance genre with a novel that should gather her award nominations."
-Affaire de Coeur

Paris, 1670

Struggling to survive on the streets of Paris, Genevieve agrees to a dangerous masquerade: She switches places with a King's Girl, a young noblewoman about to be shipped to the colonies. It's a risky venture with a high price—once overseas, Genny must marry a stranger.

PROLOGUE

Paris, July 1670

This was her only chance.

Genevieve pressed against the stone wall. The dampness seeped through her woolen dress and chilled her skin, already clammy with fear. She dug her fingers into the bundle clutched to her chest. She had come this far. All that was left was to pass the guard at the end of the hallway, and she would be free.

The distraction had already begun. A slip of a girl emerged from one of the doorways. That girl raced toward the dozing female guard and startled the woman from her nap. The guard blinked at the wild-haired creature while the young girl—a deaf-mute—gestured frantically toward the gaping door of her cell. Sighing, the stocky guard hefted out of her seat, grasped a sputtering candle, and followed her down the hall.

As soon as the guard disappeared into the chamber, Genevieve leapt out of the shadows. She raced on bare feet toward the oak doors. She would only have a few moments before the guard realized that the young woman's unspoken fears were imaginary—the crazed ravings of a simpleton, the guard would think—and then the old laywoman would shrug it off and return to her station.

But Genevieve Lalande would have already escaped.

The brass handle chilled her hand. She eased the door open to prevent the hinges from squeaking. When it was cracked enough, she slipped through and edged it closed behind her. She leaned against the door for a moment, sucking in the night air as she waited for her blood to stop pounding. But she was already late. If she didn't hurry, her second accomplice would lose courage and destroy all their plans.

She scanned the enormous courtyard of the Salpêtrière, her prison for the last three years. The night was clear but moonless. Bits of gravel scattered the starlight, making the courtyard glitter as if it were covered with frost. There was no sign of her accomplice, but she'd hoped that the girl would have more sense than to stand like a lost child in the middle of the open courtyard. She glanced at the debris scattered at the opposite end, where the church of Saint Louis was being built. There was no better place to hide than among the hewn stones, the piled earth, and the skeletal wooden scaffolding.

She clung to the walls as she worked her way

over. Chips of gravel bit into her feet. A breeze swept through the open courtyard, heavy with the stench of the Seine River. The rows of windows in the opposite building winked at her like a thousand eyes and she was so distracted that she stubbed her toe against a pick abandoned by some day worker. She squeezed her eyes shut until the pain passed. Then she limped on until she reached the shadows of the scaffolding.

Marie should have been here by now. The last note Genevieve had sent her was specific: Tonight was the night they were to meet in this courtyard to complete the plans they had so painstakingly formed over the last three weeks. She and Marie had been passing notes back and forth through the same system without fail for too long for there to be a sudden mix-up.

Come, Marie. Come.

Somewhere in Paris church bells rang. Above her, birds startled with an anxious fluttering of wings. A stream of silt filtered down from the higher scaffolding, dusting her shoulder. As the church bells faded, she saw a figure separate from one of the buildings.

Genevieve sucked in a breath and pressed back against the masonry. If one of the guards saw her, she'd be right back where she started, and who knew when she'd get a chance like this again. But as she watched the figure enter the courtyard, she realized this was no guard. It was a woman, a young woman by the quick pace of her walk, an anxious woman by the way her head pivoted back and forth.

Genevieve intercepted her near a pile of bricks.

"Marie?"

The young woman stopped short and pulled back the edge of her scarf, revealing a pale, drawn face. "Genevieve?"

"*Oui.* Come into the shadows."

She had never seen Marie before today. With relief, she noticed that they were of about the same height. Height would have been the most difficult to disguise.

As she approached, Marie loosened her head rail and pulled the scarf off her hair. "Thank God you are here. I feared you would leave. The housekeeper on my floor would not fall asleep. I had to check three doors before I found one unlocked."

Refined speech. Well, Genevieve could mimic that well enough. "You had nothing to fear," she said. "I would have stayed until dawn."

The young woman squinted at her. "I have never seen you before."

"Nor I you." She didn't bother to explain that she was housed in a separate building, isolated from women like Marie. Marie was a *bijou,* a jewel of the Salpêtrière, an orphaned daughter of the petty nobility, pampered and educated and protected.

"You write with such a fine hand," Marie murmured, glancing at Genevieve's common russet skirts. "I thought you might be one of the noblewomen housed in another building."

Genevieve felt the muscles of her neck tighten. In another time, in a better world, she might have been worthy of being called a *bijou.* But that was long ago and best left forgotten. She gestured to

Marie's skirts. "Is that what you planned to wear tomorrow?"

"Yes." Marie parted her cloak to show a dark blue traveling dress. "I've packed a small case and left it by my bed. In it, you'll find several other dresses and a few gold pieces. This is all I can give you for what you are doing for me."

Such foolish, innocent generosity. "You should have kept the money. You'll need it more than I—"

"No, that isn't true." Marie twisted her scarf in her hands. "You do know what you're doing, don't you? I couldn't live with myself—no matter how happy I'd be to escape this place—if I misled you."

"I'm the one who suggested this plan."

"But I'm going to be sent away—*you're* going to be sent away," Marie corrected. "King Louis XIV himself has dowered me. He has paid my passage to some horrible place called Quebec and he intends to marry me off to some coarse, half-savage settler—"

"I know you're a king's girl." Every year since she'd arrived in the Salpêtrière, dozens of girls had been given a dowry by the king and sent off to the Caribbean islands or to the northern settlements of New France, to marry and settle in the colonies. "I chose you because you're being sent away from here."

"Do you know anything about Quebec?"

Genevieve took the mangled scarf out of the other girl's hands to stop her from crumpling it. "I know enough."

"The forests are filled with red-skinned savages. The winters are long and frigid, and there's so much snow that it tops the rooftops." Bereft of the scarf, Marie's smooth white hands knotted and twisted and pulled at each other. "And the voyage— over the sea—halfway across the world, in storms and sickness. Why are you doing this? Why would you take my place and go to that dreadful colony and leave all this behind?"

Genevieve glared at the long buildings of the Salpêtrière and thought, *I'd rather sell my soul to Lucifer than spend another hour here.*

But Marie wouldn't understand that. She and Marie both lived in this "charity house," but they lived in entirely different worlds. Marie lived in the Salpêtrière of King Louis XIV, the charity house that succored aging servants with no pensions, old married couples of good birth, and the younger daughters of impoverished petty nobility, a charity house staffed with religious women and headed by a benign Mother Superior. Genevieve lived in a place ruled by brutal guards, a place peopled by orphans and waifs and beggars taken forcefully off the streets of Paris. Since the day she herself had been captured, three years ago, she'd found no charity in this place.

"I'm surprised Mother Superior didn't recommend you to the king himself," Marie continued into the silence. "I've been told she's having a difficult time finding enough girls of modest birth to fill the king's ship."

"I'll make a better match in marriage disguised as a Duplessis." Genevieve folded the silky scarf and laid it upon her own bundle. "Because of your birth, you'll be set aside for the wealthiest men in the colony."

Marie cast her gaze down. "I didn't think of that."

Of course she wouldn't. This woman had never tasted a stolen apple. She had never raced through the streets of Paris after cutting a nobleman's purse, fearing hunger more than the threat of capture and punishment by whipping.

"But of course, it makes perfect sense now." Marie's hands fluttered white in the starlight. "When I found your first note among my laundered shifts, I was sure someone was playing a trick on me. The girls are terrified of being shipped off to this dreadful place. They're sobbing for me and Cecile as if tomorrow the two of us will be executed in the square."

"But you won't be going now. Have you heard from him?"

"Yes. Yes." Her face lit with joy. "I received a note this morning. François is waiting for me, just inside the gates of Paris."

So that was the name of the French Musketeer Marie loved enough to risk everything to marry. Genevieve dearly hoped this François wasn't like the other strutting, shifty-eyed Musketeers she had known in her younger days. In their blue coats and shimmering braid, they had terrorized the city, taking whatever women pleased them and pulling their swords at the slightest provocation.

"We mustn't delay any longer." Genevieve nodded to Marie's cloak. "Take off your clothes."

The young woman started. "Here?"

"Quickly."

"But what am I to wear?" Marie glanced up at the skeletal scaffolding of the church and crossed herself. "I can't escape in your clothing."

Genevieve footed her bundle toward the girl. "You'll wear the clothing of a governess—a black wool skirt, a white coif, and a black mantle. Then you can walk out the front gates without being stopped."

"Where did you get it?"

"Never mind that. Hurry."

Genevieve unlaced her bodice, tugged it off, and then slipped out of her russet wool skirt. The night was balmy, and the breeze toyed with her tattered shift as she stuffed her old clothes beneath a pile of bricks. As Marie fumbled with her own laces, Genevieve scrutinized the girl more closely. Marie's tresses were long and chestnut-colored. Genevieve's own hair was a mass of copper, a gift, her mother had once told her, from the father she had never known. Marie's skin was smooth, while Genevieve had a sprinkling of freckles across her nose. Problems, she thought, but nothing that couldn't be overcome by brushing the roots of her hair with an ashy comb, covering her head tight with a scarf, and patting her face thick with powder.

Genevieve snatched Marie's bodice and thrust her arms through the sleeves. "Tell me about your family. I'll need to know their names, ages, and everything about them that's important."

As Marie struggled out of her skirt and petticoat and reached for the bundle of clothing, she told Genevieve that her mother had died in childbirth when Marie was only a few years old.

Later, impoverished by the civil wars which had flared through France, she and her father had lived on the charity of distant relatives until her father died, leaving Marie to the mercy of an unscrupulous second cousin. He refused to dower her or pay to put her in a convent, so she was sent to the Salpêtrière. Genevieve noted all the names and dates as she slipped on Marie's discarded petticoat and skirt. She would need to know as much as she could remember for when she got to Quebec.

But her mind wandered from Marie's monologue as Genevieve slipped on the blue travelling dress. The feel of the soft cloth against her skin brought a rush of memories. She blocked them out. The past was the past—it was the future that mattered now.

"Cecile awaits you tonight," Marie said as she knotted the last lace of her bodice. "She'll open the door and guide you to my bed."

"Good." In her new clothes, she twirled before Marie. "Well?"

"You have the carriage of a noblewoman." Marie plucked at her plain black robes, hesitating. "Perhaps this shall all work out as you planned."

I swear that it will.

"But," Marie began, her voice catching, "if you are caught—"

"I won't be."

"—the punishment for what we are doing is severe." Her breath came fast. "We're switching places under the very nose of Mother Superior. It's like tricking the King himself—"

"The king and Mother Superior want girls to

fill their ships, no more. They won't look too closely after counting."

"If we're caught, they could force us into a convent," Marie stuttered. "They could shut us away from the world forever."

They'd shut you into a convent, Genevieve thought, but they would find a far more painful punishment for her.

Marie ventured, "You are sure?"

"Yes." Any risk was worth the possibility of freedom.

"Very well." Marie took a deep breath. "You'll be leaving at dawn tomorrow for Le Havre. Cecile will shield you from Mother Superior as you board the carriage, but it'll be tricky."

"Mother Superior is half blind," Genevieve said. "She'll never even notice me. And I'll be crying like an onion seller into my—your—handkerchief. Will we be traveling in a public carriage?"

"Oh, no!" She rested a hand on her throat. "The carriage will be sent by the king, of course."

"Who else will be in it?"

"Some guards will ride outside to see that we are protected until we reach the ship. But there will be other girls from here, I'm told."

"Do those girls know you?"

"No. I don't know anyone coming but Cecile. But what if one of them recognizes you?"

She forced her feet into Marie's boots—a bit too small. "None of the women who live in my section were chosen, so I don't have to worry about being recognized. Go, Marie." She waved toward the gates. "Your Musketeer awaits."

Marie lurched forward and seized Genevieve's hand. "I will never forget you for the sacrifice you've made for me—oh!"

Genevieve pulled away but it was too late, for Marie had already dropped Genevieve's chapped hand like a hot poker.

Marie staggered back, her mouth falling open.

"Obviously," Genevieve said, raising her chin, "I'll need gloves. Even in Quebec, no one will believe that a fine young lady has the hands of a washerwoman."

Marie made a choked sound and then raced away. Genevieve stared sightlessly at the place where the woman had been. She'd been right, it seemed, to hide her true identity as she slipped notes amid Marie's clean laundry. Marie would never have agreed to this desperate scheme if she had known the truth.

The only women who washed linens in the Salpêtrière were the whores.

~Excerpt, *Heaven In His Arms,* copyright 2014 ~

ABOUT THE AUTHOR

Lisa Ann Verge is the critically acclaimed RITA© nominated author of eighteen novels that have been published worldwide and translated into as many languages. She started her career writing emotionally intense romance about hot men and dangerous women, and now as **Lisa Verge Higgins** she also writes life-affirming women's fiction. A finalist for RT Book Review awards five times over, Lisa has won the Golden Leaf and the Bean Pot, and twice she has cracked Barnes & Noble's General Fiction Forum's top twenty books of the year. She currently lives in New Jersey with her husband and their three daughters, who never fail to make life interesting.